SUFFER IN SILENCE

KELSEY CLAYTON

Copyright © 2022 by Kelsey Clayton

All rights reserved.

No part of this book may be reproduced in any form or by any electronic or mechanical means, including information storage and retrieval systems, without written permission from the author, except for the use of brief quotations in a book review.

Editing by Kiezha Ferrell at Librum Artis
Cover by Y'all That Graphic

To those who find beauty in the darkness.

"I loved her not for the way she danced with my angels, but for the way the sound of her name could silence my demons"

— CHRISTOPHER POINDEXTER

Chapter 1

Saxon

PAIN. IT RIPS THROUGH MY BODY WITH RELENTLESS CRUELTY. THE screaming in my head tries to drown out the silence, but it's futile. It's as if my lips are sewn shut with a fishhook and barbed wire. Not even a whimper has a chance at escaping. All I can do is get lost in the darkness. My fingernails are ripped from my skin as I drag them down the wall—his blood on my hands leaving behind evidence of my touch. It's piercingly loud and deadly quiet all at the same time, and I know with certainty that I'd rather burn alive than live one more moment like this.

A Few Months Earlier

A cool breeze blows through my long, black hair as I walk through campus. They say that on your twenty-first birthday, you feel different. More grown up. Ready to take on the world of adulthood. Personally, that's not the way I'd describe it.

My mom would say that I'm an old soul—that I've always been wise beyond my years and it's no surprise that twenty-one feels the same as twenty. And maybe she's right. Or maybe I find nothing exciting about getting older in a world I've never felt was right for me.

It's a joke, honestly. I'm Saxon Forbes—pre-med student at Columbia University, with millionaires for parents and a grandfather who owns a chunk of New York City. I've spent my entire life wanting for nothing, except feeling alive. Everything I've done, every step I've taken in my life, it's always felt so out of place. Like I've always been an inch away from falling off the edge but too afraid to jump.

"Happy Birthday!" my best friend Nessa shouts as her body collides into mine. Her arms wrap around me, and the action brings a level of comfort that I've always relied on.

I've known Nessa for most of my life, since we sat next to each other in second grade and she demanded that we share crayons. It was probably because I had the pack with every color imaginable inside, but regardless, we've been inseparable since.

I smile and lean into her touch. "Thanks, Ness."

She lets go and jumps in front of me, walking backward on the way to class. "Okay, so how are we celebrating? I'm thinking a massive party. With a seven-tiered cake with sparklers for candles. Oh! And a confetti cannon!"

Cringing, I shake my head. "More like dinner with my family."

"You're lying," she deadpans.

"I'm not."

Her shoulders sag as she stops. "Sax, I know you treat your birthday like it's an inconvenience, but we can't just not celebrate the birth of my favorite person in the world. It's a crime against humanity, or at least against me."

I raise a brow at her with a smile. "As flattering as you made that sound, don't think I'm oblivious to the fact that you're just looking for a reason to get drunk and make bad choices."

"I would never," she says in mock outrage, clutching her imaginary pearls. "Your birthday is sacred to me."

"Mm-hm. And the guy you invited to my birthday is named…"

"Jamie." His name comes out as a whine as she throws her head back. "He's in my business finance class, and he's the most beautiful thing I've ever seen."

Yep. There it is. An amused giggle bubbles out. "I thought you were talking to some guy from out of town."

The devious smirk I've come to love appears on her face. "I am."

"Nessa," I say warningly.

"What?" She feigns innocence. "He plays so hot and cold. A little jealousy will do him good."

"And how will he even know about it?"

Slipping her phone from her back pocket, she holds it up. "Social media. Duh."

I stare back at my best friend, always finding humor in her antics. When it comes to boys, we're nothing alike. I spend my lectures taking notes, while she spends her's taking numbers. But that's just Nessa, and there's no changing her.

"You're like the female equivalent of a fuckboy. You know that, don't you?"

She opens her mouth to answer, but her eyes land behind

me and she scrunches her nose in disgust. "Speaking of fuckboys..." she mutters

Before I can ask what she's talking about, two arms wrap around my waist from behind and a kiss is pressed to my cheek.

"Happy Birthday."

Ah, him.

Brad Palmer.

President of Kappa Beta Chi, weekend alcoholic, and master of all things charm. Ness isn't wrong. If you look up the term "fuckboy" in the dictionary, you're likely to see his picture beside it—smiling like the cat that caught the canary.

"Thanks, Brad," I say softly while still stepping out of his hold.

Ever since we were paired together on a philosophy project last semester, he's had his sights set on me. Now, I may not have a genius IQ, but I'm not stupid enough to think it's genuine. I simply managed to capture his attention when I refused to make out instead of working on the assignment. Apparently, that turned me into his new favorite mission.

And okay, maybe I humor him a little.

What can I say? Having Columbia's Most Wanted Bachelor's attention is nice.

"So, how are we celebrating?" he asks, and I instantly roll my eyes.

Not him, too.

Nessa throws her hands in the air. "See? A dinner with your family is *not* how you spend your twenty-first birthday. We have to at least go to the club. It's a rite of passage!"

Brad shrugs. "She's not wrong. It is."

"Thank you!" Ness says, her smug satisfaction all too apparent.

I narrow my eyes at her, silently pointing out that she doesn't even like Brad, but she just gives me a sickeningly sweet smile that fails at looking innocent.

Honestly, my ideal night would just be dinner with my favorite people, followed up by a bubble bath and ending with a soft blanket and my favorite book, but something tells me that's not happening. With these two on the same side, I may as well compromise. Otherwise, my entire day is going to consist of them trying to hijack my plans for tonight.

"Okay," I agree. "We can go out *after* we have dinner with my family."

The corner of Brad's mouth raises. "Am *I* invited to this family affair?"

"No," Ness and I answer in unison.

He pouts like a dejected puppy, but I'm not about to give on that one. The last thing I need is for my father to sit across from the guy whose sole mission in life is to steal his daughter's virtue. No part of that is a good idea.

"Sorry, but no," I repeat. "We'll meet you at The Pulse after."

Nessa purses her lips. "Decent choice, but I'm thinking something with more Gatsby vibes."

I choose to ignore her and press a kiss to Brad's cheek, just to soften the blow of my rejection. He smiles and winks at me before I loop my arm with Nessa's, walking toward Broadway.

"Where are we going?" she asks, glancing backward.

"Shopping, because I'm being forced to go out tonight against my will, and I have nothing to wear."

She puts on a shocked face with a hint of pride in her eyes. "Saxon Forbes. You're skipping class?"

I huff, but a smile forces its way through. "I mean, it *is* my birthday."

Chuckling, she pulls me closer against her. "You're damn right it is."

A MASSIVE CHANDELIER COVERS the entire ceiling of the restaurant. The lighting lands softly on my dress, causing the white fabric to sparkle. Nessa and I follow the hostess as she escorts us to the table. Once we're close enough, my father stands.

"There you are!" He greets me with open arms. "I was starting to think you got lost."

"If I had let Nessa drive, we probably would have," I quip.

Ness scoffs. "I am *not* that bad."

Turning toward Ness, I give her a knowing look. "You had to go three blocks and somehow ended up in Jersey."

She throws her head back and groans. "That was one time!"

"It was twice, and it only stopped because you gave up trying to find the place."

If looks could kill, I'd be dead with the way she's glaring at me. "Why am I friends with you?"

I gasp, looking offended the same way she did this morning, but before I can answer, my dad interrupts.

"Okay, let's not cause a scene in the nice restaurant." He moves to give Nessa a hug. "Monster."

The nickname he greets her with is one he gave her back when we were kids. He said that her name reminds him of the Loch Ness monster, and thus, Monster was born.

She grins happily and takes the seat beside him, while I

sit next to my little sister, Kylie. She looks up at me like she always does, with a broad smile that showcases the gap from where she lost two teeth. The fourteen year age gap between us might make some think we have nothing in common, but they'd be wrong. She's had me wrapped around her finger since the day she was born—when I watched her through the nursery window and refused to look away.

I nudge her with my elbow. "Hey Kyliekins. How was school?"

Looking unsure, she shrugs. "Nathan pulled on my pigtails."

"Oh really?" My brows raise. "Do you want me to fight him?"

That makes her giggle. "Saxon, you can't fight him. You're a grown up."

Her words are like a blow to the chest, and my jaw drops while Nessa laughs. "Ouch. Way to make me feel old."

Kylie shrugs. "You said it, not me."

"I knew you were my favorite Forbes for a reason," Ness tells her.

My brows furrow. "Rude. I thought I was your favorite."

Dad mirrors my expression. "And what am I? Chopped liver?"

Nessa cringes playfully and rests her head on my dad's shoulder to placate him but winks subtly at Kylie.

That's fine. She's my favorite Forbes, too.

"So, where's mom?" I ask as I glance around. "Bathroom?"

My dad gives me a sad smile. "I'm sorry, sweetie. She really wanted to be here, but something came up."

"She's at the hospital with Grandpa," Kylie blurts.

"What?"

"Kylie," Dad says sternly. "I thought we said we were going to wait until tomorrow to tell her that. Not on her birthday, remember?"

I shake my head immediately. "No. Don't do that. What's wrong with Grandpa?"

Panic starts to rise in my chest at the thought of possibly losing my grandfather. He's been my heart and soul for as long as I can remember: The guy who always snuck me alcohol during the holidays. My favorite advice giver. My biggest supporter.

I can't lose him. Not before I've barely even lived.

"It's his heart." The blasé tone he uses catches me off guard. It's almost as if he's reading a grocery list or talking about the weather to a stranger. "He's been sick for a while and now the doctors say it's starting to fail."

No. "He can get a new one. A transplant."

My dad reaches across the table to put his hand on my own. "He doesn't qualify, Sax. There's nothing they can do."

"Then we'll travel to another country and hire the best doctors money can buy. It's not like we don't have it."

The heartbreaking look on his face tells me everything I don't want to hear. "Honey, he doesn't have the time for all that. Trust me when I say your mom and I have considered every possible option, and we came to the same conclusion. I'm so sorry."

Every part of my body goes completely still as reality sets in that I'm going to lose him soon. I don't even realize I'm crying until Nessa crouches down beside me and wipes the tears from my cheeks. As I turn to face her, I don't even have to say the words out loud before she nods, standing up and giving me her hand.

"Let's go."

I DON'T THINK THERE has ever been a time when hospitals didn't freak me out. The amount of death these walls have seen... Just the thought of it makes goosebumps rise across my skin. But at the same time, they've also seen life. The miracles that save people against all odds. The babies that have been born here. It almost feels like a portal between here and whatever resides beyond our world.

A portal that will soon separate my grandfather and me.

Nessa holds my shaking hand tightly in hers as we wait for the elevator to reach the sixth floor. The whole way up, I can only imagine the worst.

I'm too late.

He's already gone.

I didn't even get to say goodbye.

The doors open, and I take a deep breath.

Every step we take down the hallway feels heavy, weighed down by the intensity of the situation mixed with the grief looming over me. I'm so lost in thought that I don't even notice as I almost walk directly into a man wearing an expensive, inky black suit, flanked by two other men also in suits. Thankfully, Nessa pulls me out of the way just in time, but my eyes still meet his.

Cold.

Vicious.

Painstakingly gorgeous.

There's something about him that sends a chill down my spine. Something that makes me want to know everything about him and run for my life at the same time. But the moment is gone as quick as it came, and he looks away and continues down the hallway.

"Here's his room," Ness tells me as we turn the corner, yanking me back to my dreaded reality.

I swallow down the lump in my throat and nod. "I can do this."

She squeezes my hand before letting it go. "Anything you need, I'm right here."

"Love you more."

"Love you longer," she recites on cue.

Walking into the room, my heart breaks a little more as I spot him in the bed. This isn't the grandfather I've known my whole life. The man who taught me how to drive the streets of New York City is strong and fearless. To everyone else, he's Silas Kingston—one of the most powerful men in the city. Someone other men aspire to be and criminals refuse to cross. But to me, he's always just been Grandpa.

Seeing him now, weak and fragile, it's a shock to my system.

He really is dying.

A choked sob escapes just before I throw my hand over my mouth, and it grabs his attention. He looks away from the TV and over at me, giving me that same loving smile I remember.

"Hey Wildflower," he greets me, using the nickname that's reserved just for him.

Tears well in my eyes and spill over the edges. I try to respond, try to gain some sort of strength, but it's useless. I don't stand a chance. Not with him in that bed, looking like he's knocking on death's door.

He reaches over to grab the remote and turns off the TV. "Come here, Saxon."

I cross the room and let myself fall into his arms. Everything I was trying to hold back comes crashing through as I break down. My tears soak the hospital gown he's wearing, but he doesn't seem to mind as he rubs his feeble hand up and down my back, whispering comforting words that walk the line between half-truths and white lies.

"It's going to be okay, Sax," he tells me. "You're going to be all right."

I pull away and shake my head. "I'm not. How could I be? You're…you're…"

"I'm dying," he admits, saying the words I can't bring myself to say. "But that's the circle of life. We're all living on borrowed time, and I've lived a very fulfilling life. *It's okay.*"

Every part of me wants to tell him he's wrong. That he's still too young. That we haven't had enough time. But just as I'm about to open my mouth, my mom walks with a Styrofoam cup.

"Saxon?" She sounds confused. "What are you doing here? I thought you were going to dinner with your father."

"You didn't tell me," I cry.

My mom exhales and her shoulders sag. "I didn't want to ruin your birthday. I had every intention of telling you tomorrow morning."

"No. We don't keep things from each other. *Especially* things like this," I argue. "You should have told me."

She nods. "You're right. I should've. I'm sorry."

"It's fine. I'm here now."

"Now hold on a minute," my grandfather interjects. "I have to take your mother's side on this one. You should be out celebrating, not sitting here watching an old man wither away."

"Dad," my mom chastises him. "Maybe choose your words a little better."

He waves her off. "Nonsense. I've never been one to sugarcoat shit, and I'm not about to start now."

"Clearly," she grumbles.

Grandpa chooses to ignore her and instead focuses on the door. "Nessa! Get in here!"

My best friend peeks around the corner and gives him a warm smile as she comes into the room. "Hey, Gramps."

"Take this girl to a bar, would you?"

My eyes narrow as my head whips back towards him. "What? No. I can't go to—you're—"

He pins me with a single look, one that always worked when I was a kid. "Saxon Royce, no granddaughter of mine is going to spend her twenty-first birthday in a hospital—unless you're getting your stomach pumped from alcohol poisoning, in which case, you're weak and I taught you better than that."

"But I—"

"But nothing," he says, one shaky finger jabbing the air at me. "I'll still be here tomorrow. Go enjoy being able to legally drink and not have to hide it under the dinner table." My mom looks surprised and slightly scandalized, but he scoffs and rolls his eyes. "Please. Don't act like you didn't know. Playing dumb is beneath you."

Mom pinches the bridge of her nose and shakes her head. "You have no filter."

"Never did, my dear. Never did." He turns his attention back to me. "Now go, unless you want me to call security and have you escorted out of here."

A part of me wants to call his bluff, but I know him well enough to know that he rarely says things he doesn't mean. So, without any other choice, I give him another hug before heading toward the door.

"Promise me that you'll still be here tomorrow,," I beg him.

He winks at me. "Have a drink for me, Wildflower."

THE TAXI PULLS UP to The Pulse at just past ten. Nessa and I climb out and step onto the sidewalk, immediately finding Brad waiting in the long line. He's being fawned over by most of the girls around him, but the second his eyes land on me, he ignores them all.

"Well, at least he's punctual," Nessa murmurs.

I exhale slowly and start to walk toward him when a guard steps in front of me. He's tall, probably about six foot four, which towers over my five foot two and a half inches. And yes, that half inch counts, thank you very much.

"Miss Forbes?" he asks.

Craning my neck to look up at him, I answer hesitantly. "Uh, yes?"

"I've been given strict instructions to escort you and your friends to your VIP table," he informs me. "Please, come with me."

I turn and give Nessa a look. "The person you were texting in the cab?"

She smiles guiltily. "He was demanding your mom find out where we were going. Did you want me to deny him his God-given right to spoil his granddaughter *and her best friend*?"

"Yes," I deadpan.

The man is quite literally on his deathbed and still ordering people around. His body may look different, but the man inside is still very much the same Silas Kingston the city sees him as.

Reluctantly, I grab Brad and pull him away from his own personal harem. They all give me dirty looks as he wraps an arm around my shoulders and we skip the line, following the bouncer into the club as everyone groans and complains behind us.

"I was waiting in that line for damn near an hour," Brad says. "How'd you get us in so quick?"

Nessa runs her fingers through her hair and looks around as she answers for me. "Her grandfather owns the place."

Brad's eyes widen in surprise. "Well, damn. Not just a pretty face, are you, Saxi?"

I cringe at the nickname. He thinks it's cute, with it sounding like sexy, but it just makes him look even more like the tool he is. And that's not even touching on the fact that he thinks all women need to be is pretty. I mean, shouldn't misogyny be long gone by now?

Wrapping my fingers around Nessa's wrist, I pull her close to me and speak into her ear. "Get me a drink. A strong one."

She turns to me with a broad grin. "Coming right up."

As she heads for the bar, I give myself a chance to take everything in. The place is visually interesting but not tacky. The walls are a sleek black that the lights paint with color. The white VIP tables, including the one we were given, are in the upper back corner of the club, with their own private bar. The platform is eye level with the DJ, both looking over the dance floor from opposite sides of the club.

Two hands land on my hips, and Brad's chest presses against my back. "You look so fucking good tonight, Sax."

I roll my eyes. "I'm sure you say that to all the girls."

"Yeah, but with *you*, I mean it."

Gag. This idiot sounds like something out of a 90s soap

opera. And after the night I've had so far, I can't be bothered with his bullshit.

Nessa comes back holding a drink in each hand, and I sigh in relief as she hands me one. Tilting the drink back, I down the whole thing in one go. Brad watches in disbelief while Nessa whines.

"You bitch. I wanted to get a picture of you with your first legal drink."

I shrug and hand Brad the empty cup. *"Babe?* Mind getting me another?"

His brows raise at the pet name. "Coming right up."

Ness and I both watch as he walks away, grabbing the attention of every girl he passes by. The second he's out of earshot, she comes closer to speak directly into my ear.

"Keep drinking like that and your v-card will replace the condom in his back pocket."

I snort. "Absolutely not. I did not grow up with a strict father cockblocking me at every chance only to lose it to a wannabe Hugh Hefner."

She chuckles and runs her fingers through her hair. "Accurate description. Does that mean I need to stay sober to keep you from making a drunken mistake?"

Giving her my best smile, I wink at her. "Consider it my birthday present."

A long exhale emits from her nose. "You're lucky I love you."

SPOILER ALERT: SHE MUST not love me as much as she claims she does, because it only takes an hour before she's just as drunk as I am—two hours before she makes me look sober. She's swaying to the music in the middle of the dance floor, completely off beat but without a care in the world.

Sometimes I envy that about her. The way she can just be and not care who is watching, including Jamie, who is, in fact, just as gorgeous as she described and probably why she almost failed business finance. He stands behind her, holding her hips just to keep her steady on her feet.

"Where's your fuckboy?" she slurs as she looks around the room.

To be honest, I don't know the answer to that. "He disappeared after the third time you told him he's not allowed to deflower me tonight."

And yes, those were her actual words, because apparently, her filter goes out the window a little more with every shot she takes. Honestly, he probably found some girl who's eager to jump into bed with him and take care of the hard-on he got within three seconds of grinding against me.

Better her than me.

A drunken hiccup bubbles out of her. "Well, he's not. You deserve better. The best. I'm talking wine and rose petals and to be serenaded on a balcony under the starry night sky. Real big-spender romantic level shit."

I spare a quick glance at Jamie who is trying not to laugh before looking back at Nessa. "Okay, Nicholas Sparks, I think you've had enough. Maybe we should head home."

"No. A few more songs," she whines and grabs my wrist. "Dance with me. It's my birthday."

Confused, Jamie turns his attention to me. "I thought it was *your* birthday."

"It is," I confirm with a fond smile. "But you try telling her that. See how that goes for you."

Instead of fighting a pointless battle, I decide on the easier option, moving my body and letting myself get lost in the music. My eyes settle closed, and my head falls back as I feel the vibration from the bass against my body. For once, I don't think about school, or Brad, or the impending death of my grandfather. I just…let go.

The DJ transitions the music into another song, keeping the tempo but upping the energy level. I can feel as my serotonin level rises, and maybe Nessa was right. Maybe this was exactly what I needed.

My body keeps moving to the music as my eyes open and lock with *his*. In an instant, I'm stone cold sober. The man holds the same frigid gaze he had at the hospital earlier, only this time, there's something darker there. He's leaning against the wall with a glass of amber liquid in his hand as he watches me.

His breathing steady.

His body still.

His gaze unwavering.

He raises the glass to his mouth and watches me over the rim as he takes a sip. Every ounce of my attention is locked on him, as if I can't look away. His brown hair is carelessly pushed back and out of his face. His shoulders are squared, showing he never lets his guard down. His knuckles are white as he grips his drink so tightly I'm afraid the glass might shatter at any given moment.

The fleeting glance of him I got a few hours ago was nowhere near enough to take in all of him. He looks like he was carved from stone—hours upon hours spent turning him into an artist's most prized masterpiece. With confidence that demands the attention of everyone around him and a smoldering gaze that could melt ice, he's nothing less than utter perfection.

"No," Nessa says as she steps in front of me and blocks my view. "Nuh-uh. Over my dead body."

I try to look around her, but she moves with me. "What are you doing?"

"Keeping you alive."

"Please. He's harmless." It's probably a total fucking lie, especially with the vibes he gives off, but maybe if I say it, it'll be true.

She scoffs. "Sure, if you consider a grenade with the pin pulled out *harmless*. I'm telling you, Sax. Not him. Literally anyone but him."

I look past her to see him still watching us. "Who even is he, anyway?"

"Kage Malvagio," she tells me as she glances back at him. "Cruel, heartless motherfucker who takes no mercy on anyone. Rumor has it he killed his own parents."

Okay, *that* sounds a little extreme. "How do you know him?"

Hesitating for a second, she trains her expression and waves it off. "I've just heard things. Come on. You were right. It's time to go home."

With a grip on my wrist, she drags me with her and heads for the exit.

And me? I can feel his gaze lingering on me the whole way out of the club.

CHAPTER 2

KAGE

I'VE ALWAYS PRIDED MYSELF ON BEING A MAN IN control.

One that's confident.

One that doesn't panic.

One that smiles in the face of chaos.

It's something I've needed since I was a kid. The way I coped with loss and dealt with the pressures of what I knew my future would hold. Being in charge is not just a preference, it's fucking vital.

So, you can imagine my dismay as I pace in the basement of The Pulse—my phone pressed firmly to my ear as I listen to my underboss, Beniamino, update me on Silas Kingston's condition.

"It's not looking good, Boss," he says gravely. "The doctor doesn't think he has more than a couple of days."

Fuck. I pull my phone away from my ear as I grip it tight enough to crack the case. "What about the treatment they were going to try?"

"It's scheduled for tomorrow, but they're not as hopeful about it as before."

Leaning with an arm on the wall, my fingers tap on the concrete one at a time, back and forth. It's a technique I learned a long time ago, one of the only things to calm me down when my anger threatens to take over. Acting out of rage only ever leads to mistakes, and in my world, mistakes get you killed.

"And what about Dalton?"

He must step into an empty room because the background noise fades. "We've had intel that he's been hanging around Mari Vanna increasingly within the last week."

Of course, he has. Mari Vanna is the main headquarters for the Bratva scum. There's only one reason he would be there, and it's no secret as to what that is.

His loyalties don't lie with us.

"All right," I murmur with a newfound determination. "Call Mauricio and tell him to put a rush on that paperwork. I don't care how much it's going to cost or what he wants in return. It needs to be his number one priority. I want them written up, signed, and notarized before he takes so much as a nap."

"Yes, sir," Beni responds.

Without saying another word, I hang up and slip the phone into my pocket.

The rapid decline of Silas's health has not only been an unexpected shock, but one that threatens to destroy the empire my father worked so hard to build. Dalton Forbes, the piece of shit that Silas's only daughter was all but forced into marrying after she wound up pregnant at sixteen years old, is days away from inheriting damn near half of the city, and we can't let that happen.

A couple months ago, it was brought to my attention that Dalton was spotted hanging around a few of the local *Bratva* haunts. Now, usually I wouldn't give a damn what any of that scum does with their shady business. The Italians have run this city for decades. But when Silas's health started to take a turn for the worst, I knew.

Nothing with Dalton is ever a matter of happenstance.

Slipping my phone back into my pocket, I focus my anger on more pressing matters and push through the door. The room is small, with soundproof walls and a metal chair cemented to the middle of the floor. The man tied to it has his head down, but I can see the blood dripping from his nose. Glancing over at Nico, he's scrolling through his phone without a care in the world.

"Mancini," I growl.

He looks up at me and smirks. "What? He's a mouthy motherfucker."

The guy lifts his head, spitting on the floor. "Fuck you, prick."

Nico makes a move toward him again, but I raise my hand, stopping him in his tracks. He exhales slowly and takes a step back. I let my eyes graze over the man. His clothes that were in perfect condition last night are now stained a deep red. Sweat forms on his forehead and drips down his face.

He's scared.

He should be.

"What's your name?" I ask him.

He snarls. "Fuck you, too."

The corners of my mouth raise. I reach over and grab his wallet off the table, inspecting his license.

Brad Palmer.

Twenty-two years old.

And judging by the college ID behind it, he's a student at Columbia University.

"You know, *Brad*, I don't think I've ever met a Sagittarius I actually like," I tell him as I pocket his license and toss the wallet back down on the table. "That remains true."

He tilts his head back and narrows his eyes on me. "What do you want?"

"Tell me who you were with last night."

A dark laugh emits from the back of his throat. "No way, asshole. That untouched territory is *mine*."

"Is that right?" I crack my neck by turning it side to side, noticing the way his words grabbed Nico's attention.

Before he has a chance to answer, my fist collides with his face, sending blood and one of his teeth flying across the room. It takes him a few moments to recover as I go back to leaning against the table. Nico chuckles quietly as he scrolls through his phone.

Brad groans and stretches his jaw out. "You piece of shit! Just wait until I'm out of this fucking chair."

Aw. He thinks he's going free. How adorably naive.

"I'm going to try again," I tell him, reaching over and grabbing a pair of pliers. "The girl's name."

"Nessa."

Now he's just playing games. "Wrong answer."

With a nod toward Nico, he moves to stand behind him. He grips Brad's head and jaw, forcing his mouth open while I take the pliers and pull out his front tooth. Brad screams in pain and thrashes around as I yank it from his mouth. When I'm done, I wipe the blood off the tool, using his shirt.

"You're asking questions you already know the fucking answers to," he roars.

Good. He's catching on. "Tell me her name."

"Saxon." The name comes out with a lisp from the new gap in his mouth. "Saxon Forbes."

"How do you know her?"

He hesitates, but as Nico goes to grab him again, he sings like a bird. "She's my girlfriend."

Another lie.

I flip open my lighter, holding it to his face. He tries to turn away from it, but he can only go so far.

"Try again," I order as the flame licks at his skin.

He winces from the pain. "Fuck, okay! We had a class together. My frat has a bet going on how long it'll take me to sleep with her."

Pulling the lighter away, I flick it closed. Brad sighs in relief, but that feeling is quickly ripped from him as I backhand him with a closed fist. I grip him by the hair and pull his head back, forcing him to look at me.

"You think it's okay to drug women to get what you want?"

His eyes widen as he realizes why he's here.

Why he was ripped away and thrown into the basement by three of my men.

Why I want nothing more than to paint this room with his blood.

"I-I wasn't going to—"

His words are cut off as I toss the lighter behind me and wrap my hand around his throat. "Lie to me again, you piece of shit, and I'll cut off your dick and make you choke on it."

Complete terror fills his expression for the first time since I walked in the room. The same terror that courses through me when I think about what would've happened if I wasn't there last night—if my men hadn't intercepted the drink before it got to her. If I wasn't so fucking drawn to her after nearly colliding with her in the hospital that I followed her to the club.

I may be a mystery to Saxon—something I don't intend on changing—but I've known her for years, after she swept into her grandfather's house unannounced. I stayed out of view, yet was unable to take my eyes off her. But Silas was right when he said my world isn't one she belongs in, and I won't be responsible for ruining her.

Neither will Brad.

"You want Saxon?" he asks urgently as I lighten my grip on his neck. "You can have her."

That makes me laugh.

Look at this fucker, giving her away like he has any right to.

"I'm serious. No pussy is worth dying over." He's resorted to begging. "Just let me go and she's yours. I'll make sure of it."

"Well now you're just making promises you can't keep."

I lick my lips and smirk as I pull the switchblade from my pocket. Brad starts to shake his head rapidly the moment he sees it, but there's nothing he can do to change his fate now.

"You don't have to do this," he pleads. "You can just let me go. I won't say a word to anyone, I swear."

I hum, and my mouth forms into a sick and twisted grin. "Shame. I liked you better when you were an arrogant prick."

Just like that, my resistance snaps, and I plunge the knife into his abdomen. Brad screams as I pull it out, only to do it over and over again.

Once for making the bet.

Once for slipping a drug into her drink.

Once for thinking he deserves to even breathe the same air as her.

Blood splatters against my suit, staining the white shirt underneath, but I don't relent. Not until he's hunched over, the only thing holding him upright is being tied to the chair. When he's just as lifeless as he was evil.

Only then do I stop.

I stand up straight and toss the knife onto the table before walking out the door. Nico follows behind me as we make our way up the stairs, the two men guarding the door waiting for my instruction.

"Go clean that up. Burn the trash and pour the ashes in the sewer."

They both nod and immediately go to do as they're told, while Nico and I leave through the back. He glances over at me and cocks a brow.

"Spit it out," I tell him.

He smirks. "She's still a virgin."

I press my lips into a line and swallow harshly. "On second thought, keep your mouth shut or I'll turn your insides into minced meat, too."

Chapter 3

Saxon

I pull my sunglasses over my face in an attempt to shield myself from the sun, but it's no use. The pain that shoots through my head is unforgiving. That, paired with the utter exhaustion from not getting enough sleep last night, is a cocktail for misery.

"Never again will I go out on a school night, my birthday or not," I tell Nessa as she leans against me.

She grunts. "I might fight you on that later, but right now, my hangover very much agrees with you."

"Saxon," someone yells.

We stop and turn around to see Grady and Logan, two guys from Brad's frat, jogging toward us. My brows furrow as I glance at Nessa, but she looks just as lost as I am.

"Hey, have you—"

"Shh!" Ness and I shush him in unison.

I press two fingers to my temple. "Lower your voice, Grady."

He chuckles and drops the volume a few levels. "Sorry. Have you heard from Brad today?"

"Not that I know of." I pull my phone from my pocket, but the only notification I have is a text from my mom. "No. Why?"

Grady and Logan share a frustrated look. "He didn't come home last night, and his phone is off. We have a group project due tomorrow morning and he hasn't given us his part."

"Sounds like him," I joke. "But I haven't seen him since he disappeared on me last night at The Pulse, but if I hear from him I'll tell him to call you."

Grady nods. "Okay. Thanks, Sax."

The two of them walk away, discussing where else they should check for Brad, while Nessa gives me a look.

"You don't seem all that concerned," she notes.

I shrug. "Why would I be? It's Brad. He probably found some girl last night who was willing to spread her legs. He'll show back up when he gets bored of her."

She seems lost in thought for a moment but then shakes herself out of it. "Yeah. Yeah no, I'm sure you're right."

"Aren't I always?" I tease. "Now, come on. We have to suffer through three lectures."

Throwing her head back, she whines. "Do I have to?"

"If I have to, so do you. Last night was *your* idea."

"Ugh. You're the worst," she groans, but she follows me anyway.

THE DAY DRAGS, MAKING me wish I had stayed home to sleep instead of even attempting to go to school. But finally, my last class lets out, and I muster all the energy I can manage to hail a taxi. I get in, tell him my address, and then rest my head against the window, watching as the city passes me by.

As we drive by The Pulse, my mind wanders to last night. More specifically, the man from last night.

Who is he?

Why was he watching me?

And most importantly, how does Nessa know who he is?

Seeing him at the hospital and then again at the club could have been a coincidence. For all I know, he might have been staring at me because I nearly barreled into him. I would have if it wasn't for Ness paying more attention than I was. But it felt like something else.

Like he was watching me with a purpose.

It should've made me uncomfortable. He looked so intimidating, like he could burn me alive with just his stare. But I don't think I've ever felt more protected and safe. Despite Nessa's warning, I wanted to stay. To keep breathing the same air as him. To spend the rest of the night basking in his attention.

"Miss?" the driver asks, pulling me from my thoughts. "We're here."

I look out to see we're parked in front of my building. Pulling more than enough money out of my wallet, I hand it to him. "Thank you."

"Have a good one, ma'am."

"You, too."

With my books securely in my arms, I get out of the cab and head inside. The doorman, Levi, opens the door for me with a smile—the same way he has since I was younger.

"Miss Forbes," he greets me. "How are you today?"

"Tired. And you?"

He radiates a comforting warmth. "I'm just fine. Do you need help carrying those books up?"

I shake my head. "I think I've got it. Thanks, Levi."

"It's my pleasure."

As the elevator opens to our penthouse, I can already hear my mom's sniffles echoing from the kitchen. My heart hurts for her. The pain of knowing I'm going to be losing my grandfather is hard, so I can't even imagine if it were my dad. And yet, she's trying so hard to stay strong for Kylie and me.

I place my books and my purse on the coffee table and then go find my mom. As expected, she's sitting on a barstool at the island—her head in her hands and tears streaking down her cheeks. I walk over and wrap my arms around her from behind.

She startles slightly before realizing it's me. "Oh, I'm sorry, honey. I didn't hear you come in."

Watching as she starts wiping her face and pretending she's fine, I grab her wrists and stop her. "Mom, you don't have to do that."

"But I do," she sighs. "I'm your mom. I'm supposed to be strong for you."

"Being strong doesn't mean you're not allowed to be human."

Her lips form into a sad smile. "I know. You're right. It's just hard, and I'm so emotionally drained. I've been trying to get all the funeral arrangements figured out so I don't have to do it while grieving. And of course, your grandfather wants a say in all of it. That man can never let anyone do anything for him, even when it comes to his afterlife. It's just been a lot."

I rub her back and look around the room. "Where's Dad? Shouldn't he be helping you with all of this?"

"Oh, honey," she says with a sigh. "You know how your father is."

But that's the thing. *I don't.* Not the way she does, at least. Ever since I was little, I've always been treated like his little princess. He's always put me first. Done anything I wanted. And until now, I thought he was the same way with Mom. I guess I never looked close enough to realize I was wrong.

I press a kiss to the top of my mom's head and step back. "Let me get changed and I'll go with you to the hospital."

"I'm sure Grandpa will love that," she replies, but I can see the relief in her eyes.

ARRIVING AT THE HOSPITAL, I can already feel my heart rate spiking. I honestly don't feel like there will ever be a time where I don't get anxious at this place. As a distraction, I take my phone out of my pocket and realize I have a couple text messages from Grady and one from Nessa, both telling me the same thing—Brad is still yet to be found.

"You go ahead," I tell my mom. "I'll meet you up there."

She nods and disappears into the hospital while I let out a deep exhale and dial Brad's number. I swear, if I have to listen to pornographic moans, someone is going to pay.

But it doesn't even ring.

It just goes straight to voicemail.

I wait for the beep and then speak quietly into the phone. "Hey, Brad. Listen, I don't really know where you disappeared to last night, but your friends are worried about you. So, call them when you get this, okay? Thanks."

There. I tried.

Putting my phone away, I take a deep breath and head into the hospital. The security guard checks my license and prints me out a visitor's pass before telling me where to go. I thank him and follow his directions since Nessa was the one who guided me to his room last night.

The elevator feels like it takes forever to get to the sixth floor, stopping at both the third and fifth to let off other visitors. On the fifth, I notice the labor and delivery ward.

People being born on one floor, and others dying on the floor above it. Circle of life.

It's a morbid thought, and one that a therapist would probably want to dig deep into. But that's the beauty of thinking things. As long as you don't say them out loud, it's your little secret.

Making my way down the hallway, the sound of someone sobbing grabs my attention. I turn to the left to see a young woman crying, her head resting on a patient's bed. The man lying in front of her can't be much older than she is. He has a tube down his throat, the ventilator breathing for him. He looks completely lifeless, other than the forced rise and fall of his chest.

A nurse murmurs a quiet apology before stepping outside the room. She smiles kindly at me, but it doesn't reach her eyes. How could it, when you just had to give someone the worst news of their life?

Not wanting to be rude, I continue to make my way toward my grandfather's room, but my mind is still with the woman back there.

What happened?

Is he going to make it?

Who am I kidding? Of course, he isn't. And if he is, it'll be as a vegetable and not as the man she fell in love with in the first place. Regardless of what happens from here, she has lost the love of her life, and that's heartbreaking to me.

Feeling sad for a woman that I don't even know, I go to turn the corner when my body collides with something soft yet firm. I almost fall backward but two hands grip my hips, holding me in place.

Fire courses through me, everything going boiling hot and ice cold all at once as I look up and find the pair of eyes that are becoming increasingly familiar with every time I see them. His fingers rest against my bare skin between where my crop top ends and my sweatpants begin.

His touch is like nothing I've ever felt before.

It's branding me.

Embedding itself into my skin and attaching itself to my nerve endings.

It's everything, and then it's gone.

He releases me and steps back. "Are you all right?"

His voice is deep, yet smooth and silky, and has me practically tripping over myself. "F-fine."

That's apparently all he needs to know before he sidesteps and heads down the hall.

Nessa told me I should stay away from him, and she's probably right. After all, I can't remember a time where she ever gave me bad advice.

And then there's the part of me that needs to know who he is. Where he came from. Why he keeps watching me.

And that's the part that wins, but when I turn back around, he's gone. There's nothing left to remind me he was there but the lingering feeling of his touch and the way my heart pounds beneath my ribcage.

He's just *gone*.

CHAPTER 4

KAGE

IT HAPPENS ON A FRIDAY.

Before I can get everything in order.

Before any of us are mentally prepared.

Before his family has the chance to say goodbye.

Chaos brews as my phone vibrates on the table in front of me. Raffaello's name appearing tells me it can only be about one thing, because he knows not to call me while I'm working. I grab the device and excuse myself from the business meeting, stepping outside to take the call.

"How?" I ask before saying anything else.

The man who has acted as my father over the last couple decades sighs. "Heart attack. His heart was too weak. He never had a chance."

Fuck! I grab the closest thing to me—a small glass vase holding a couple flowers—and crush it in my grip. The glass shards slide across my skin, slicing through my palm without mercy. My jaw locks at the sting and I open my hand, letting the pieces fall to the floor, but the pain is grounding. It gives me something to remind me that I'm alive. That I have a reason to fight.

"Can you meet me at my place in an hour?"

His answer comes without hesitation. "I'm already on my way there."

"Good. Call Mauricio and have him there, too."

Hanging up, I make a pitstop at my office to grab my briefcase and head down to the lobby. My driver, Killian, waits out front, always ready to go at a moment's notice. As he spots me, he opens the door.

"Early day today, sir?"

I huff exasperatedly. "You could call it that. I need to get back to my place as fast as possible."

He nods once. "Yes, sir. I'll have the pilot ready and waiting."

As he shuts the door and makes his way to the driver's seat, I'm typing an email to the executives at my company, letting them know that I will be out of the office for the foreseeable future. They won't be happy about it, but they don't get a say in the matter.

That's one of the perks of being the boss.

BY THE TIME THE helicopter lands at my house, a

large, castle-like structure in the Hamptons, everyone is already there. The cars that fill my driveway tell me that everyone is inside and most likely panicking.

Silas passing before we had a chance to transfer all the properties over to me was not part of our plan, but I can guarantee it was part of Dalton's.

He needed it.

He relied on it.

He made it happen.

What kind of scumbag kills his wife's father? Not to mention his children's grandfather. Dalton fucking Forbes, that's who. The same piece of shit who preyed on someone who was, for all intents and purposes, a child. At sixteen years old, Scarlett couldn't even drive a car, but he deemed her old enough to bear his spawn.

There's nothing anyone can say that will convince me this wasn't his doing. Not with everything I know. I've had surveillance on him for months now, and everything points to him. I just wish I was fast enough to get ahead of his plan. Instead, I have to do damage control, because we're not going down without a fight.

I straighten the sleeves on my suit and climb out of the helicopter. With all the confidence in the world, I walk across the yard and into my house. The commotion is loud: Men blaming each other for this, like we had any hand in it. Capos and *soldati* from all of our territories fill the room. Some look scared while others are just angry.

Shutting the door harder than necessary, they all go silent when they notice my arrival. Raff sits across the room, and a smirk makes its way to his face. He always has loved the way I can control a room. After all, he's the one who taught me. I just perfected it.

"Stop freaking out like a bunch of bitches with late periods," I demand.

Beni, who has been leaning against the island with the

same calmness that made me choose him as my underboss, chuckles and shakes his head. Meanwhile, everyone is completely silent.

Everyone but Enzo.

"Boss, with all due respect, this means we've lost ownership of all our New York properties, along with some in other territories."

Just what I need right now—a know-it-all who states the obvious. "You're wrong. This is a blow, yes, but it's not nearly the end. I will have a plan in place and executed by the end of the week."

Some people relax at my words while others seem just as tense. But I'm not responsible for coddling them like their fucking mother.

Just when I think things have calmed down, Nico speaks. "What about Plan S?"

My whole body goes tense. "What about it?"

"It's strong and bold. We should start with that to set an example that we aren't to be messed with."

No. Absolutely not. "Plan S is not on the table."

"Why the hell not?" he barks. "You know damn well it's the best option we have."

My eyes narrow on him. "Shut your fucking mouth, Mancini. No one will be making a call like that except me, and I said it is *not* on the table. And if this becomes another instance where you go rogue, I will personally make sure it's the last thing you do."

Everyone glances between the two of us, but no one dares to speak up or take his side. My decision is firm, and it is final. After a moment, he backs down and looks away.

"Now that that's settled and before anything else, we need to pay our respects to the man we lost today."

With a nod at Romano and Cesari, they disappear into the other room to get things ready while I make my way over to Raffaello.

"Raff," I greet him.

He smiles warmly at me and shakes my hand. "My boy."

Raffaello Mancini is the only man—other than Silas Kingston—that I hold the utmost respect for. It's the only reason I haven't riddled his son's head with bullets yet, though I've come very close. Nico just never knows when to shut his mouth. He thinks that because we were raised in the same household that we have the bond of brothers, and that it gives him permission to do things others wouldn't.

It doesn't, and I'm not afraid to prove that.

"How are you doing?"

Raff was my father's best friend, along with Silas. The three of them spent the earlier decades ruling the city with an iron fist, with Silas handling the business aspect and Raff and Armani handling, well, everything else. Silas was a silent partner. Keeping everything in his name gave them an advantage on their enemies. For the longest time, no one that wasn't a part of the *Familia* knew what cards we held. And that made them untouchable. That is, until the death of my father. It shook the whole dynamic of the Familia and changed the course of my life.

"Everything is ready, Boss," Cesari tells me.

We all make our way into the dining room. The table is lined with shots of Cognac, and in the middle is a framed picture of Silas and my father from the eighties. They're sitting at a bar with their arms around each other and broad smiles on their faces.

I take a shot in my hand and raise it up, waiting for everyone to follow. "To Silas. May him and my old man be reunited in peace."

"To Silas," everyone says in unison, and we take our shots.

Setting the glass down, I turn around and walk toward my office. I don't need to glance behind me to know that

Raff, Beni, and Mauricio are trailing behind. As soon as we all step inside, they close the door behind us.

"How far did you get with the paperwork before he passed?" I ask my lawyer.

Mauricio pulls a stack of papers out of his briefcase. "Not far enough, but once you sign these, you'll gain ownership of a few properties. The Pulse, your penthouse, and a nail salon on 33rd street."

"The fuck am I going to do with a nail salon?"

Raff smiles. "That was one of the first businesses your father laundered money through. Silas saw it as sentimental, I'm sure."

"Fantastic," I scoff and sign my name on the line.

Once I'm done, I put the pen down on top and let Mauricio do his thing. He labels a few things and slips them back into his briefcase. Meanwhile, Beni chimes in.

"So, where exactly do we go from here? Should we go in hot and attack or try something on the more subtle side?"

"Well, Dalton won't be stupid enough to just rip everything out from under us," Raff answers. "He knows it would get him killed."

"Something I've already been considering," I say, and Raff gives me a look. "What? It's not like the piece of shit deserves to be alive."

Mauricio crosses his arms over his chest. "Well, he couldn't do that anyway. Everything will have to go through probate. I've seen the will, and it's pretty cut and dry. At the time it was drawn up, he left everything to his wife, but since she predeceased him, it will all go to his daughter, Scarlett. However, there was also a clause that if Scarlett was married at the time of his passing, it all goes to him."

"He assumed any man she married would become family," Raff acknowledges. "And Dalton played the role well until Silas became sick."

He's right. Dalton never played a very strong role in our

world, but he never went against us either. He was there when we needed something from him and never showed signs of being a traitor, but I could always tell he hated me since the day I took my place as the Don.

As soon as Silas became sick, everything from Dalton went radio silent. We became unable to reach him, and only a few weeks later, he was spotted with a few members of the Bratva. It didn't take long to piece everything together—this was a plan long in the making.

"So, how long would you think we have before he takes ownership?" I question.

"In normal circumstances, I would say anywhere from six months to a year, but these are not normal circumstances," he answers. "Dalton has probably already started filing the necessary paperwork, and with money on his side, I'd say six months is a stretch."

Fuck me. "Well, part of his plan was to give us barely any time to react. Let's show him and the Bratva scum that it doesn't matter if we were given six years or six minutes. The Familia is not to be underestimated, and we will give up control of nothing."

SCREAMS OF AGONY FILL the room, ricocheting off

the walls but being drowned out by the noise above us. One of the best parts of doing business underneath a nightclub is that when the place *does* have people present, they're also accompanied by music that tends to be deafeningly loud. The second you're down here, all hope is lost.

"I'm going to ask you again," I tell the Bratva prick we snatched off the street. "What are they planning?"

Instead of answering, he gathers the blood pooling in his mouth and spits it at my feet. I can feel the rage building inside of me as it hits my shoe.

Beni hums. "Bad fucking move, my man."

"Screw you," he sneers.

I've had enough of his shit. "Lay him down."

With Beni on one side and Nico on the other, they lift him up and throw him to the ground, pinning him by his hands. I grab the metal bucket containing two rats. He watches with wide eyes as I come closer and cut his shirt open with my knife.

"Have you ever wondered what it would feel like for rats to eat their way through you? For them to be so desperate to escape that they will chew through your skin and your organs if it means finding a way out?" I flip the bucket upside down and hold it firmly as I heat the top with a blow torch. "You're about to find out if you don't tell me what I want to know."

He thrashes around as the two rats begin to eat through his flesh. When the pain becomes too much, he turns his head to the side and vomits, earning a kick in the face from Nico for nearly getting it on him. I turn off the blow torch and grab him by the chin.

"Last chance before I give them the dinner of a lifetime."

A menacing smile stretches across his face, his teeth covered in blood, and he laughs. "Your days are numbered, Malvagio. It's only a matter of time now before the Italians no longer rule the city. You and all your men will be no more, just like your weak prick of a father."

My restraint snaps, and I knock the bucket to the side. The rats run free as I dig my knee into his new wound and my fist slams into his face. Swing after swing, my hands become covered in blood, and when I've had enough, I wrap my fingers around his throat. With every second, I watch as the life leaves his eyes, and his pulse stills beneath my touch.

"Give me the branding iron," I order Nico.

He walks over to the table and holds it out to me. Heating it with the blow torch, I take it and press it into the piece of shit's stomach, leaving the initials K.M. burnt into his flesh. I want them to know *exactly* who did this.

"Dump the body behind Mari Vanna," I instruct Beni. "Make sure they find it before some unsuspecting soul does."

"I'm on it," he replies.

I wipe my hands clean on a towel and leave the room with Nico behind me. I can feel his eyes on my back, judging my methods and having his doubts. Hell, I can't blame him. It's been three weeks since Silas passed, and we're not even an inch closer to stopping Dalton and the Bratva.

I'm frustrated.

On edge.

Losing sleep.

I've killed a total of four men just this week, and it's done nothing. We've gotten no answers. There's been no retaliation. Not even the simplest acknowledgment of the lives we've taken from them. Which can only mean one thing.

Their plan is more important to them and more lethal to us than we assumed.

"Mal," he says, shortening my last name, and I stop in place. He comes up next to me and places his hand on my shoulder. "I know it's the last thing you want to hear right now. Trust me, I get it. But it's time for Plan S. We have to get ahead of this before it's too late."

My blood boils as I shove him off me. I storm up the

stairs and out the back door, getting in the car and throwing my phone across the back seat. It lights up on the floor, with the screen cracked down the middle, and as I stare at the picture of my father and me from when I was younger, I know he's right.

And that fucking sucks.

THE WHISKEY SWIRLS AROUND in the cup as I sit at my desk. It's well past three in the morning but my mind is wide awake. The knowledge of the call I have to make sits heavy on my chest, making it hard to breathe.

I wanted to leave her out of this, not only for me but for Silas. If he knew what I'm about to do, he'd kill me himself—his relationship with my father be damned. He was right when he told me there is no part of her that belongs in this world.

She's too innocent.

Too perfect.

Too good to be tainted by all of this.

And yet I have no choice but to drag her into it—kicking and screaming, I'm sure.

There used to be a time when I would imagine another life for myself. One where I wasn't the leader of one of the most powerful organizations in the world. One where a family was in the cards for me. One where she wasn't the most forbidden thing in my life.

I used to close my eyes and live in that false reality for as long as I could. But it was exactly that.

A daydream.

An imagination.

An impossible outcome for how my life will go.

And after I do this, I'm only sealing that fate. But as much as it pains me to admit, Nico was right. This is our only option at this point. I will not lose everything my father worked so hard to achieve.

I grab my phone and down the rest of the glass as I dial the number. It rings three times before a voice comes through the other side. Sleep laces Beni's tone as I pull him out of a peaceful slumber.

"Boss?" he asks.

Closing my eyes, I utter the words and kick into action a plan I'd hoped would always be theoretical. "Execute Plan S. Let me know when it's done."

Chapter 5

Saxon

I RUN MY FINGERS THROUGH MY LONG, BLACK HAIR as we make our way through campus. Nessa keeps her eyes focused down at her phone, pouting because she doesn't want to go to class. That's always been our friendship, though. I'm more of the responsible type, while Ness thinks life is a party and we shouldn't take anything too seriously.

"You're typing a novel," I point out.

She presses send and smiles as she slips the phone back into her pocket. "Not everything can be said in a few words, Sax."

"Fair enough. So, who is it this time? Jamie?"

Scrunching her nose, she shakes her head. "No. Jamie was simply to make the other one jealous."

Of course. "And did it work?"

A wide grin stretches across her face. "You bet your ass it did."

I roll my eyes but can't help the chuckle that bubbles out. Ness is a little much sometimes, but all I ever want is to see her happy. And apparently, this guy does that for her. I could probably judge her methods of using poor Jamie, because he seemed into her, but I don't think he's all that heartbroken over it.

"When do I get to meet this new *love of your life?*" I question. "Isn't that the next step? Introduce him to the best friend?"

She bites her lip, but as she goes to answer, someone interrupts.

"Miss Forbes?"

Nessa and I turn to find two detectives standing no more than ten feet away. They're dressed in suits, with their badges on their belts and sunglasses covering their eyes. Ness grabs my arm as if they're about to take me away, and my brows furrow.

"Yes?"

The one moves his sunglasses to the top of his head and reaches to shake my hand. "Agent Lynden with the FBI. We'd like to have a word with you privately."

I glance back at the building behind me. "I actually have a class."

"Your professor has already excused you and promised to provide you with the notes from today."

Pressing my lips into a line, I have to keep from laughing. "So, you were just asking to be nice when really I have no choice in the matter."

He shakes his head. "You can decline, but I wouldn't recommend it. We just want to ask you a few questions."

It doesn't take a rocket scientist to know what they want to talk to me about. It's been almost a month, and Brad is still missing. I know I could plead the Fifth and refuse to go with them, but that would only make me look guilty. Honestly, I'm surprised it took them this long to approach me, being as I was one of the last people to see him.

"Okay," I agree. "Lead the way."

"Sax," Nessa says warningly. "Shouldn't you call your dad before you're questioned?"

I shrug. "I've done nothing wrong."

"That's what we like to hear," Agent Lynden says.

Taking a step toward him, Nessa reluctantly releases my arm. I hold my head high and keep my composure, despite the part of me that is freaking out at the fact that I'm about to be interrogated. I give him a confident smile and gesture for him to go ahead.

Let's get this over with.

As I follow them towards the main building, I can't help but notice the brightly colored flyers with Brad's picture. I mean, there isn't one tree or pole that isn't covered in them. His fraternity has been looking non-stop. The media is clinging to the story.

Golden Boy goes missing after late night partying.

I really thought he would show up a day or two later with some insane story about a threesome with two of the hottest girls he's ever seen. Or that he got so drunk and woke up in Vegas or something. But his phone never turned back on, and he never showed back up.

"Right this way, Miss Forbes." Agent Lynden directs me into a conference room.

I give him a shy smile. "Saxon is fine."

He nods once. "Saxon. You're a very hard woman to get ahold of."

"I didn't know you were trying to get ahold of me."

"We went to your penthouse a couple of times over the last few weeks," he informs me. "Your father told us you were not interested in speaking to us."

Strange. Why wouldn't he have told me they came by? Unless…He doesn't *actually* think I had something to do with Brad's disappearance, does he? He can't. Can he?

"Well, anything I can do to help find Brad," I reply sweetly.

The three of us sit down at the long table, with me on one side and both of them on the other. Agent Lynden pulls something out of his bag, while the other one grabs a notepad and a pen.

"Do you mind if I record?" Lynden asks.

I shake my head. "Go ahead."

He presses play and the interrogation begins. "So, Miss Forbes. Sorry. *Saxon*. We just want to get your input on the disappearance of your boyfriend, Brad Palmer."

"He wasn't my boyfriend," I correct him. "Brad and I were just friends."

"And how did you meet Brad?"

"We had a philosophy class together last semester. We were paired together on a project."

He nods. "And how was your relationship with Brad?"

I shrug. "It was fine. He was a little more into me than I was into him, but he was never rude or anything like that. I just don't think it was ever going to go where he wanted it."

"So, he never went too far or pushed too hard?"

"No. Never," I answer. "He was respectful of my boundaries. Just a little cringey at times."

Agent Lynden hums. "Can you give me an example of that?"

Leaning back in the chair, I sigh. "Like he used to call me Saxi because it sounded like sexy. Stupid things like that."

"I see." He glances beside him to make sure that the other detective is writing everything down. "And the night he went missing, you two were at The Pulse celebrating your birthday, correct?"

"Yes, though he disappeared halfway through the night."

"And it didn't concern you where he went?"

"Not really," I tell him honestly. "I just assumed he met someone else and went off with them."

"Is that something he would do?"

"He's got the reputation of a God around here. What do you think?"

The quiet detective snorts while Detective Lynden watches me intently. "I think I didn't know him as well as you did."

I cross my arms over my chest. "I didn't know him very well at all."

The corner of his mouth raises, as if he finds me amusing, before he sits up. "Only a few more questions and we'll get you out of here."

Thank fuck.

A FEW QUESTIONS ENDS up taking another hour, and by the time they let me go, class is long since over. Nessa is waiting for me outside, sitting at the bottom of the steps. The second she sees me, she sighs in relief.

"Thank God," she says, wrapping her arms around me. "I can't believe you agreed to talk to them without a lawyer present."

"Why? It's not like I'm a suspect." I run my fingers through my hair but stop when I see the way she's looking at me. "What?"

Ness gives me an uneasy look. "I've heard that there isn't any footage of him ever leaving The Pulse, so they're looking at anyone who was in the club that night."

"As in the cameras weren't working that night?"

She shakes her head. "As in he just never left."

Goosebumps rise across my skin. How is that even possible? It's been weeks. He clearly isn't hiding out in there. Someone would have seen him by now, and what reason would he have for that? I mean, it wouldn't be the most surprising thing if he was doing it for attention, but he would have gotten enough of that by week two. I feel like if he was okay and this was his doing, he would have popped up by now with some insane story about how he was kidnapped and kept alive by drinking his own piss or something just as dramatic.

"We should go there tonight," I tell Ness as we walk to our next classes.

She stops short. "What? Why would we do that?"

"To figure out what happened. Someone had to have seen something."

"If they did, they're probably not talking for a reason," she argues. "Besides, I thought you didn't like Brad."

I roll my eyes. "And neither did you. That's beside the point. I just want to know what happened. Give his friends and family some closure."

Nessa isn't having it as she looks at me like I've lost my mind. "You know how you rely on me to tell you when something is a bad idea?" I nod. "This is one of those times. You talked to the detectives. You did your part. Let them do theirs."

"Oh, come on," I press. "Since when do you shy away from a mystery?"

"Since this one isn't safe." She turns and starts walking again.

I jog to catch up to her. "What do you mean *it's not safe*? How could going back to the club and looking around not be safe?"

"Drop it, Sax."

Drop it? "No. You're being weird." I grab her arm to stop her. "Tell me what's going on."

She looks anywhere but back at me and exhales heavily, then looks me in the eyes. "Just stay away from The Pulse. I've heard he's not the only one to go missing from there."

My eyes widen. "There are others?"

"It's just what I've heard," she answers with a shrug.

And as she takes two steps backwards before turning around and heading to class, I know the topic is no longer up for discussion. Still, that doesn't stop me from wondering what happened. If anything, it only makes me more curious.

More determined.

I'm going to find out what happened to Brad, with or without Nessa's help.

THE DRESS CLINGS TO my body in all the right places, except it's about four inches too short. I tug it down my legs to shield myself from the perverted eyes of the creepers. You know the ones. They're the same guys who would try to say if I didn't want it, I shouldn't have dressed this way. Like my body is up for the taking if I show too much skin.

Bullshit, that's what that is.

If my father knew my location right now, I can practically hear what he'd tell me.

The streets of New York are no place for a lady, Saxon.

He honestly believes that his drivers should escort me everywhere I go. The problem with that being I don't want him knowing my plan for tonight. He would never let me go, and even if I get there before he finds out, he'd drag me out by my hair.

I stare up at the neon sign after walking seven blocks.
The Pulse.

It's a clever name for a club. You know the feeling, when your whole body experiences the pulse of the music. The beat that vibrates the floor. The one you can feel in your chest. You don't just hear the songs, you experience them.

Skipping the line, I walk straight up to the bouncers. "Saxon Forbes."

The bigger one's brows furrow. "Is that supposed to mean something to me, little girl?"

I scoff and straighten up. "It should. My grandfather is Silas Kingston. *Was* Silas Kingston."

It may be a dick move, throwing his name around after he's gone. I never did it while he was alive. I never wanted to make it seem like I was better than anyone else. But desperate times call for desperate measures, and I *need* to get in that club without having to wait in line all night.

The bouncers share a look, and the one puts his hand out for my ID. He looks over it and uses his earpiece to communicate with someone inside. Once he gets the answer he's looking for, he grabs the rope to let me in.

"We're deeply sorry for your loss, Miss Forbes," he says solemnly as he hands me back my license. "Mr. Kingston was a great man."

I smile in response, not because I don't appreciate his words but because I can feel the lump in my throat threatening to build, and crying in the arms of a bouncer is not on my list of aspirations. It's been a few weeks, but I'm still not nearly over the loss that shook my whole world.

The club looks the exact same way it did the last time I was here, but it feels...different.

Colder.

Darker.

Dangerous.

A part of me expects to see Brad sitting in the same VIP area we had for my birthday. Like he's been there and waiting for me this whole time. But instead, it's filled by a group of older gentlemen who watch the dance floor like it's a Broadway musical. Their eyes stay fixated on women half their age with dresses so short they may as well just be wearing a shirt.

No Brad in sight.

I push through the crowd to the bar and lean up against it. When the bartender, a younger guy with spiked brown hair, sees me, he smiles. The drink in his hand gets put in front of another customer, and he makes his way over to me.

"What can I get for you?" he asks.

I press my lips together as I try to think. Every time I've drank, I've had Nessa with me to order them. She knows what I like, so I've never had to worry about it, until now.

"Something sweet and fruity?"

He bites his lip and looks me up and down, clearly flirting. "I've got you."

As he goes to make the drink, I glance around the club once more. There are couches below the VIP tables, outlining the back of the dance floor. They're filled with couples who are far too into each other to be socially appropriate but way too intoxicated to care.

For a moment, I imagine Brad sitting there. Some girl in his lap, her tongue down his throat as he holds her by the waist. Last time I saw him, he was going to buy me a drink. It would make sense if he ended up on one of those couches, only to leave with some drunk girl who wanted in his pants too much to wait until the end of the night. What I can't fathom is the lack of proof that he ever left at all.

"Here you go," the bartender says as he places the drink in front of me, pulling my attention back to him. "Let me know if that's what you had in mind."

It's pink, with a piece of an orange and a flower sticking out of it. The only thing it's missing is a little umbrella and I'd think I'm back in Turks and Caicos on vacation. I pick up the glass and bring it to my lips, taking a generous sip.

It's definitely strong, but Nessa would tell me that's a compliment. A bartender adding more alcohol to your drinks means he likes you. Though, the more than obvious flirting was enough to tell me that.

"It's really good," I tell him honestly.

He grins. "Does that mean I get to know your name?"

Now it's my time to blatantly check him out. My eyes skim the stubble on his face then move down to his shirt, which is tight enough to see how muscular he is underneath. Honestly, if he flexes the muscles in his arms, it may rip the material. When I make my way back to his face, he raises his brows, his question still looming and unanswered.

"No," I finally reply, "but you can tell me where the bathroom is."

He chuckles. "As if that's some kind of special privilege."

I shrug. "I mean, I could go ask someone else."

This is amusing him, the chase. He's attractive, so he's probably used to girls throwing themselves at him. But me? I'm different than what he's accustomed to. And that is enough to keep him interested.

"Down that hallway and on your right," he tells me.

I grab my drink off the bar and smile sweetly at him. "Thank you."

He smirks. "Mm-hm."

Following the directions he told me, I end up at the back of a line of women. They're all on their phones or whining about how long it's taking. Some even discuss going to use the men's room, since there is no line for that. Personally, I'd pass. I've seen co-ed bathrooms. Men can't aim to save their lives, and their bathrooms are usually horrid.

As I'm waiting, a man in a suit walks by. The silver watch on his wrist glistens in the light, and he makes eye contact with no one as he goes further down the hall and turns left. He reminds me of the guy who made me forget all about Brad on my birthday. The one I haven't seen in weeks, since I quite literally ran into him in the hospital.

Kage Malvagio.

It's not him. This man's hair was shorter, and he wasn't as tall, but he might lead me to some answers. It might be a stupid idea. Scratch that. It's *definitely* a stupid idea, but it's all I've got.

I swallow my nerves and step out of line before following him. As I get to the front of the line, a girl grips my arm before I pass.

"Do you have a death wish?"

What? "Why? What's down there?"

She looks like she wants to tell me something, but her friend interrupts. "Come on, Alyssa."

Sighing, she follows her friend. "I'm trying to keep her out of trouble."

"Don't," her friend answers. "Don't get involved."

Alarms are going off in my head. They're red and screaming that I should turn around. But I've come all the way here. I can't leave without at least having a look around.

I have to do this for Brad.

If we hadn't come here for my birthday, maybe he would still be here and not a picture on a neon-yellow poster. I at least owe it to him to try to find out where he went or what happened. I can't just give up on him. Not without trying.

I muster up all the courage I can manage and continue down the hallway. The one that he turned down leads to three more hallways, and being as he's long gone now, I can only guess and take my chances.

The first one leads to a few small, empty offices, making me turn around and try again. I look between the second and third, but something about the second one is calling to me. It's a long hallway with nothing on the walls and turns to the right at the end. It chills me from the inside out, and that's exactly the thing that makes me choose it.

My feet feel like they're in quicksand as my nerves tell me to turn back, but I can't. I won't let myself. I make it to the end of the hallway and turn the corner to find two doors. The first has an exit sign above it. My guess would be it leads to the alley. But the other one is intriguing.

A dark steel door with a keypad next to it.

What could be in there? What is honestly worth putting at the end of some weird hallway and behind a door that looks bulletproof?

Maybe it's a panic room, or this place used to be a bank or something. But it doesn't look like either of those. It looks like something else.

A red light stays lit on the keypad to show that the door is locked, and I start to wonder what the code could be.

1 2 3 4. *Wrong.*

Okay, of course they wouldn't make it that easy. Next, I try the address to the place.

5 7 5 7. *Wrong again.*

Every time I hit a button on the keypad, it makes a noise, and if I don't act fast, someone might catch me. I wrack my brain for what it could be when a thought occurs to me.

This place was owned by my grandfather.

My birthday.

0 3 2 7.

A beep sounds and the light turns green as the sound of a click tells me it's unlocked, but before I can open it, the other door opens and a tall, beefy guy comes in. He looks between me and the keypad.

"What do you think you're doing?"

My mouth opens and closes as my chest feels like it's going to cave in on itself. I should've listened to Nessa. She was right. This was a bad fucking idea.

As a last ditch effort, I blurt out the first thing that comes to mind.

"The bartender sent me to get smaller bills," I lie. "He ran out and it's really busy out there, so he didn't want to leave the bar. I-I think I might be lost though."

He doesn't look like he believes a word that comes out of my mouth, but he also doesn't look like he wants to kill me for sport anymore. He grabs me by the wrist and mutters, "Come with me" as he drags me back toward the club. As we turn the corner, he releases me, but the look in his eyes tells me it's only so onlookers still waiting for the bathroom don't see anything suspicious.

"Enzo," he roars as we get back to the bar.

The bartender looks his way, but when he sees me, he's more intrigued. "What's up, Ces?"

"This little thing claims you sent her to the back to get more small bills," he growls. "That true?"

I give him a pleading look, silently begging for him to cover for me. He watches me for a moment before the corner of his mouth raises and he trains his expression to something more in character.

"Yeah," he replies. "If you or Ro had answered your damn phones, I wouldn't have had to use her. I need singles and fives."

Ces, as the bartender called him, releases me immediately and grumbles under his breath as he heads for the back again —probably getting the small bills he doesn't actually need. I sigh in relief once I'm out of his clutches and take a seat at the bar.

"Thanks for that," I tell him.

He cocks a brow at me. "What happened back there?"

Taking a sip of my drink to buy me some time, I swallow. "Your directions were shit. I got lost."

"Right," he drawls, clearly not believing a word of my story. "But now you have to tell me your name. It's only fair and all, being as I saved your ass."

Okay, fair enough. "Saxon."

His face pales. "As in Saxon Forbes?" I cringe and nod. "Silas's granddaughter, Saxon Forbes?"

"See, this is why I didn't want to tell you," I say, exasperated. "Now it's weird."

He shakes his head. "It's not. I just never would have guessed that."

"Oh yeah? And what would you have guessed?"

Looking me over once more, he shrugs. "An influencer trying to make it in modeling and using the big city to get you there."

An involuntary laugh bubbles out of me. "More like your everyday pre-med student with a billionaire legend for a grandfather."

"Sounds a lot more interesting to me," he muses.

I SPEND A COUPLE hours at the bar, talking to Enzo in between customers. He's funny and knows how to hold a conversation. And if I wasn't the jealous type, I'd probably let him buy me dinner. But there is no part of me that could handle the amount he gets hit on every night by drunk women. I'm way too possessive for that.

I'm on my fifth drink when I finally have enough courage to ask the question that's been on my mind all night. Enzo is just coming back from getting some guy a beer when I catch him off guard.

"So, what's back there, anyway?" I question, trying to sound nonchalant.

His eyes narrow. "Back where?"

"Behind the steel door that only opens when you put in my birthday."

All the color drains from his face, but he plays it off pretty well as he composes himself. "I think you shouldn't worry your pretty little head about it. It's nothing interesting."

"Try me," I press.

He smiles, as if he likes that I challenge him, but he doesn't fall for it. Pushing off the bar, he nods toward the other side of the bar where a customer is waiting, but I open my mouth again to stop him.

"Is that what everyone is so afraid of? And why people keep going missing?"

His eyes meet mine, and while they're almost begging me to stop looking, there is also a warmness in them. "You should go home, Saxon."

No. Not yet. "What if I don't want to?"

But the topic isn't up for discussion as he takes out his phone. "I'll get you an Uber. It's on me."

A part of me wants to hate him for all but kicking me out. Who is he to tell me when I should or shouldn't go home? But at the same time, the room is practically spinning. The drinks he made me were generous on the pour and it's all rushing to my head at once.

"Fine, but I'm coming back tomorrow," I tell him.

He smiles, thankful that I'm agreeing to leave. "I hope you do."

As I turn to leave, my mind wanders to Kage again. The way he leaned against the wall, just watching me like I was the most interesting thing in the world. There was something dark in his stare, but while it looked intimidating, it only intrigued me. I wanted to know more about him. Wanted to hear the thoughts that ran through his mind as he kept his gaze focused solely on me.

While I came here to look for any signs of Brad, I'd be lying if I said I wasn't hoping I'd find Kage right where I left him. That I might get a chance to actually say something to him this time. But as I spare one last glance toward the place he stood I quickly come to terms with the fact that he's not here. Running my fingers through my hair, I make my way out the door.

The cold late-April air kisses my skin and chills me in an instant. I wrap my arms around myself as a car pulls up and rolls the window down.

"Saxon Forbes?" the driver asks.

I nod and open the back door to climb inside. "Thank you for being so fast. It's cold out there."

"Enzo is a good friend," he tells me. "I always put his rides at the top of my list."

"That's sweet of you."

I stare down at my phone as I rattle off my address, only looking up when he hands me a bottle of water. I take it from him cautiously when he answers my unspoken question.

"Have to keep your electrolytes up."

I chuckle, knowing *that* was probably Enzo's doing as well. He seems like the type to look out for everyone, even when he's the one serving the drinks that could make your breath flammable.

I take a sip and continue my scroll through Instagram. I stop on a picture of Nessa, all dolled up and ready. She must have gone out with her new boyfriend tonight. The broad grin on her face makes me smile. She deserves to be happy. I hit like on it and glance up from my phone. As we drive past campus, I realize we're headed in the total opposite direction.

"You're going the wrong way."

The driver looks at me through the rearview mirror, but he doesn't answer. That's when the panic sets in. My chest tightens as I realize I'm in danger. I tug on the door handle, just trying to escape, but it won't budge.

"What are you doing? Let me out!"

Fuck. Fuck. Fuck. This is everything I've been warned about, and I just walked right into it. Great fucking job, Sax. Way to keep your guard up and your safety first.

"Let me out of here!" I scream as I pound on the windows, but it's no use.

Everything around me starts to blur. My head feels like it wants to cave in on itself. I focus on my phone as hard as I can in an attempt to call 911, but before I can dial a single number, the driver reaches back and grabs my phone.

"You won't be needing this," he tells me.

"No," I plead. "Don't."

I don't even have the energy to hold onto it. He gently slips it out of my now-limp hand. My whole body weakens and goes numb as I start to slip into the darkness.

"Don't worry, Miss Forbes. Everything will be okay."

Somehow, I doubt that.

CHAPTER 6

KAGE

I'VE NEVER LIKED THE CONCEPT OF VIDEO CALLING. It's too vulnerable. Not nearly secure enough for the kind of information we speak about. I'd much rather fly out places and have these discussions in person, but situations beyond my control are preventing that from happening at the moment, so this will have to do. At the very least, I had a private server installed in my home office for this very purpose.

Salvatore, my Capo residing in Vegas, and Giovani, my Capo in Chicago, are both sitting in their offices on the other side of the computer screen. Keeping them in the loop has been imperative, being as Silas owned all of our Vegas properties and a few of our Chicago ones. If anything goes down, they need to be prepared.

"I want at least two men at every location at all times," I tell them. "No exceptions. We cannot be caught defenseless."

They both nod agreement, though I expected nothing less. If their territory gets taken over, they'll have me to answer to.

The Bratva will have to rip these companies out from under my cold, dead body.

Two knocks sound against the door before it opens, and Beni appears. He doesn't need to say a word. Just him being here tells me what it's about. I turn my attention back to Sal and Gio.

"Excuse me. I have other business to attend to," I tell them. "Keep me aware and updated of anything and everything that goes on. More than usual. If someone walking by looks suspicious, I want to hear about it."

Before they can answer, I press a button and the screen goes black. I stand from my chair and straighten my suit jacket before walking toward the door. Beni holds it open for me and follows me out.

As we walk across the house, I try to prepare myself for seeing Saxon again. I've done my best to avoid this moment, even choosing to stay unnoticed during her grandfather's funeral. We paid our respects but did it without potentially causing a scene.

The closer we get to the room I've prepared for her to be kept in, the louder it gets. My brows furrow in confusion as I hear her voice clear as day. I wasn't interested in the details of how they were going to take her, just that she was not to be harmed in the process. However, I don't know how they got her out of the city without ringing alarms if she's being this combative.

I glance up at Beni questioningly, and he exhales. "The drugs wore off halfway through the drive. She's been putting up a fight ever since."

I fight off a smile at the thought.. I always knew Saxon was a firecracker. She is Silas's granddaughter, after all. If she didn't try to defend herself, I'd be disappointed. She's not the kind of girl to just lay down and take it. She can't be.

Arriving outside the door, she's shouting obscenities and screaming at the top of her lungs—doing all she can to try to get the attention of someone who could rescue her. Unfortunately for her, there isn't a neighbor around for at least half a mile. No one is going to hear her.

It goes quiet for a brief moment before Carmine yells. He comes out of the room, holding his arm and looking like he's ready to throttle her. When Beni cocks a brow at him, Carmine's expression turns sour.

"The fucking bitch bit me."

I don't hide my amusement and neither does Beni, which only seems to piss Carmine off more, but he'd never dare say anything about it. Instead, he storms off to clean the blood that's dripping down his arm.

She got him pretty good.

Footsteps in the room tell me she's trying to find a way out. I can hear as she opens the closet door as well as feels around on the floor to see if there is some secret hatch. As if we'd put her in a room with an escape that easy.

For a moment, I honestly believe she's not stupid enough to try the door, but when it flies open, I realize I was wrong. My body fills the doorway and as her eyes meet mine, she stumbles back. I take a step into the room, swinging the door shut behind me.

"Kage," she breathes.

Now that's a surprise. "You know my name."

I take another step toward her, and she takes one back, bumping into the dresser. She jumps as if there is someone behind her. I use the few seconds she looks away from me to take in what she's wearing, but the second I do, I wish I hadn't.

Fuck.

Bringing myself back to safer ground, I move again so she focuses all her attention on me. There's rage in her eyes, but it's mixed with something else: a level of fear she refuses to show, but it's looming there in the background —threatening to break her at any given moment.

"What else do you know about me?" I ask.

She swallows harshly. "My best friend said you're bad news."

I bet she did. "Your best friend should mind her fucking business."

"So, she's wrong?" she challenges.

I chuckle darkly. "No. She's spot on."

Walking around the room, I take in every little detail. I chose this one specifically to keep her in due to its location in the house. In order to escape, she would need to run through the entire place to get to an exit, not to mention passing my office. There are cameras all over the house, but this room would give my men the most time to get to her before she makes it out.

A queen-sized bed juts out from one of the walls, and a dresser filled with clothes in her size with a mirror sits beside it. While I'm sure one would expect just a mattress on the floor, I wasn't about to treat her like garbage. She *is* Silas's granddaughter, after all. It's bad enough I've taken her. I'm not going to disgrace him further.

"What am I doing here?" Saxon asks, both scared and curious as I run my finger over the white wood dresser. "What do you want from me?"

That is a loaded question, and one I don't plan on answering in any capacity. She will be here until she serves her purpose. After that, I will vanish from her life like I was never there in the first place—the way it was always intended to be. And what she does then is none of my business.

I turn toward the door and grip the knob. "Let's hope you live to find out."

She shouts for me to wait as I leave the room, but before she can reach me, the door is shut and locked.

"Please, no!" she begs and pulls at the door, but it's not going to budge.

There are three different locks holding it shut, each of

which needs a key on either side to open. The single window is made of bulletproof glass and sealed shut. There is no escaping for her, not without my permission—something she won't get unless her father cooperates.

Carmine stands beside Beni, holding a paper towel to his arm. As amusing as it is that she's been here less than a half hour and she's already injured him, it also shows how weak he is. Carmine wasn't my first choice for a soldier. To be honest, I find him arrogant. While it's useful to play dirty occasionally, he tends to do it all the time, regardless of if you're on his side or not. If he doesn't watch himself, he's going to be staring down the barrel of my gun.

"She is not to leave that room unless it's to shit, piss, or shower," I tell Beni and then turn my attention to Carmine. "He is your boss when it comes to her. You do nothing without his approval. Understood?"

He nods once. "Yes, sir."

I glance at his covered wound once more with a look of disgust before my fist pummels into his face. I feel as his nose breaks against my knuckles. Blood instantly starts pouring out and over his mouth while his hands move to cover his face.

"Next time don't be such a pussy. Weak men have no place in La Familia, and if she were a Bratva, you'd be dead right now. Your guard is never to be down, not even in your fucking sleep."

Leaving Carmine's groans and Saxon's unanswered pleas behind me, I make my way back to my office. I sit down at my desk and turn on the oversized monitor. Immediately, video feeds from all over the house come to life. I can see Beni lecturing an injured Carmine, the chef preparing my dinner, and a few of my men playing poker in the basement. But my attention is only on one.

I watch as Saxon paces back and forth across the room, tugging at her hair and trying and failing to pry the window open. When she realizes her efforts are futile, she collapses onto the floor and curls into a ball. I snap a picture of the screen and send it with a single message.

She's alive...for now.
Meet our demands or that will change.

I CHECK MY WATCH as the car drives through the city. One thing that has always bothered me about this place is the traffic. I'm already fifteen minutes late, and there is nothing I can do about it but sit and wait. I rub my palms against my pants before taking my phone out and requesting an update from Beni.

Saxon has been anything but a cooperative little captive since she arrived late last night. She didn't sleep a wink. Instead, she's spent the last twelve hours screaming until her voice gives out and pounding on the door. Judging by the look on Carmine's face this morning, he was less than amused.

A response from Beni is almost instant.

Beni: Still the same as last night. Girl has got a set of lungs on her.

That she does, and for a split second, my mind wanders to what she would sound like underneath me. If I hiked that skintight dress up over her hips and buried myself inside of her. Would she be just as loud as she's being now, or is she more of the breathy moan type? And if I wrapped my hand around her throat, would her eyes widen in both fear and lust?

"Sir," Killian says, grabbing my attention. "We've arrived."

"Thank fuck," I murmur under my breath.

He climbs out of the car and walks around to open the door for me. As I step out, I straighten my suit and put all thoughts of Saxon out of my mind—exactly where they belong in the first place.

Walking into Eleven Madison Park, a fancy restaurant in New York City that overlooks Madison Square Park, I see Raffaello sitting at a table in the back corner. I nod politely at the hostess as I pass and head straight to Raff.

"Kage," he greets me.

I pull myself out a seat. "Raff. How are you?"

"A little bit older, but none the wiser."

I hum in response. It's the same phrase he's used for years, but there's something different behind it today—something colder in his voice. Not being the type to avoid confrontation, I'm about to ask what's going on when the waitress comes over.

She's a tiny thing, with long blonde hair and a shirt two sizes too small for her disproportionately sized breasts. Her eyes skim down my body, and she pulls her bottom lip between her teeth.

"What can I get you today?" she asks with a flirtatious tone to her voice.

There's no bigger turn off than when a woman throws herself at you. Before, I might have considered taking her in a back room and giving her what she's silently begging for.

Only once and never more. But now, I couldn't be less interested.

"I'll take a bourbon on the rocks," I order.

Mandy, according to her nametag, smirks. "Would you like a twist with that?"

"No. That's okay."

"Are you sure?" she teases. "I can be quite flexible."

I lean back in my seat and place my hands on my thighs. "I'm sure you can. What's that saying? Practice makes perfect."

Raff does well at disguising his amusement, but I do see a hint of a smile on his face as he stares down at the menu. Mandy, however, can't seem to figure out if she was just delivered the complement of a lifetime or a harsh insult.

"I'll have the same, sweetheart," Raff says with a friendly grin.

She nods. "Coming right up."

As she scurries off, Raff gives me a look.

"What?"

He chuckles and shakes his head. "Have you ever gone a day without being an asshole?"

I purse my lips and rub my chin thoughtfully. "I don't think I've ever gone an hour without being an asshole."

"And what about with Saxon?" he questions, making his opinion known by his tone. "Are you being an asshole to her?"

"Ah. So that's what this is about."

I honestly can't say I'm surprised. Raff has watched Saxon grow up. Sometimes from a distance, sometimes while she was with Silas. But he was always willing to hear about the little girl who stole her grandfather's heart right out of his chest. And if it was anyone else who took her, he probably would have had them dead within the hour.

He takes a sip of water. "Do you know what you're doing, boy?"

"Don't I always?" I counter. "And besides, what are you coming at me for? It was your fucking son's idea."

"As far as I'm concerned, you're *both* my sons," he corrects me. "And like you said, you're the one calling the shots."

My jaw clenches as the table goes quiet. What he doesn't know, what no one knows, is that call is one of the hardest I've ever had to make. And goddamn it, having her in my house is no walk in the park either. Knowing she's so fucking close after all these years of keeping my distance—it's intoxicating. I don't think I slept for a single second last night. I laid in bed and recalled every detail of the dress she had on.

The way it clung to her in all the right places.

How if she bent over, I'd get the perfect view of her pussy.

Seeing her nipples harden through the fabric while I was standing in front of her.

It's all I could think about, and it fucking tormented me for hours. I've spent years dreaming of this woman, repeatedly convincing myself that I'm no good for her. That she's too good for my world. And now she's in it anyway, but I still can't have her.

"I trust you, Kage," Raff says, breaking the silence. "All I'm saying is I hope you can stay levelheaded with this."

Levelheaded. Right.

I nod but say nothing else. Raff has never questioned my methods before, but I can respect why he's doing it now. Silas is probably rolling over in his grave. If he was alive to see me take his perfect granddaughter, he would slit my throat himself.

But if he were alive, we wouldn't be in this mess.

"And Kage?" He grabs my attention once more. "She is not a toy. Not for you or anyone else. Silas's granddaughter deserves the same respect we gave him."

"That won't be an issue."

And even my demons laugh at that.

Chapter 7

Saxon

Being alone is nothing new for me. With parents who travel more than they're home, I grew up with a plethora of nannies—all of whom had no issue letting me entertain myself. And yet, I don't think I've ever felt *this* lonely.

Hours feel like days, and I'm stuck in an everlasting limbo. All I can do is sit here in this room, with only my thoughts to keep me company—mainly those of Kage.

Who exactly is he?
Why did he bring me here?
What the fuck does he want from me?

Those are just a few of the things that run through my mind on a constant basis.

When I woke up, still in the backseat of that SUV with my hands tied behind my back and my ankles tied together, I wracked my brain on who could be responsible for this. My first guess was Brad. I thought I was going to end up wherever he ran off to, and he was going to tell me to stop looking for him. But never, out of all the scenarios I imagined, did I consider Kage a possibility. Why would I? I hadn't seen him in weeks.

Seeing him walk into the room was a shock to my system. My attention was completely and undividedly stuck on him, the same way it was the night of my birthday—only this time, the intrigue was mixed with fear.

Fear that Nessa was right.

Fear that his attention is not something I want.

Fear that I won't make it out of here alive.

The locks turn one at a time and then the door opens. A man I've seen but never spoken to comes in holding a plate of food. He's tall, with light brown hair and blue eyes that look so much softer than his demeanor.

"Dinner," he tells me and places the plate on the end of the bed.

It's not the kind of food you'd think a bunch of intimidating men would feed their victim. This stuff looks like it was made by a professional chef. Just the smell of it is mouthwatering, but I refuse to give them what they want.

I look away. "I'm not hungry."

Sighing heavily, he runs a hand through his hair. "You haven't eaten a bite since you got here."

"And?"

"*And* you need to eat."

I scoff and turn to glare at him. "Would you be hungry if you were being held prisoner? If you were ripped away from everything you knew and locked in a room without even being told why?"

He walks to the side of the bed and crouches down, showing me his wrists. Scars tarnish his skin in a full circle, as if he was tied up with barbed wire. The story behind them is probably just as painful as they look, and I'm almost curious enough to ask, but I don't.

"I wasn't," he clarifies. "But I also refused to let them win."

Moving my attention back to the food, I pick up the plate and let myself enjoy the scent for just a moment before I throw the whole thing across the room. Food flies in all directions and the plate shatters against the dresser. Just like that, the whole meal is ruined.

"This *is* me not letting them win."

To my surprise, he drops his head and lets out a breathy laugh. The door opens and Carmine comes in, looking alarmed at the scene in front of him. He scrunches his nose at the mess that now covers half of the bedroom and rolls his eyes.

"Ro, come on," he says. "If she wants to fucking starve, let her."

The name piques my interest, as if I've heard it before, but I can't pinpoint when or where. Ro stands up and pats the bed twice. With a smirk, he follows Carmine out of the room and leaves me with the mess that is bound to stink by morning.

WHEN I WAS LITTLE and I couldn't sleep at night, my mom would tell me to lay there with my eyes closed and imagine I was somewhere else. I remember thinking of places like Disney World or the beach—or my personal favorite, Grandpa's house. So, as I lay here in this personal hell, I imagine I'm anywhere but here.

Playing Barbies with Kylie just to see her smile.

Having a sleepover with Nessa as she talks about falling in love with every guy she meets.

Going out to dinner with Dad on our monthly daddy-daughter date that never seems to stop no matter how old I am.

I wonder if they're holding up okay. I can almost picture my dad, all stressed out as he reports me missing. And poor Nessa. She's probably beating herself up over not coming with me to the club that night.

Tears leak from my closed eyes at the thought of my family. It's not that I ever really took them for granted, but I don't think I hugged them nearly enough. I'd give anything just to wrap my arms around them again. To feel the comfort that they bring once more.

My skin crawls as thoughts of being trapped in here creep in. I've never been one for claustrophobia, but I've also never been locked in a room with no end in sight until now. My breathing becomes labored, and I can't seem to sit still.

I need to get the fuck out of here.

Screaming at the top of my lungs, I jump out of bed and start pounding.

On the walls.

On the door.

On the window.

Anything to get the attention of the men I know are standing right outside that door.

"I can't breathe!" I shout. "I can't breathe! Somebody help me!"

I'm starting to get dizzy when the door opens. My whole body goes ice cold and I freeze in place when a familiar face steps in. If I had anything in my stomach, it would be all over the floor as the need to vomit starts to rise in my throat.

"You," I hiss.

Enzo sighs and lets his shoulders sag. "Saxon."

He goes to take a step toward me, but I hold my hands up. "No! You're a traitor. I fucking trusted you!"

"I know. I'm sorry."

"You're sorry?" I scoff. "You called me a car and let me walk out of that club, knowing this would happen! Knowing they were going to kidnap me! And all you have to say is that you're sorry?"

He looks away and down at the floor, almost like he's ashamed of himself. I glance at the door and notice that it's still open a crack. If I can manage to subdue him, I might be able to make it out of here.

I exhale and act as if I'm calming down. Dropping my head, I walk over to the nightstand and start to sob.

"I just have to get out of here," I tell him. "I'm only twenty-one. I don't want to die."

"Don't," he pleads. "Don't cry. You're too pretty to cry."

I can hear as he starts to step behind me, and the second I feel his touch lightly graze across my lower back, I know it's now or never. I grip the lamp in my hand and swing it around. My intention is to smash it into his head. That would at least knock him dizzy for a moment so I can run, but it's as if it happens in slow motion. I'm so weak from not eating that he has more than enough time to catch the lamp before it hits him.

Shit.

A darkness I haven't seen before fills his blue eyes. His hand tightens around the lamp, and he throws it into the corner, pieces flying as it shatters against the wall. He takes a step closer to get in my face and grips my hair, pulling my head back.

"Try that again and I promise it'll be the last thing you do," he threatens.

Oh, how I wish that were true. "Fuck you. I'd *rather* you kill me."

I clench my fist, and with all the energy I have, I swing

directly into the side of his face. He releases me instantly and pushes me onto the bed while he stretches out his jaw. I roll to the other side and run toward the door, but Enzo is faster. He slams it shut and towers over me, his whole body shaking as he tries to resist giving me a taste of my own medicine.

"Sit back down, Saxon," he orders.

"Screw you."

He chuckles darkly and shakes his head. "Don't you get it? This isn't about *you*. You're going to get yourself killed if you keep pulling this shit."

My brows furrow. "What do you mean this isn't about me?"

"It's your father we're after," he admits. "He has something we need, and you're the leverage we're using to get it. So, if you'd just calm the hell down and do as you're told, you might make it out of here alive."

Everything to just come out of his mouth was a total mindfuck. There is so much to pick apart in that statement, but there is one word that stands out and makes my stomach churn.

"M-might?" I croak.

Enzo pinches the bridge of his nose and groans. "You will," he corrects, but it's too late.

"You said *might*. I *might* make it out of here alive."

I take a step back, avoiding his touch as he reaches toward me. Everything runs through my mind a mile a minute. The room is spinning as the backs of my legs hit the footboard and I nearly fall over.

What am I going through all this for if I'm just going to die anyway?

Why deal with all this torture and misery only to lose in the end?

What's the point?

Tugging on my hair, my jaw clenches and my blood runs hot. They say when you're faced with danger, you go into fight or flight, and being as flight isn't an option I was given…

I grab the small nightstand next to my bed and throw it at Enzo with all my might. His eyes widen as he dodges it, and I watch as it hits the mirror. The sound of a crash fills the room as shards of glass scatter amongst the floor. Enzo watches as I notice one, and before he can get to me, I grab it and hold it to my neck. His body halts immediately.

"Let me out of here, or I swear to God, I'll kill myself," I threaten.

He puts his hands up—whether in surrender or defense, I'm not sure. "You don't want to do that."

"The fuck I don't," I counter. "I'm going to die here anyway. May as well be on my own terms."

"Saxon," he pleads, but before he can say another word, the door opens again and Kage steps in.

I haven't seen him since the night I was dumped in here, and yet my body still reacts to his. He has a way of calming me and exciting me all at the same time. His whole demeanor radiates violence and danger, and yet the confidence he maintains is gripping. I find my breath catching at the mere sight of him.

"Out," he demands.

Enzo keeps his worrisome gaze on me as he backs out of the room, leaving Kage and me alone. He looks to the sliver of glass in my hand and glares at it, as if the risk it poses to me is personal to him.

He moves to take a step closer, but I press the shard against my skin.

"Don't, or I'll slit my wrist right now," I tell him firmly.

Kage moves his gaze to my eyes but stays in place. "Put it down, Forbes."

"Let me out of here."

He shakes his head. "I can't do that."

Without hesitation, I press the shard against my forearm

and quickly drag it down, the adrenaline pumping through my veins masking the pain. It's a warning shot, but his attention moves to the blood that trickles down over my hand.

"Try again," I order.

His jaw ticks, but he doesn't answer. I move the glass closer to the center. Closer to the spot that with one deep cut would have me bleeding out in minutes. I slice another gash into my skin, keeping my eyes locked on Kage.

A sort of peace sets over me as I come to terms with the fact that dying is my only way out of here. That the only way to end this torment is to end myself. It's clear now that the plan never involved me making it out alive, but they can't use me if I'm dead.

I'll be back with Grandpa.

I close my eyes and tilt my head back as I move the shard to the right place, but just as I go to cut, I'm shoved backward. As I'm pressed against the wall, Kage's knee presses high between my thighs and his one hand grips mine while the other is on the wall beside my head. A subtle moan vibrates in my throat, and I need to resist the urge to grind against him.

There's a fire in his gaze I've never seen before. It's intimidating and beautiful at the same time. My heart pounds against my ribcage as I breathe in his cologne—a strong tobacco scent with vanilla undertones. He keeps his stare locked with mine as he lifts my hand with the glass and moves it to his neck.

"I've spent my whole life around blood, princess," he tells me, dragging the shard over his skin and cutting the right side of his neck. "You don't scare me."

I watch as his blood flows from the cut and disappears beneath his suit, but not before staining the white collar of his shirt. Swallowing harshly, I move my gaze to his eyes to find his pupils blown wide. As I'm lost in the trance that is

Kage Malvagio, he moves again, this time shoving a needle into my arm. As he pushes down the plunger, I immediately go weak. Everything becomes blurry, and I'm having an issue keeping my eyes open. What little strength I had is gone. The glass falls from my grip, and I start to fall forward. Kage scoops me up in his arms and whispers something I can't understand as everything around me goes black and I slip into the darkness.

I was almost free.

CHAPTER 8

KAGE

I AM NOT A SENSITIVE PERSON.

I never have been.

In the last twenty-four years, I haven't felt a single ounce of remorse for anything I've done. All the men I've killed. All the torture I've inflicted. It's been without guilt every time. I saw a therapist once, thinking maybe I was a sociopath. She was a very smart young woman, with more than enough credentials to diagnose me, and while I'm sure she thought I was batshit crazy, she said that being able to feel the loss of my father ruled it out.

Still, I'm known as an emotional black hole. So, explain to me why I'm pacing back and forth outside of Saxon's bedroom, digging my nails into my palms as I wait for the doctor to finish with her.

The sight of blood is something I'm used to. I've literally grown up around death and destruction. I've stood in the shower and watched as the water washed the aftermath of my father's murder from my body. But the sight of her blood? That's something I never want to see again. Not like that.

I lift my head and square my shoulders as Dr. Ferro steps out. He's an older man in his late fifties that we've held on retainer for years. One of the best in the country and takes discretion seriously.

"The cuts weren't fatal, but they were deep," he tells me. "I've stitched them up and given her fluids, as well as put in the feeding tube you requested."

"Thank you, Antonio."

He nods once. "She's in very bad shape, Mr. Malvagio. I agree with you that sedation is necessary at this point, but please remember that it cannot be for long. Muscular atrophy will become a problem if you keep her in bed for too long."

"I understand," I reply.

The last thing I plan on doing is discussing anything more than Saxon's medical condition with him, and I think he knows that as he ends the conversation there.

"Have someone give her more fluids in a few hours, and I'll be back tomorrow to monitor her and administer more medication."

"Will do. Goodnight, Doc."

"Goodnight, sir."

As he leaves, I find myself leaning against the doorway, just watching as Saxon sleeps. Her skin is pale, almost blending with the white gauze wrapped around her forearm. I knew she was refusing to eat, but I had no idea it was this severe. She must've lost fifteen pounds since she got here. And for someone that started at a hundred pounds soaking wet, that's a problem.

Her black hair is splayed across the pillow, lacking the liveliness it once held. Even as she sleeps, I can see the bags under her eyes and the hollows of her cheeks. She just barely resembles the woman I watched in the club that night. The one who held my intense gaze with just as much confidence as I'd expect from her.

My jaw twitches at the voice inside, telling me I caused this, but I don't let it stay for long. I shut the door behind me and lock it, just in case, before heading to my office. As I step inside, however, I groan when I find Nico sitting with Beni.

"How's the drama queen?" he asks.

I ignore him and focus on Beni. "She needs her fluids checked regularly. I want you to do it. Don't pass it off on someone else. I don't trust them enough to do it."

He nods dutifully. "You've got it."

"I'm just a little surprised she tried to kill herself already," Nico chimes in again. "I thought she'd be stronger than that."

I lean against my desk, and the corners of my mouth twitch. It's instinctive. A smile that I don't stand a chance at fighting when I relive the last few hours in my mind.

"She *is* strong," I tell them. "Saxon Forbes is a goddamn spitfire, refusing to play the part that we want."

Nico crosses his arms over his chest. "I'm not sure I follow."

Of course, he's not. He's a glorified moron.

"She was willing to die if it meant fucking us over," I clarify. "She's even stronger than I thought."

Beni hums. "A little kamikaze maniac."

A small chuckle bubbles out. "Exactly."

"Well, if you ask me, I think you should've just let her do it," Nico says, as if he's discussing the weather or a choice in golf clubs.

My hand grips the desk with force. "That's why *no one fucking asks you.*"

"Down boy," he jokes, making the desire to punch him in the face only ratchet higher. "I'm just saying, he's been silent. He hasn't demanded we give her back or insisted we negotiate. There has been no response at all. It's almost like he isn't taking it seriously."

As much as it pains me to admit this, he's right. It's been a week since we took Saxon and hand-delivered a letter explaining to Dalton exactly what the terms are to get her back. I expected outrage. After all, he's always acted like she's his pride and joy. But it's been the opposite—he's completely indifferent.

He needs incentive.

Something that scares him.

Something to make him believe she's in danger.

"Get me the dress she was wearing the night we grabbed her," I tell Beni. "And four vials of her blood."

He gets up from his seat, immediately going to follow orders, while Nico scoffs. "A dress? That's your master plan?" He throws his head back dramatically. "You are losing your touch, brother."

"Mind your business, Mancini," I order, but if anyone loves to disobey me, it's him.

Rolling his eyes, he gets up from his seat. "Oh, come on. Where's the guy who ripped out a man's intestines and wrapped them around his neck like a noose before dropping him off at his brother's doorstep? A bloodstained dress is child's play to you."

Everything in me goes ice cold and boiling hot all at the same time. If there's anyone I want to reenact that scenario with right now, it's the fuckwit in front of me who doesn't know when to shut his damn mouth.

I count to ten and then back down again, trying the methods I've been taught to calm myself down. Raff would be a bit disappointed if I slit his son's throat in the middle of my office, though it's not much of a loss, if I'm honest.

It's finally starting to work, but of course, he still doesn't know how to read the fucking room and know when to stop talking.

"All I'm saying is you need something a little more intense. Cut off a finger or an ear even. She's doped up enough. Probably won't even feel it."

My hand grips the letter opener on my desk and not even divine intervention could hold me back from slamming him into the wall. As I press the point of the letter opener to his jugular, he swallows nervously.

"No one is laying a fucking finger on her," I sneer. "Not a goddamn person. So, take your opinions and all your ideas and shove them up your ass, because I'm not fucking interested. She's. Off. Limits."

Nico grunts to let me know he understands, but the second I slip the letter opener into my pocket, he smirks. "Not even a week in and she already has you bitch whipped."

That's it.

I clench my fist and spin around, driving one firm punch to the side of his face. His whole body goes motionless as he falls to the ground—out cold, but alive. Beni walks back into the room and eyes Nico's motionless body on the floor.

"The fuck did you do to him?" he asks.

I wave it off dismissively. "He didn't know how to shut his mouth, so I did it for him."

He bends down to check for a pulse and when he finds one, he chuckles and hands me the things I asked for. "Where do you want me to move him to?"

"The doorstep," I answer, no hesitation.

Beni snorts. "Seriously?"

I shrug. "I wanted to say the ocean, but I figure Raff would be a little upset if I drowned his prized moron."

"Fair enough."

As he drags Nico out of my office, I spread the dress out on the table in my office. It's an art form, cutting the fabric and soaking it in her blood to make it look like she was stabbed in the stomach, but I make it work. When I'm done, I hang it up to dry, making the excess blood drip down the dress—the same way it would if she were stabbed while wearing it.

Beni comes back into the room and looks at my twisted artwork. "Not going to lie, that looks pretty real."

"And if they DNA test the blood, it'll be a perfect match to Saxon."

It's a solid plan.

Let's just hope it works.

ONE THING I'VE ALWAYS prided myself on is the ability to remain stone-cold in any situation. It's useful in so many different scenarios. It keeps enemies from sensing fear —or at least it would if I had any. It masks my feelings when I'm on the edge of losing control. And it makes me a kickass poker player.

I never show my hand.

Beni sits across the table from me, trying to read my face even though this has proven futile countless times before. Romano and Cesari sit on either side of him and snort when he gives in. He curses under his breath and tosses his cards face down onto the table.

"I fold."

Smirking, I look to Ces and Ro. They glance at each other

before simultaneously agreeing with Beni. Once everyone at the table has folded, I place my cards on the table face up and gather my winnings.

Beni gapes as he glares across the table. "You've got to be kidding me. A pair of threes? You looked like you had a royal flush!"

"No one said I play fair," I quip. "Besides, you should know by now you'll never get a read off of me."

He flips me off and tosses his cards toward the center of the table, showing he had a full house. If he didn't get in his own head, he would have beaten me. But overthinking got the better of him, making me ten grand richer.

As Enzo goes to deal us in again, my phone starts to vibrate. The name that appears on the screen is not one I expected, though it never is. After delivering Saxon's bloody dress to her father by personal courier two days ago, I thought we would at least see him falter a bit. But instead, he's acting as if everything in his life is business as usual.

It's fucking infuriating.

"You should answer that, Boss," Beni tells me as he glances at my phone. "You know how she gets when you don't."

I lean my elbows on the table and narrow my eyes at the device as it goes from ringing to a missed call notification. I'd like to just leave it where it lies. Pretend I didn't see it and go about my poker game. But Beni is right. Not answering is not the answer.

Not with this one.

I CHECK THE CLOCK for the fifth time since I got here, now seeing it's forty-five minutes since the time we agreed to meet. I'm not stupid enough to believe her being late is an accident. Nothing she does is unintentional. Keeping me waiting is a power move. A grasp at any control over the situation she can get, because she has none. And that won't be changing, no matter how much she wants it to.

When the clock hits eight, I stand up to leave, and the familiar face I've been waiting on walks through the door. Her long brown hair cascades over her shoulders in waves, and the peach-colored dress she's wearing stands out against her skin that's been kissed by the Italian sun.

The hostess attempts to greet her, but her hazel eyes meet mine from across the room and she smiles before heading my way. Tossing her designer handbag onto the chair beside me, she throws her arms around my neck and pulls me close.

"Do you have any idea how much I've missed you?" she coos.

I grunt. "So much so that you were an hour late."

She puts a hand to her chest and feigns ignorance. "Was I? I could have sworn we said eight o'clock."

"Viola." Her name rolls off my tongue with a warning behind it—one she knows better than to mess with.

A guilty smile spreads across her face as she takes a seat. "Are you saying I'm not worth waiting for?"

"I'm saying you pull that shit again and this dinner will be our last."

Viola Mancini is everything mothers warn their sons about. She's physically flawless and mentally deranged. The absolute epitome of the phrase heaven on the eyes and hell on the heart. She may be Nico's twin sister, but while he got sarcasm and stupidity, she got every psychopathic trait known to man. He could only dream of being as insane as she is.

It's probably why Raff had her sent to Italy for the last year to spend *quality time* with her aunt, who is currently battling leukemia. If you ask him, he will just tell you that family is the most important thing and you can never go wrong being there for one another. I don't think Viola agreed with that statement as she held her aunt's hair back and watched her empty the contents of her stomach.

"You would never fulfill that threat," she says confidently. "Your life would be much less fun without me in it."

I huff out a laugh. "My life is much less fun *because* you're in it."

"Now that's the first lie you've told tonight."

Good. She knows I wasn't bluffing.

Apart from Cecilia, Raff's wife, Viola is the only woman I've ever let myself get somewhat close to after my mother's death. I always felt more connected to her, and she doesn't make me want to wring her neck as much as her brother does. Whether or not that's because I think she would literally cut my balls off for sport, who knows.

"So, Nico told me you have the Forbes girl locked up in your castle like some storybook princess."

"Nico needs his mouth permanently sewn shut," I grumble.

She's been back in town for less than forty-eight hours

and already he's singing like a bird. I can only imagine how chatty he gets when he's drinking. It's the main reason we don't give him bartending shifts at The Pulse. He'd end up giving tours of the basement just to look like a badass.

"Any other secrets he so generously shared?"

She shrugs and takes a sip of her water. "He may have mentioned that you went all out on her boyfriend."

"Brad wasn't her boyfriend," I snap back.

The corner of her mouth raises. "Maybe not, but you instantly knew who I was referring to."

I roll my eyes. "Nice try, but he's the only guy that had anything to do with her. And I'll have you know he was attempting to drug her before we stepped in."

Viola scoffs. "Please. At least fifteen women get drugged in that club every week. Don't act like it wasn't personal."

I put my glass down and look her dead in the eyes. "It *wasn't* personal."

"Sure, babe," she says with a wink. "Whatever you say."

"When did you say you're going back to Italy?"

"I didn't."

"You should," I counter. "Make it two years this time. Better yet, make it permanent."

She giggles and shakes her head as she looks back at the menu.

Too bad I was only half joking.

THERE IS NOTHING MORE frustrating than a lack of control for a man who feeds off it. I need it to function. I need it to breathe. And when I don't have it, things can turn volatile if someone so much as breathes in my direction.

It's been nearly two weeks since I sent Dalton his daughter's dress. In those two weeks, he's been seen at work, at Kylie's school concert, and at a gala that he attended with members of the Bratva—as if he doesn't have a care in the world. And fuck if I don't want to put a bullet between his eyes for that sole reason.

Killing him is something we've considered. It honestly was higher on my list than taking Saxon. The problem is he's too protected. Offing him would start a war with the Bratva that I'm not confident we're equipped to handle at the moment. Therefore, he's safe.

For now, at least.

I'm looking through footage from a security camera at the gala venue when there's a knock at the door.

"What?"

Beni stands in the doorway, feeling the tension in the room. "Dr. Ferro wants to speak to you if you have a minute."

Shit. I was hoping we'd be further along by the time she

was healed enough to be taken off the sedatives. She hasn't been completely unconscious the whole time, but she has been medicated enough to stay in bed, staring at the wall and not attempting to off herself with the closest weapon she can find.

Ideally, I would've liked for her to be going home when we took her off everything. But nothing about this has been going my way, so of course, this won't either.

I get up from my desk and Beni steps to the side so I can leave my office. He follows behind me as we walk through the house and into Saxon's bedroom. Dr. Ferro is sitting beside her, and my chest tightens at how much better she looks.

Color has returned to her face.

Her arm is no longer wrapped up.

The feeding tube is gone.

She looks *good*, just sleeping peacefully.

"Antonio," I say with a nod. "You wanted to see me?"

He nods and stands from his seat. "I feel it's time to wean her off the sedatives. As I told you in the beginning, muscular atrophy is not something to be underestimated. Her wounds are healed. She's hydrated and fed. I'm afraid anything beyond this point is unnecessary and could lead to her needing physical therapy to walk again."

Walking to the side of her bed, I watch as she sleeps. She looks so calm. So serene. If it wasn't for the IV in her arm, I'd think she was just taking an afternoon nap, with her hair brushed neatly to the side and her plump lips begging to be kissed.

She's beautiful.

"I want all of the furniture taken out of the room," I tell Beni. "Nothing is to be left but the mattress and a pillow."

Beni nods while Dr. Ferro seems hesitant. "Are you sure that's necessary? It sounds a little overboard."

I grunt out a humorless laugh. "I'd have my men pad the walls if I thought they were a danger to her."

He steps back and drops his head. "My apologies. I assumed she was just leverage."

She is.

Or at least she should be.

Beni clears his throat and murmurs something about going to get help with the furniture while my gaze stays on Saxon. My hand twitches with the need to touch her. I stretch it out and slip it into my pocket. As I watch her sleep, I think about what she might be like when the sedatives wear off. A part of me hopes she's more submissive. More willing to obey.

But then again, I hope she's not, because the fire that burns inside of her is what makes her so extraordinary.

Chapter 9

Saxon

A STABBING PAIN SHOOTS THROUGH MY SKULL. Everything is blurry but slowly comes into focus. I don't know how long I've been out. It all started to blend together after a while. I was strong enough to open my eyes, to see the IV in my arm and the feeding tube that went from a machine and up my nose, but wasn't strong enough to do anything about it. I couldn't fight. I couldn't move. All I could do was lie there, but at least I was calm. It was a refreshing change, albeit frightening.

As my vision starts to clear, I realize something feels different.

There are no more machines.

No feeding tube.

No IV.

My breath hitches as the room around me doesn't even look the same, but as I try to sit up, the pain in my head gets worse.

"Ow," I groan, pressing two fingers to my temple.

A chuckle from across the room grabs my attention. I look

up to see Beni leaning against the wall, his legs crossed in front of him and his phone in his hand. I don't know much about him, other than he's the boss of everyone but Kage. He gives an order, and everyone listens, but Kage gives an order, and *he* listens.

Second in command.

Carefully sitting up, I look around to see all the furniture has been taken out and the mattress is now on the floor. There isn't even a sheet or a pillowcase. Just a thick blanket, a mattress, and a pillow.

I guess I should be grateful for even that in this personal hell.

"Hey, Kamikaze," he teases. "Have a nice nap?"

Pinching the bridge of my nose, I close my eyes and take a deep breath. "Headache."

"Yeah, the doc said that could happen."

He goes over to the door and knocks twice, making me wince at the noise. It opens and he's handed a bottle of water and a small paper cup. He comes closer and hands me the paper cup first and holds out the water.

"It's Advil," he answers, obviously hearing my silent question.

I cock a brow. "And I'm supposed to just trust you on that?"

He shrugs. "I mean, you don't have to, but if we didn't want you awake, you wouldn't be. It's as simple as that."

If I wasn't so miserable, I'd probably question it more. Maybe even fight him on it a bit just to piss him off. But I don't doubt for a second that he would take it away just as fast as he gave it to me. Unfortunately, I'm living in a reality where simple headache relief is a luxury.

As I crack the seal on the bottle, I can't help but chuckle as I realize they've been careful not to give me anything glass. "You walk around in Armani suits and drink out of plastic bottles?"

He snorts. "Nope. Boss had those bought just for you. *We* don't try to kill ourselves with everyday objects."

I swallow the pills down and hand him back the cup. "You might if you were being held against your will."

"Probably not even then. Sicilian men don't quit."

He heads for the door, but before he leaves, I need to know something.

"Wait," I plead. Thankfully, he stops and gives me a questioning look. "How long was I out?"

Shrugging, he smirks. "Not too long. Just a couple of weeks."

Weeks? "Oh, is that all?" I sass. "How nice of you to let me come back to consciousness so I can enjoy the facilities."

He looks at me like I'm the most amusing thing he's seen in months, then with a wink and a sarcastically blown kiss, he knocks once on the door.

"*Aprire*," he says in Italian.

The door opens and he slips out, and just like that, I'm left alone again in this prison.

THIS ROOM IS DRIVING me insane. Like, officially losing my mind level of crazy. I can't force myself back to sleep, because I've slept for practically the last two weeks. I can't play with the string on my sweatpants because they took that away. I can't even bite my nails because they cut them down short enough to make sure I don't scratch my skin raw.

The deep red stain in the corner taunts me, reminding me that I was almost out of here. That I almost won. If only I had just done it. No warning shot. No hesitation. Just one fast, deep cut, and I could have been gone.

Who am I kidding? Kage is never going to let me go.

He'd manage to keep even my soul hostage.

I perk up at the sound of the door being unlocked. Carmine steps in, holding a paper plate. As he kicks the door shut behind him, someone else locks us in. He comes closer and hands me what I can only guess is my dinner—mashed potatoes, peas, and chicken cut up into pieces small enough for a toddler.

Carmine sits across the room from me and rests his back against the wall. "I'm not allowed to leave here until you eat, so I suggest you get to it."

My brows furrow. "With my hands, like some kind of barbarian?"

"You tried to kill yourself with a broken piece of a mirror," he points out. "You're lucky Boss isn't making you drink your food. He's sure as shit not going to trust you with utensils."

"How would I hurt myself with a spoon?" I deadpan.

He snarls. "I'm sure you'd manage."

I can already tell this is an argument I'm not going to win, and while someone else's company might be a welcome change, Carmine's is not. I swallow my pride and eat willingly for the first time in weeks.

Besides being a little cold, the food is actually delicious, which tells me it's the same thing everyone else had. The chicken has just the right amount of spices added and the mashed potatoes are the homemade kind, instead of out of a box. It's better than it could be, that's for sure.

After five short minutes, the plate is clean, and I toss it

across the room at Carmine's feet. His nostrils flare as he looks between me and the garbage in front of him. He obviously sees me as an inconvenience, one he would like nothing more than to be rid of, but he's not stupid enough to let me go. He'd be killed immediately, though I'm not sure that would be much of a loss.

"*Butana,*" he growls, rising from his spot and angrily snatching the plate up off the ground.

The same word Beni used before comes out of his mouth as he pounds once on the door, and someone on the other side unlocks it. It's clear they're no longer allowed to trust me enough to have a key with them, which only makes it more difficult to plan an escape.

Getting past one is hard.

Getting past two would be damn near impossible.

THE LONGER I SIT in this room with nothing but a bed, the more I wish they had just kept me sedated. Days turn to nights, where I toss and turn repeatedly until the sun rises again. They haven't even let me go to the bathroom, demanding I use a bucket instead. It's the most degrading thing I've ever had to do. With every day that passes, I feel less like myself.

I've broken down to the point where I just stare at the window all day, watching through the tinted glass as the sun moves across the sky. I tried keeping track of the days by pulling small threads from the blanket, but it quickly became more depressing than useful. Now I just stick to counting the freckles on my arms and pretending I can feel the breeze in my hair as it blows through the trees.

The only thing I refuse to do is give up hope.

Hope that I'll escape.

Hope that I'll make it out alive.

Hope that there's a future for me that doesn't involve rotting in this room.

WITH MY HANDS CUFFED in front of me, Enzo leads me out into the hallway. He's one of the last people I want to be around right now, only second to Carmine the ogre, but it's been weeks since I've seen an actual bathroom, and the thought of a real shower instead of bathing myself with a washcloth and a bowl of cold water is more than enough incentive to behave.

He opens the door and I step inside, allowing enough room for him to step in as well. I'm not about to assume I get any sort of privacy in a room that isn't my four walls of hell. Sure enough, he shuts the door behind us and gestures to the shower.

"There's shampoo, conditioner, and body wash already in there," he tells me. "A towel and a change of clothes are here on the sink. When you're done and dressed, you can brush your teeth and your hair, and then we'll go back."

Once he's finished explaining, he turns around to face the corner. Relief rushes through me as I realize he won't be watching me. Having to be in here is one thing, but him seeing me undressed is something else entirely.

I quickly strip down to nothing and turn the shower to almost scalding hot, excited to feel the water wash over my body. Maybe it can wash away the feeling of loneliness that has been overpowering lately, or at the very least give me some sense of normalcy.

I step in and hiss as the water burns against my sensitive skin. The sound is enough for Enzo to take notice.

"Everything okay?" he asks.

"Yes," I reply. "Just not as adjusted to the heat as I was before."

He grunts in response but doesn't say anything else.

I turn around and tilt my head back, feeling the water run through my hair. It's the little things in life that you take for granted—the small luxuries you don't appreciate until they're ripped away from you.

Taking my time, I shampoo and condition my hair twice. The need to get myself as clean as possible is more than just a preference. If I could scrub the remnants of this place from my skin, I would, but something tells me I won't be given this privilege again if I even attempt it.

As I grab the body wash, Enzo's voice echoes through the room. "You almost done in there?"

I sigh, knowing this heavenly experience is ending faster than I'd like. "Yeah. Just washing my body."

A subtle whimper emits from the back of his throat and grabs my attention in an instant. I peek my head out of the shower to see him pressing his palm against his crotch—almost as if he's attempting to relieve the pressure.

Oh my God.

I always knew that Enzo had a thing for me. Since the night I was taken, before he even knew who I was, he was intrigued. He let his eyes linger for a little too long and flirted a little too hard for it to be unintentional.

He wants me.

The idea that immediately comes to mind is a risky one, but it's all I've got. This is the only time I'm ever with only one guard, and in a room that doesn't have three deadbolts holding it shut. This may be the only chance I get.

I breathe slowly, calming my nerves as I rub the washcloth over my skin. The risk I'm about to take is not lost on me. If this doesn't get me out of here, I can only hope it gets me killed. Otherwise, this may only get worse.

After letting myself enjoy the shower for one more moment, I shut it off and wring out my hair. As I step out, I see Enzo is still facing the wall, though his hand is now by his side.

"Do you mind handing me that towel?" I ask innocently.

He reaches back without turning around and feels for the cloth. When he finds it, he holds it out to me, careful to keep his eyes on the wall.

"Thanks."

I dry myself off, giving extra attention to my hair so it's no longer dripping, and then it's time to put my plan into action. The towel falls to the floor, leaving me completely bare. I bite my lip and run my fingers through my hair.

"You can turn around," I tell him.

He does, and the second he sees me, his jaw falls slack. His gaze rakes over my body, taking in every inch of me as I stand there for him to admire. Bile rises in my throat, but I swallow it down as he exhales.

"Fuck, Saxon," he moans. "What the hell are you doing?"

I take a step toward him. "What does it look like?" Raising on my tiptoes, I move my lips to his ear. "I want you, Enzo."

"Y-you do?"

"Definitely." I run my hand down the front of him. "You always take such good care of me, but who takes care of you?"

His breathing quickens, and as I grip his hard cock through his pants, his whole body twitches. "We s-shouldn't be doing this."

"Why not?" I ask seductively. "No one has to know. It's just you and me in here."

My hands move to undo his belt as I press a soft kiss to his neck. He runs his fingertips lightly over my skin, like I'm fragile. Like if he leaves a mark on me, it'll cost him his life.

"Let me repay the favor," I whisper.

He doesn't stop me as I drop down to my knees, undressing him from the waist down. His cock springs free, and I look up at him through my lashes. As my hand wraps around his length, I kitten lick the tip. He throws his head back and bites down on his lip to keep from making too much noise.

"Don't be a tease," he begs.

It takes everything in me not to vomit on the spot. "Don't worry. I don't plan on it."

With a firm grip on his dick, I take him into my mouth. It's my first time doing this, which is almost pathetic at twenty-one years old. My stomach churns as I realize I'll never get this moment back. My first sexual experience is forever tainted by this place, along with the rest of me. A single tear slides down my cheek—the only sign of weakness I'll ever let show. And then, I use all the strength in my jaw and dig my teeth into him.

Enzo roars as I feel tissue rip beneath my grasp. The metallic taste of his blood fills my mouth and the gag that forces its way out lightens my grip. He throws me off him as he collapses to the floor, curling into a ball and holding his now bleeding cock. Once he's down, I get up and leap over him.

"Bitch!" he shrieks as he writhes on the floor.

I rip open the door and run down the hallway. The scream he let out was loud enough for someone to hear. It's only a matter of time before someone comes our way.

The house is a fucking maze. I turn one corner and then another, glancing back every few seconds to make sure no one is behind me. If I don't find an exit soon, fucked will be an understatement for what I am.

I keep running, not stopping for a single second as I try to find my way through this place. There has to be a way out. It doesn't even have to be a door. An open window would do. I just need to get outside so I can run as far from this place as possible.

As I turn around another corner, my stomach drops as I realize I'm right back where I started. Enzo, with one hand still wrapped around his injured dick, is hobbling out of the bathroom. I turn around to run the other way, but instead, I'm ripped back by my hair and thrown against the wall.

Kage towers over me, with one hand still laced in my hair and the other against the wall, keeping me in place. The way he's glaring at me threatens to set me on fire, and as he looks down, I'm suddenly aware I'm still stark naked.

My nipples perk at his attention. I want to crawl into a hole and never come out as I watch him notice. For a second, he looks tempted. Conflicted. Like he's battling with some internal struggle and the rational side of him is about to lose. But then, he looks over at Enzo, seeing the state he's in, and suddenly, dying seems like a likely possibility.

CHAPTER 10

KAGE

Rage flows through me like it's the only feeling I'm capable of. And at the moment, it is. My jaw locks and my grip on Saxon's hair tightens at the same time as I take in the sight of Enzo.

His pants around his ankles.

How his hands cover his junk as he drips blood onto the carpet.

The fear in his eyes as he stares back at me.

It doesn't take a rocket scientist to figure out what happened. Even Nico could read the fucking room right now if he were here. Though, lucky for him, he isn't. If I had to listen to a smartass comment out of his mouth right now, all the respect for Raff in the world wouldn't be able to keep me from slitting his throat.

"You're bleeding on my floor," I snarl. "Go get that looked at while I take care of this, and then clean up your goddamn blood. Come to my office when you're done."

Enzo nods, having enough sense not to say a word as he hobbles away. Once he's gone, my attention fixates on Saxon.

She swallows harshly and bites her lip out of fear, but it only makes me notice Enzo's blood that still lingers in her mouth. With my grip on her hair, I drag her toward the kitchen.

"Do you think I don't have cameras in every inch of this place?" I growl as she stumbles through the door. "This is *my kingdom* you're in. You don't get out of it until I let you out. *If* I ever let you out."

Grabbing the bleach from underneath the sink, I take her chin in my hand and force her mouth open. She fights me by trying to turn her head but she doesn't stand a chance. As soon as I pour enough inside, I grip her throat to keep her from swallowing.

"Rinse," I order.

Her eyes close and she cringes as she swishes the bleach around inside her mouth. When I feel like it's enough, I bend her over the sink and force her jaw open again so it spills out. The second I release her throat, she gags and spits out the remainder.

"Fuck you," she slurs.

And oh, she doesn't know how much of a possibility that is right now. The bathroom is the only place where I don't have cameras, so my mind is running wild as it imagines what exactly happened between those two. The thought of his hands on her skin makes me want to slaughter the entire world around me.

As I spin her around, I'm surprised when she doesn't try to avoid my gaze. She keeps her head held high and stares back at me with the same intensity I feel right now. She's fuming. I'm livid. And she's still not wearing any goddamn clothes.

"Look at you, trying to use that pretty mouth as a weapon." I take my thumb and wipe away the drops of Enzo's blood from the corner of her lips. "Pull some shit like that again, and I'll have your jaw wired shut. We've already proved you can survive with a feeding tube."

Before I can do something I'll undoubtedly regret, I turn her back around and hold both of her wrists behind her back, pushing her out the door. Every step we take is one where I need to resist the growing urge to take in every inch of her. To see if her ass jiggles as she walks, or run my hands over the curve of her hips.

As we reach her room, I kick the door open and shove her inside. She falls to the ground and turns around to glare at me, but I'm already swinging the door shut. I ignore the way she pounds on the other side, screaming obscenities as I pull the key out of my pocket and lock all three of the deadbolts.

THE SHOWER RUNS ICE cold as I step inside, barely taking the time to strip off my clothes before I let it hit my skin. Everyone in this place is at risk of being killed unless I get my anger under control. I'd slit all their throats and use their blood to paint the walls if given the chance right now.

I always knew Saxon had the fight in her. That she wasn't someone to be underestimated in any sense. She's smart and vindictive and can be absolutely brutal if faced with the need to be. But I don't think I ever believed she would go that far. According to the call I got from Beni as I paced around my bedroom, she damn near castrated Enzo with her teeth. They needed to sedate him to sew the lacerations shut. I said to leave them, but they mumbled something about the Hippocratic Oath and the call disconnected.

If it wasn't for the fact that she had someone else's cock in her mouth, I might even be turned on. The fight she has inside her—the absolute refusal to break—it's the most attractive thing I've ever been faced with. It makes me want to set us both on fire just to feel the way she clings to me as we burn alive together.

As I close my eyes, images of Saxon's naked body run through my mind. The way she subtly arched her back when I let my eyes graze over her. All the water that dripped from her hair and onto her tits—I wanted to suck it off her like it was a spring in the desert.

My cock strains despite the frigid shower. It's painfully hard and angrily red. I press my back to the wall and wrap my hand around it. Moving my hand up and down the shaft, I tighten the grip like I'm holding her throat—withholding air like she withholds my ability to think clearly.

Images of what she must have looked like on her knees make me throw my head back. For once in my damn life, I'm jealous of one of my men. The concept alone disgusts me, but fuck I want to know what she feels like. The sounds she would make. If her eyes would water as I thrust into the back of her throat.

My whole body is tense and shaking as I reach up and grab the shower head with my free hand. The pain is excruciating yet phenomenal as I come close to the edge. I just need a little more to push me over the edge. To send me plummeting back into a world where my thoughts aren't taken over by a black-haired beauty with the fire of a thousand suns.

And then the shower head breaks right off the wall, and the thought of feeling the same thing as I snap her neck for wrapping that sinful little mouth around someone else does me in. I slam my head back against the wall as I roar, and cum shoots in streams of white ecstasy all over the shower floor.

My labored breathing starts to settle as I slide down the wall. The lust, the overwhelming thirst, it's all gone, and what I'm left with is the wrath that all but screams the reality back at me.

That one of my men betrayed a direct order.

That Saxon is a force to be reckoned with.

And that despite how much I may want her, she will *never* be mine.

I launch the broken shower head across the room. It hits the glass door at full speed and the whole thing shatters into a million tiny pieces. And all I can think about is how I want Enzo to lick it up off the goddamn floor.

BENI SITS IN THE chair in front of my desk, watching me like I could self-destruct at any given moment. He's had years to learn the signs of my breaking point, and judging by the way he's looking at me right now, I'm guessing he's seeing some of them.

"You sure you're good?" he asks with a quirk of his brow.

I shoot a glare his way. "If you ask me that one more time, I won't be."

He chuckles. "Fair enough."

Raff always hoped Nico and I would grow up tight like brothers, and I'd eventually make him my underboss, the same way Raff was my dad's. However, I don't think he realized at the time that giving his son any position of power over a soldati would be a grave mistake. He's too reckless. Too impulsive. And far too selfish.

I was an angry teenager, getting into fights at school on a weekly basis for no reason other than they looked at me funny. I didn't need anyone else. There was no part of me that wanted a friend. I was perfectly okay going it alone. And it wasn't until I picked a fight with the wrong guy that I realized being alone might not be the best after all.

He was one of those guys who looked like a badass but also looked like he tried too hard. There was an arrogance about him that pissed me off. And when I caught him telling his friends how he was going to bone Viola just to teach her not to be such a tease, I lost my shit.

It would have been a fair fight. Fair for me, anyway. He looked like he could at least hold his own for a bit. But as I swung an uppercut directly into his jaw, I wasn't aware of the blade he had in his jacket pocket.

Beni just happened to be leaning against the lockers when the chaos broke out, and when he saw the piece of shit about to fight dirty, he stepped in. He broke his hand with one hard grip, and when the knife fell onto the ground, he kicked it away from him and let me finish kicking his ass.

The only man I've ever called a friend earned my trust that day, and he's had my back ever since.

A knock at the door brings a smirk to Beni's face, but my muscles tense with the need to take care of business.

"Come in," I call out.

Enzo steps in with a sheepish look on his face and an

icepack pressed to his groin. The sight is honestly pathetic. For a woman to put a made man into this condition is laughable. But then again, Saxon is anything but your average woman.

"Boss," he says, timidly. "You wanted to see me?"

I give him a friendly smile. "I did. Have a seat, Enzo."

Beni huffs out a laugh as he pinches the bridge of his nose and looks away. Enzo, however, relaxes slightly at my tone. He walks over and takes the seat beside Beni. I get up from my chair and walk around to lean on the front of my desk.

"What did the doctor say?"

Enzo deflates. "The damage is horrifying, but as long as I avoid getting a boner for the next few weeks, it should be business as usual soon enough."

I hum. "That's good news for you."

"Yes, sir."

The sound of a commotion makes its way down the hallway. Saxon's yelling gets louder as they get closer to my office, until the door opens again and Carmine tosses her into my office. Thankfully for me, and for everyone else within a hundred feet of me, this time she's fully clothed.

"Get your fucking hands off of me," she shouts.

Enzo snarls at the mere sight of Saxon, and her eyes widen as she sees him sitting there. But for me, the party is only just getting started.

"Good. You're here," I greet her cheerfully. "Go stand in the corner."

Her lips curl upward. "Go fuck yourself."

I chuckle as I grab the gun off my desk and point it at her head. "I said, go stand in the goddamn corner."

She flinches, and while a part of her looks like she wants to fight me on it, she obeys instead. Once she's in her place, I nod at Enzo.

"Stand up," I order.

He does as I say, albeit wincing as he stands. Dropping

the icepack onto the seat, he waits for my next command—the same way he was trained. If only he had listened to his training earlier.

Spinning the gun around in my hand, I hold it out for him to take. He furrows his brows at it, as if he's unsure of what I'm doing, while Saxon's breath hitches in terror. Looks like someone fears death after all.

"Kage," she pleads.

My head whips toward her and I level her with a single look. "Don't you dare say my fucking name like I owe you any loyalty."

Saxon wraps her arms around herself as she starts to cry. Meanwhile, Enzo is still yet to take the gun from my hands.

"What is that for?" he questions.

Ugh, moron. "What do you think it's for? If someone bit my dick, I'd rip their head off their fucking shoulders."

Grabbing his hand, I place the gun in it and wrap his fingers around the handle. I nod toward Saxon, and he turns to face her. I step up next to him and ignore Saxon as she begs for her life for the first time since she got here.

"She made a joke of you," I tell him. "Disrespected you. Nearly robbed you of your manhood."

He raises the gun and points it at her, and I smirk. Saxon is now crying hysterically as she stares down the barrel of a .45. She holds her hands up, as if the bullet won't go right through them. Just the sight of her in fear threatens to turn me on again.

"She made her bed. Now make her lie in it."

I watch carefully as Enzo's hand trembles. He's angry, and he's hurt that she betrayed him like that, but you can almost see how he's trying to talk himself into actually killing her. Finally, I watch him move his index finger to the trigger, but right before he shoots, I pull the gun out of my back pocket and point it at his head, pulling the trigger without an ounce of hesitation.

Saxon screams as blood spatters against the bookshelf and Enzo's lifeless body falls to the floor. She collapses, sobbing in what could either be horror or relief. But as I point my gun at her this time, she freezes.

"I'm not kidding when I tell you that you're out of strikes. Pull shit like you did today again, and I'll put a bullet right between your fucking eyes," I growl. "Your games and your attempts at escaping will *not* be tolerated. You'll leave this house in a body bag, delivered right to your daddy's doorstep, if you underestimate me again."

She's trembling, and when Cesari and Romano come in to take her back to her room, she stays completely pliant. Not a single word comes from her mouth as she's escorted out of my office.

Good. I want her scared.

Once she's gone, Beni steps up beside me and looks down at Enzo, who is currently bleeding out all over my white rug.

"See? This is why white is not a suitable color for you."

I purse my lips and tilt my head.

He may have a point.

THE GRIP ON MY mouse turns my knuckles white as I stare at the screen, seeing Salvatore on the other side with battle wounds on his face and chest. We had assumed the first attack the Bratva would initiate would be in New York. After all, it's where the majority of our properties are located. We should have known they would start small first.

Last night, they decided their first point of action would be on a club in Vegas, one located off of the strip and in a more secluded area. It also happens to be where some of our men were having a drink after work.

It was a firefight that we were unprepared for because we never thought they would start there. When it was clear there was no winning, Salvatore was able to escape, but we lost six of our men last night.

The thought that lives are being lost at the hands of my enemies while I have the daughter of one of their own is rage-inducing. They should be bringing the fight here, where we stand a better chance than they do. At least then I'd at least be able to get my hands dirty and take some of my frustrations out on Bratva scum.

"I'll have Giovani send you some of his men to make up for the ones we lost," I tell him confidently. "But you're officially in a dry spell. I don't want a drop of alcohol to be consumed until we have this under control. They *will not* catch us off guard again."

Sal nods once. "Yes, sir."

My phone vibrates against the desk, and I reach for it as I see the name appearing on the screen. "I've got to take this. I'll call you after I talk to Gio."

Without waiting for a response, I end the video call and answer my phone.

"What did you find?"

Mattia sighs. "Nice to hear from you too, Kage. I'm great. Thanks for asking. How are you?"

I roll my eyes. "Impatient and my trigger finger is twitchy. Now, answer the question."

While Mattia is a vetted confidant, he's also the best

private investigator money can buy. He's been on my payroll for the last five years, and while he likes to think we're friends, I'd prefer to keep our relationship strictly professional. It's how I work best.

"I believe this is more of an in-person kind of conversation," he tells me, which means he has something big. "Can you meet me in the city tomorrow night for dinner?"

The prospect of getting something useful from him instantly improves my mood. The last month and a half have been nothing but disappointments. While now may be the worst time in history, since I'm busy babysitting a prep-school princess, it's still better than nothing at all. This could be my plan B.

"Dates aren't exactly my thing, Matt," I joke.

"Well, it's a good thing you're not my type," he claps back. "So, Eleven Madison Park at seven o'clock sharp?"

Not soon enough. "You can't fly out here tonight? I could have a helicopter waiting for you within the hour."

"No can do, Boss. I've got to do a little more digging on this lead."

I groan, running a hand through my hair and leaning back in my chair. "Fine. Seven tomorrow it is."

"Perfect," he replies. "I look forward to seeing you."

As I go to hang up the phone, my whole body freezes as the video feed in Saxon's room grabs my attention, and the ear-piercing scream that echoes down the hallway sends goosebumps across my skin.

Chapter 11

Saxon

Darkness fills the room as the sun sets and the natural light starts to fade, but my mind stays wide awake. No matter how hard I've tried the past few days, I can't close my eyes. When I do, images of Enzo's lifeless body haunt me.

The way his blood sprayed out of the side of his head.

How his body immediately fell onto the floor.

The look in his eyes as they stayed locked on me, dead and lifeless.

What happened in Kage's office that night is what nightmares are made of. To honestly feel like you're going to die at someone else's hand leaves a lasting memory. Before my near escape, I was ready to die. But getting a feel of that freedom, even the slightest taste of it as I ran through the house, it sparked a will to live inside me that I was sure had vanished.

And then watching Enzo be executed right in front of me showed me my fate.

I lay my head back against the pillow as I force myself to

think of the only other thing that can distract me from the thought of death—Kage. If I ever make it out of here, I'm going to need a live-in therapist to make sense of the feelings that rush through me when it comes to him.

He makes me feel dead and alive all at the same time.

Like I want to fight him with everything I have and obey his every word.

After I was kidnapped and thrown in this prison, I convinced myself that the reason he was watching me on my birthday was because he was stalking his leverage. Planning my capture. But after the way he looked at my body, like he was starving for it, I'm not so sure.

There are so many layers to Kage that I would love to peel back. To see what makes him tick. To learn how his mind works. He's so dark that it's almost as if he lacks any empathy at all, and yet, I'm still alive. A little voice in my head tells me that it's only because of my father, but I don't buy it.

There's something else there.

I can feel it.

The door opens and rips me from the thoughts that make my head spin. For a second, it's a welcome intrusion, until I see Carmine step through. Knowing Enzo's ultimate fate, if I could go back, I would've made *him* my target instead. Enzo was an easier mark, but something tells me all of these men are lacking in the sexual aspect of life. It would have been worth the extra effort to be rid of him.

"Time for your shower," he tells me, holding out two pairs of cuffs.

Since I tried to escape, any time I'm taken out of this room is now with my wrists and my ankles cuffed, like a goddamn death row inmate. Not that I would ever try that again anyway. I'll have to find some other way out of here.

SHOWERS USED TO BE my safe space, before kidnapping. I used to sit in them for over an hour and just feel as if the water washed away any worries in the world I had. Though, all those worries seem like jokes after the shit I've been through lately. I could really use a long, relaxing shower, but this one is not what I had in mind. Not with Carmine making me feel increasingly uncomfortable as he sneaks glances in my direction. He's not even subtle about it, which is somehow worse. It's like he thinks he deserves the ability to look.

I manage to keep the towel wrapped around me as I get dressed, careful not to give him the show he's so desperately hoping for. When I'm done, I stand at the sink and start to brush my teeth. The taste of bleach still lingers, even days later, though I think that might be better than the taste of Enzo's blood.

"Okay," I tell Carmine, holding my wrists out in front of me. "I'm finished."

He gives me a dirty look but says nothing as he cuffs me again.

The walk back to my room is fast, only being down the hall, and as he opens the door for me to step inside, I feel like I'm going to vomit. I'm convinced there is nothing worse than the feeling of isolation. The silence. The boredom. The lack of anything to keep your mind off your worst nightmare. It very well might end up actually being the death of me.

Carmine unlocks the cuffs but instead of leaving, he throws them out the door and glares at me. "What? Am I not good enough for you, princess?"

My stomach drops. "W-what?"

"You're all for seducing Enzo, but not me?" He takes a step closer, and I take one back, but my heels hit the mattress and I fall backwards.

"I-I was just doing what I was told," I choke out. "I was behaving."

He scoffs. "Sluts like you don't *behave*. Your little stunt got him a bullet in the head, and he didn't even get to fuck you." Taking another step toward me, he starts to undo his belt. "But don't worry. I'll do it for him."

"No. Please," I beg, scrabbling backward on the bed.

My virginity cannot be stolen by a man who looks like Shrek doused in self tanner. I won't live through that.

He takes out his nub of a dick, and it disappears inside his hand. "Shut up, bitch."

I try to spin around to get up, but he grabs my ankle. Screaming as loud as I can, I try to fight him, but there's no use. He uses his hold on my sweatpants to pull them right off me, leaving me in only my panties and a T-shirt. His knees land on mine as he comes down on the mattress, holding me with my legs spread open. Everything is just his for the taking.

"This will be a lot easier for you if you don't fight me," he growls, but somehow, I doubt that.

In a last-ditch effort, I reach up and jab my fingers into his eyeballs. They feel soft under my touch, and he yells out in pain as he smacks my arm away from him.

"You little cunt!" His hand raises, and he backhands me across the face. "You're going to fucking pay for that."

He rips my underwear off one leg and uses a hand on my

chest to keep me pinned down as he aligns himself at my entrance. I'm trying with everything I have to fight him off, but I can't. He's three times my size. I don't stand a chance.

He's going to win.

He's going to rape me.

Tears stream down my face, and I squeeze my eyes shut as I finally break. He's going to steal everything from me. I always knew that if I were to ever make it out of here, it wouldn't be unscathed. But this, this is going to ruin me. I'll never be the same.

His hand grips one of my breasts through my shirt as I feel him against me, but just before he pushes in, he freezes. He lets out a strangled noise, and I open my eyes to see blood flowing from his neck, and Kage looming behind him.

Carmine falls backward off me and chokes as he bleeds out onto my floor. I scramble back into the corner and use the blanket to cover me. Kage's whole body is tense as he watches me intently.

"Are you okay?"

But I can't answer. I can't say a single word, because as soon as I open my mouth, I need to scurry to the end of the mattress and empty the contents of my stomach onto the floor.

Kage exhales slowly as he looks away, and then focuses his attention on Beni and Romano as they come into the room.

"Get him out of here," he orders and heads for the door. "There have been too many fucking bodies to clean up lately."

It takes both of them to drag Carmine's body out of the room, but they manage. And then I'm left alone again with the puddles of blood and vomit. There's so much blood that not even the carpet can absorb it all. It just sits there, taunting me, and there's only one thing I feel.

Pain.

It rips through my body with relentless cruelty. The screaming in my head tries to drown out the silence, but it's futile. It's as if my lips are sewn shut with a fishhook and barbed wire. Not even a whimper has a chance at escaping. All I can do is get lost in the darkness.

My fingernails are ripped from my skin as I drag them down the wall—his blood on my hands leaving behind evidence of my touch. It's piercingly loud and deadly quiet all at the same time, and I know with certainty that I'd rather burn alive than live one more moment like this.

The panic attack comes without warning, crippling me down to nothing. No matter how hard I try, I can't seem to get enough air in. My chest tightens, and I feel like I can't breathe. I'm hyperventilating, and when everything starts to go hazy, I wonder if this is what death feels like.

It's too much.

It's too hard.

I can't do this.

Falling onto the floor, my whole body starts to go numb, and all I'm left with are the shallow breaths that aren't nearly enough. And then, it all goes black.

I'M WALKING THROUGH A meadow, one filled with tall grass and wildflowers. The sun beats down on me, heating my skin in a way that isn't uncomfortable. It's relaxing. My family is off in the

distance. I see Kylie spinning around in circles as she smiles at me, but as I try to run to them, they keep getting further and further away.

"Come on, Saxon," my dad calls.

Can't he see that I'm trying? Stop moving away from me!

"Saxon," he repeats.

I'm trying with everything I have to get to them, but my body just won't move. It's like I'm standing in cement, stuck in place.

A hand on my shoulder has me spinning around, and suddenly, my dad is standing there, but he's not the same. His eyes are black as he glares at me. As if he hates me. As if he never loved me.

"Wake up, Saxon," he says, but his voice doesn't sound like his anymore.

It sounds like…

"Wake up."

I jolt awake to see Kage standing beside me. He's dressed in his usual suit, but something about him is different. He looks more formal than he usually does. His sleeves aren't rolled up and his shirt is neatly tucked in. But that isn't the only thing off about what I see.

Rubbing my eyes as I sit up, I look around. This isn't the same room I've spent the last month and a half in. For one, the door is on the other side. And I can see a bathroom attached, the entrance to it on the far side of the room. And this one is furnished.

I'm sitting on a bed with a headboard and footboard made of cherry wood. There's a matching dresser on the wall across from it, and what looks like the hookups for where a TV was mounted on the wall.

"Where am I?" I ask, my voice rough.

"I had your room switched," he replies simply.

My brows furrow. "Why?"

He stares at me, completely void of any emotion. "Because your old one needs new carpeting, and I don't particularly enjoy picking unconscious women up out of a puddle of blood."

Eyes widening, I inspect myself for any signs of blood, starting with my hands and arms, then moving to my hair. Before I can look any further though, Kage shakes his head.

"Rosalie cleaned you up," he answers the unspoken question.

"Who is Rosalie?" Throughout the whole time I've been here, I've never seen another woman.

"She's my housekeeper. I figured after the recent events, having Beni or Ro do it was a bad idea."

And that's when it all comes flooding back.

Carmine unbuckling his belt.

Pinning me down.

I shake the thoughts from my head and dig my nails into my palm to remind myself that I'm okay. I'm safe, or at least safer than I was. Kage stays in the same place, unmoving and just watching me.

Breathe, Sax. "How long was I out?"

He slips his hands into his pockets. "A little over eighteen hours. You had a panic attack that made you pass out. Judging by the way you haven't been sleeping lately and the events of late, I figured you could use the rest, so I had Beni administer a sedative."

I look up at him through my lashes as my mind locks onto one part of that statement. "How do you know I haven't been sleeping lately?"

Staring back at me, I can't read the expression on his face. It's not angry, but it's not happy either. It's almost like disbelief. Like he's caught. But instead of answering the question, he just looks down, and the corner of his mouth twitches.

"There's a dress hanging on the door inside your bathroom," he tells me as he heads for the door. "I need you to be ready to go in an hour."

His words wipe my original question right from my mind as my attention piques. He's letting me leave the house? I'm not stupid enough to think he's letting me go, especially not if he's having me wear a dress, but just the thought of breathing in fresh air again is enough.

"Where are we going?" I ask eagerly.

"Manhattan," he answers. "I have a dinner to attend, and I've lost too many men lately to think I can trust you with another. Therefore, you're coming with me. Now get dressed. I don't have all night."

As he shuts the door behind him, I feel something for the first time in a while.

Something that awakens the will to survive that I thought I'd lost.

Something that heals little broken parts of me.

Something that could destroy me even more if it fails.

I feel hope.

CHAPTER 12

KAGE

I PACE BACK AND FORTH ACROSS MY OFFICE. THE risk I'm taking by bringing Saxon into the city is a big one. It not only opens up the opportunity for her to escape, but if she gets away, there's a good chance I won't find her until she's already back in the protection of her family. Her father may not give a shit now, but if she's standing in front of him, he's damn well going to pretend.

I'd much prefer to leave her here with Beni, and that was my first choice, until he told me that he has other business to attend to. Business that has to come before babysitting Saxon. He suggested I reschedule my dinner, but I'm a very impatient man. I didn't want to wait the one day I had to. There's no chance I'm waiting longer. I want to know what he found out.

That leaves me with only one option—she's coming with me.

Looking at the clock, I decide she's had more than enough time to get ready, and I start to head her way. It isn't until

I'm halfway there that Beni comes running down the hallway. My brows furrow as I stop and look at him.

"I thought you were halfway to Montauk by now," I say.

He exhales. "I was on my way, but I turned around. You have to see this."

Taking out his iPad, he flips to a video from the gala Dalton attended recently. Beni mentioned having one of the IT guys he knows work to clear up the audio on it. I wasn't optimistic and didn't think it would amount to anything.

The video starts to play, and you see Dalton with Saxon's mother on his arm. They both smile as they greet a man dressed in a dark blue suit. I don't recognize him, but judging by the comfort level between them, they already know each other.

"Dalton. Scarlett," the man greets them. "How are you both?"

"We're doing well, James. And you?"

He raises his drink toward the dance floor. "I'm here with my beautiful family. I don't think it could get better than that."

Dalton chuckles. "I hear you there."

"Are your daughters here with you tonight?" he asks, glancing past Dalton.

He shakes his head. "No, Kylie is still much too young for an event like this, and Saxon recently moved. She got into the pre-med program at Duke University."

"That's fantastic," the man says, impressed. "I've heard their program is one of the best in the country. Good for her. That girl is going places."

Dalton plays it off like a professional as he grins. "That she is, James. That she is."

The video stops, but I can't look away from the carefree expression on Dalton's face. He's lying to everyone. He has them all convinced nothing is wrong and Saxon is just off living her best life at a new college.

I playback the video one more time, watching Scarlett for any signs that she knows the truth, but I find none. I don't know what he did to get her to believe Saxon would just up and leave without saying goodbye, but he's gotten away with it...for now.

Taking a deep breath to keep the frustration at bay, I realize now is the perfect time to bring Saxon into the city. I wasn't sure before, just dealing with the hand I was given, but I definitely am now. She needs to be seen. His plan needs to crumble, and then the empire he's attempting to build will go down with it.

WALKING OUT TO THE helipad with Saxon, I can barely even look at her. The second I saw her wearing the dress I chose, I instantly regretted it. I should have chosen something more conservative. More nun-like. Not something with a neckline that plummets into her cleavage, shows off her curves, and has a slit on the side that damn near reaches her hip.

I half considered having her change back into a pair of sweats and a T-shirt but I need her to fit in. I can't be seen at an expensive restaurant with a girl who looks homeless. Hell,

I don't even think they would let her inside. So, I'll be spending my night avoiding all glances in her direction.

The second we step out the door, I hear as Saxon takes a deep breath. The heels she's wearing are four inches tall, but she still only reaches my shoulders. She throws her head back and takes in the fresh air, but her steps don't falter as she keeps up with me.

"Mr. Malvagio," Killian says respectfully. "Miss Forbes."

She gives him a sheepish grin and turns to me. *Good girl.* I nod once and she turns to him with a smile.

"Hello."

Her mood is infectious, and Killian must feel it too because he instantly warms toward her. They briefly talk about how beautiful the weather is and how it looks like it will be a clear night, making the sight of the skyline gorgeous from the air. However, I don't have all night. I gesture for her to climb inside the helicopter and focus my attention on my driver.

"Please have the Bugatti ready," I tell him. "I'll be driving us tonight."

"Very well, sir. I'll have it waiting for you."

"Thank you, Killian."

THROUGHOUT THE DURATION OF the helicopter ride, Saxon's eyes stay fixated out the window, and yet mine stay fixated on her. Don't get me wrong. I try to look away. I try to focus on anything else. But she's fucking magnetic. A temptress whose sole intention is to drive me over the edge. I can't help myself.

As we start to fly closer to the city, she puts her hand up against the glass. I can see in the reflection as the smile falls off her face. She misses home, and I'm teasing her with the taste of it.

The helicopter lands safely and I climb out first before giving her my hand to help her. The gesture is not what she was expecting, given the shocked look on her face, but she takes it anyway. Once she's safely out, she goes to release me, but my grip tightens. It's then that everything becomes clear for her.

It's so she can't run.

Waiting a mere fifty feet from the helicopter is my black-on-black Bugatti Divo. It was my birthday present to myself when I turned thirty, though I don't get to drive it nearly as much as I'd like. A man standing by the helicopter hands me the keys, and the lights flash as I hit the unlock button.

Saxon's eyes widen. "You're driving *that* in the city?"

"Yes?" Isn't it obvious?

She looks at me in disbelief. "Are you insane?"

I tilt my head from side to side. "It depends who you ask. The general consensus is presumably yes, though. Now, get in. We're going to be late."

As we get in, I realize one thing that doesn't bode well for me. There is only one thing that looks better than Saxon in that dress, and that's Saxon, in that dress, in this car. Her head rests back and she stares out the window, but I still notice the smirk as she hears the engine roar to life.

I wait until we're out of the parking lot to speak. "I don't think I need to remind you of what will happen if you try anything while we're here."

She glances over at me. "I wasn't planning on it."

"Sure you were," I tell her. "I'm just making sure you know it won't work."

Running her fingers through her hair, she looks forward. "Contrary to what you may think, you don't actually know anything about me."

Now *that* makes me smile. "Your name is Saxon Royce Forbes, which is pretentious as hell, by the way. You were born on March twenty-seventh after an excruciating thirty-two hour labor. You have a younger sister named Kylie, whom you adore. And you study pre-med at Columbia University. Or, at least you did when you weren't locked in a room in my house."

She rolls her eyes and scoffs. "That's nothing a twenty-minute internet search can't tell you."

I hum. Okay, if she wants to play that game, we can play.

"When you were a child, you took horseback riding lessons," I start. "Those stopped when you were nine and you fell off, resulting in a concussion. You refused to go back, and it's something you regret. You tried finding the horse years after he was sold, but your searches came up empty."

Sparing a glance her way, I see I'm hitting my target. I continue.

"You met your best friend Nessa when you were in the second grade, and you have been close ever since. You have five credit cards, all of which are for the best designer stores in the city, and you use them regularly. Oh, and you broke your left wrist when you were thirteen trying to do a back handspring you had no business attempting."

As silence fills the car, I turn to find her gaping at me.

"Still want to say I don't know anything about you?"

She forces herself to turn away and shifts—whether it's

because she's uncomfortable or because she's intrigued, I don't know.

"So, you're a stalker on top of a kidnapper," she quips. "Got it."

I can't help but chuckle. "You don't even know the half of it, princess."

Saxon flinches at my words, and within a single moment, her mood changes. I can practically see the way she's retreating into herself. I keep my eyes on the road, but still manage to pay close enough attention to her.

"Spill it," I order.

Her voice is quieter as she responds. "What?"

"Your mood dropped faster than a girl at her first frat party. I want to know why."

She shakes her head, and after a few seconds, when I think I'm going to have to force it out of her, she starts talking. "Car..." She pauses, unable to say his name. "*He* called me princess when he..." Her whole body shivers as the thought of what Carmine attempted plays through her head. "Just don't call me that."

Honestly, the events of last night are something I've been trying to forget all day. She doesn't need to know that I sat in my office until three in the morning and watched her sleep through the camera feed. Or that my mother was raped when I was younger, and that it's ultimately one of the things that caused her suicide. None of that would change what he did.

Killing another one of my men was not something I intended on doing, but it needed to be done. What he did was unforgivable. He not only betrayed the same direct order that Enzo did, but he tried to steal something that wasn't his to take. The only regret I have is that he died too quickly. If I could go back, I would make it slower...more painful, with a lot more torture.

"So, who are we having dinner with?" Saxon asks, changing the subject.

I don't really know what to tell her, so I keep it as vague as possible. "A friend."

"*A friend.* Right." She presses a fist to her mouth as she laughs. "Well, I'm sorry. I'm not fluent in hit man so you'll have to translate."

Now it's my turn to scoff. "A hit man would imply I'm doing someone else's dirty work. Believe me, Givenchy. Every life I've taken has been personal."

"Even Enzo?" she asks without hesitation.

I can feel her eyes burning into the side of my face, but I refuse to meet her gaze. My grip tightens around the steering wheel.

"Especially Enzo."

As the car coasts down the street, Saxon looks around with a conflicted look on her face. I don't have time to question it, though, before we're pulling up to the restaurant. I climb out of the car and run around to the passenger side. To anyone else, it looks like I'm being a gentleman, but she knows the deal.

"Let's go, Prada. I'm not getting any younger."

She allows me to help her out of the car, but she looks completely unamused at the nickname. I give her my best panty-dropping smile and ignore the way it makes her breath stutter. Putting out my arm, she takes it, and the two of us walk into the restaurant.

"Ah, Mr. Malvagio," the hostess greets me. "Your dinner guest is already here. Let me show you to your table."

"Thank you, Hannah."

With a hand on the small of Saxon's back, I lead her through the place as we follow Hannah to our table. The whole time, I'm mentally begging her not to try anything. At least not before dinner. I'm not in the mood for this information to be delayed any longer.

Mattia stands as he sees us. He gives me a confused look when he notices Saxon, but he recovers nicely. I thank

Hannah once more and then extend my hand for Mattia to take.

"Mattia, this is my girlfriend, Saxon," I say with my best playboy smile. "Saxon, this is Mattia."

Saxon trips up on the title I introduced her with, though I expected that. I considered giving her a warning beforehand, but this way felt much more fun. The reality is, Mattia would not expect me to bring anyone less than that to dinner with me. I trust him, but not enough to think he wouldn't try to pull some heroic shit to save her.

"It's nice to meet you," she says.

"You as well," he replies and turns to me. "I had no idea you were seeing someone. She's beautiful."

I play the part by looking over at Saxon and taking in the sight of her. She's on the verge of crumbling under my gaze, but exactly as I thought she would, she holds her head high and doesn't look away.

"That she is." And if I'm being honest when those words leave my mouth, no one has to know.

The three of us sit down, and Mattia pulls a large envelope out of his briefcase. As he folds his arms on the table, he glances at Saxon and then back at me.

"May I speak freely?" he questions.

No. "We're in the middle of a restaurant, Mattia. Discretion is always a requirement."

He seems to get what I'm trying to convey. "Very well. I have some intel on the ones you have been looking for."

Pulling out a few pictures, he passes them to me and my whole body goes tense. I'd recognize those three men anywhere. Their faces have been burned in my mind since I was ten years old. Saxon glances over my shoulder, and I'm too frozen to stop her.

"That's from the city," she points out. "A couple blocks away from Central Park, behind that hole-in-the-wall restaurant no one goes to."

Mattia looks impressed. "You know the area well."

She smiles. "I grew up here. My best friend used to live over that way. I'd recognize it anywhere."

"They're here." The words are meant to come out calm, but they end up sounding more like a low growl. "All this time, I assumed they were hiding out in Russia. You mean to tell me they've been right under my nose?"

"Not exactly." He slides paperwork over to me. "It looks like they may have come back in anticipation of something."

The revelation almost sends me into a fit of laughter. This whole time I thought everything with Dalton was the worst thing to happen since my father's death, but it might just help me achieve the goal I set out to accomplish twenty-four years ago.

I'm going to find them. I'm going to scare them out of whatever shithole they're hiding in, and then I'm going to rip them limb from limb. Now that they're in my territory, they won't be leaving. Not alive, anyway, and probably not dead either. I want nothing more than to throw them through a wood-chipper and watch as tiny body parts shoot out the other end.

I guess Dalton was good for something, even if it wasn't intentional.

"Follow the lead," I tell Mattia. "I want eyes on them whenever possible, and I don't care if you have to do something to shut down the airport, the tunnels, and the bridges. They don't leave the city."

The corner of his mouth raises. "Yes, sir."

THE ELEVATOR OPENS TO reveal my penthouse, and Saxon and I step inside. The massive living room has floor to ceiling windows that overlook the city. To the left is the kitchen, something I don't think I've ever personally cooked in, not in the six years I've owned this place. To the right is a hallway that leads down to my bedroom. There's another set of bedrooms past the kitchen where my men reside when they need to stay here with me. Beni's is one of them.

"Tired?" I ask as Saxon covers a yawn.

She nods. "I don't know why though. I woke up like six hours ago."

"The sedative can make you groggy for a day or two," I tell her. "Come."

With a hand on her lower back, I lead her down the hallway and into my bedroom. She looks around as we enter, her eyes focusing on the king-sized bed that sits against the far wall. It's covered in black satin bedding and is just as comfortable as it looks.

I watch as she walks over and sits down on the edge. She's hesitant to touch anything, but her hand lightly skims the duvet. As I pull a drawer open to the dresser, I fill the silence.

"Beni will be meeting us here in the morning."

She hums. "Are we staying here long?"

I shake my head and hand her a T-shirt and a pair of my sweatpants. "We'll be heading back early afternoon."

"Oh." Her voice has a melancholy tone to it.

Honestly, I can't say I blame her. Ro has told me things about the time he was held prisoner by the Bratva. If he was on the verge of breaking, I can only imagine the way she's feeling. Giving her a taste of freedom is cruel, but was unavoidable.

"You can change in the bathroom." I gesture to the en suite.

She glances over to it and back to me. "Y-you're sleeping in here, too?"

I cock a single brow at her. "You think I'm going to allow you out of my sight while we're here?"

"I was hoping," she replies, that teasing smirk appearing on her face once more.

As she goes to change her clothes, I let out a heavy breath. Having to watch her in that dress all night, seeing her flirt with me to play the part in front of Mattia, it was fucking torture. I almost considered letting her go just to keep me from crossing the line I've drawn for myself.

I hang my suit jacket on the back of a chair and then unbutton my shirt. It falls from my shoulders, and an almost inaudible gasp sounds from the bathroom doorway. My body heats as I see her staring, her gaze on my bare skin. I stay completely still until she makes the first move.

She comes closer, her footsteps slow and tentative. "Are those tattoos?"

I look down at my torso and see the six bullet holes I had inked into my skin the day I turned eighteen. She reaches up as if she's going to touch the one right over my heart, but I catch her wrist before she can make contact. Her eyes meet mine, all demanding and confident, yet concerned.

"What are they for?"

In an instant, I'm catapulted back to when I was ten years old again.

The ringing in my ears from the loud gunshots.

The sight of my father falling to the ground.

The carnival lights casting a cheery glow on the horror before me.

"What do we do about the kid?" one asks as the other two run away.

"Leave him," he shouts back. "He's harmless."

I run to my dad, trying to help him as he struggles to breathe. There's so much blood. It's staining the boardwalk and covering my hands. I try to stop it with my body, laying on top of him to keep it all inside.

"Someone help!" I scream. "Please! Anyone!"

But everyone hangs back, and in a few moments I feel his body still beneath me. When the police finally arrive, I fight with everything I have as they pull me away from his lifeless body—promising myself that I will show the monsters who did this just how harmless *I can be.*

"They're nothing," I say, ending the conversation before it even becomes one. "And don't ever try to touch me again."

Chapter 13

Saxon

THE SUNLIGHT PULLS ME FROM WHAT WAS EASILY the best sleep I've gotten in weeks. For a second, I let myself get lost in a dream that I'm free. That I'm not locked in a room, with three different deadbolts and an endless supply of made men keeping me from the outside world. But when I hear the clang of metal as I go to move my arm, I'm ripped back into reality. The one where I'm literally handcuffed to the currently sleeping god of a man who holds the key to my fate in his hands.

I can't help but stare at him. His perfect skin with a jawline that could cut glass. How he can pull off facial hair better than anyone I've ever seen. The way his chest rises and falls with every breath he takes. He looks so peaceful, as if he's not handcuffed to someone he's holding prisoner.

Prisoner. Right.

Just being in his general vicinity does things to me. Makes me forget there's a reason why getting all wrapped up in him like I did on my birthday is *not* an option. It can't be. Not if I want to escape. To regain my freedom. To get away from this hell.

As I look past him, my breath hitches when I see his gun sitting on the nightstand—just there and ready for the taking. It almost feels too good to be true, and it might be. Kage doesn't seem like the kind of man who would do anything unintentionally, but I can't not try.

I focus my attention back on him, wondering if he's a heavy sleeper. His breathing is still even, his face unmoving. This may be the only chance I have, and I need to take it.

Imagining I'm weightless, I hold my breath and carefully move toward him. Any change in him would have me stopping in an instant, but he stays exactly the same. I use my free hand to reach up and over him, but before I can even get close, cold fingers wrap around my wrist.

My eyes go to Kage's, only to find they're darker than usual. Angry—no, *livid*.

"What do you think you're doing?" he asks, voice thick with sleep, and fuck, I should not find that so hot.

I try to pull my hand back, but he won't budge. "Let me go."

"What were you doing, Saxon?" he says again, only this time it's more demanding.

Swallowing harshly, I try not to show him fear. "You know exactly what I was doing."

A deep chuckle vibrates his chest as he reaches over and grabs the gun. "Is this what you wanted?"

Shit. "Y-yes."

He sits up and throws one leg over me, straddling my waist. "And what would you have done if you got your hands on it?"

Everything in me is screaming not to move. Just the slightest arch of my back would grind me against him. My skin is tingling. My breathing is becoming erratic. And why the hell is the way he's looking at that gun so fucking attractive?

When I don't answer, he looks down at me and tilts his head to the side. "Well?"

"Nothing," I choke out.

The corner of his mouth raises. "You're not a liar or a pussy. Don't become one now."

His words strike a nerve, but he's right. "I would have shot you."

"That's better."

He looks menacing as he runs the barrel of the gun down my cheek. My fingers twitch with the urge to try to grab it, but I'm at least smart enough to hold back. I stay completely still as he runs it over my lips and then pulls it away. He turns it so the barrel is facing himself.

"Go for it."

My throat tightens. "What?"

He gestures for me to take the gun. "You want to shoot me. Go ahead. I'll give you one shot."

It's a test. It has to be. Trying to take him up on this would be a mistake. And yet, I'm tempted.

"Better hurry up," he tells me. "Beni should be here in about an hour, and you better be gone before then because finding his best friend dead might spark his temper."

I give myself all of three seconds to weigh my options before I take the gun from him and point it at his chest. My hand trembles under the weight of it. Kage stares down at me with his icy green eyes, taunting and tempting me.

He glances at the gun and then back at me. "Go ahead, Gucci. Shoot me."

The look on his face tells me he doesn't think I'll do it. He's either underestimating me or *over*estimating the hold he has on me. Big mistake on his part, because I like my freedom a hell of a lot more than I like him.

My finger moves to the trigger, and without a second thought I pull it.

Nothing.

No.

No, no, no.

Dread courses through me as the darkness intensifies in Kage's eyes. He rips the gun from my hands and grins darkly as he turns it to the side.

"Daddy dearest really should have taught you about guns, Hermes," he mocks. "Had the safety not been on, I would've been dead."

I swallow harshly. If I'm being honest, that was the first time I've ever held a gun, let alone tried to shoot one. I've never had a reason to. At least not until now. And my lack of knowledge may have just made everything ten times worse for me.

Lying completely still, my gaze doesn't leave Kage's as I wait for his next move.

"That's what you wanted, isn't it?" His voice is deeper than normal. More frightening. "You wanted me bleeding out on the floor while you searched my body for the key that'll free you from me, didn't you?"

My eyes blink but I don't say a word. I know better than to try lying, but I'm not brave enough to speak the truth. And yet, my silence only fuels his anger.

He wraps his hand around my neck. "Answer me."

Between the thought of him cutting off my air supply and the way his movements cause him to grind down on me slightly, there's nothing I can do to keep my body from reacting. My hips arch up to rub against him, and an involuntary moan slips from my mouth.

Fuck.

We both freeze, neither one of us saying a single word for what feels like eternity. I half expect him to get off. To be disgusted that I would be turned on in what must be one of the most fucked-up moments of my life. When I finally get the courage to look back at him, he looks like he's battling between two emotions. But then his eyes fall closed for a moment, and when he reopens them, his pupils are blown.

"Not the innocent angel everyone thinks you are," he muses.

Taking the gun that's still firmly in his grip, he slides it in between my breasts. I squirm once more, looking for friction, and that's when I feel it. Kage's dick is rock solid inside his sweatpants.

I did that?

He bites his lip and tightens his grip on my throat. "I'm going to need you to stay still, Versace."

Yeah, right. I've never been one to listen to him, and I sure as hell don't intend to start now. Not when we're doing…whatever this is. Even if I wanted to, my body seems to have a mind of its own right now.

"Kage," I breathe. "Please."

I need it.

I don't know exactly what *it* is, but I fucking need it.

He groans and drags the gun down my stomach until he pushes it between him and I—giving us both the friction we need. When I thought about my first sexual experience, I never thought it would involve grinding against the barrel of a gun like it's the best sex toy known to man, but I'd be lying if I said this wasn't hotter than the Sahara. Kage watches me with a small smirk splayed across his face as I let myself give in to the moment.

"You like that, don't you?" he murmurs. "Like the way my gun rubs against your clit."

"I'm imagining it's you."

My honesty catches him off guard, and when he doesn't respond, I use my free hand to reach for his waistband, but he grabs my wrist. I huff and whine, but that only amuses him more.

"Absolutely not." He places the gun back on the bedside table and reaches inside it to pull out a handcuff key. "Didn't anyone ever teach you not to touch someone without their permission?"

I snort. "Now who's the innocent one?"

"Trust me, Balenciaga," he says as he releases the cuff from his wrist and then proceeds to cuff both my wrists to the metal headboard. "There's nothing innocent about me."

Once my hands are secured above my head, he drags his touch down my body. As his fingertips graze my nipples, I can't help but hiss at the contact. Even through my shirt, they're so sensitive. It's like every nerve ending is on overdrive.

Sirens going off in my head tell me what a fucked-up situation this is. He's my captor. My potential future murderer. Enemy *numero uno*. But tell that to my body as it hangs on his every move, just waiting for him to touch me exactly where I'm craving it the most.

"Fuck, Saxon," he groans as I grind against him once more.

I pout. "I don't like these handcuffs. I want to touch you."

He smirks but shakes his head. "That's exactly *why* you're handcuffed."

Much to my dismay, he moves so he's no longer straddling me but instead lying beside me. His hand skirts across my stomach, lifting my shirt just slightly. His mouth is so close to mine I could kiss him, but I resist. As our eyes stay locked on each other, he dips his hand inside my waistband.

My whole body tenses as I wait for the moment he touches my clit, and the second it happens, the mewl that comes out of my mouth is damn near pornographic. I press my head back into the pillow and bite my lip to try to suppress it, but it's useless.

I'm at his fucking mercy.

"You're so wet for me," he murmurs, his breath hitting my lips. "I could just slip right in."

His finger teases my entrance, and as he just barely pushes in, I whimper as I stretch around him. It's official. Even if I make it out of here alive, I'll never be the same again. He'll leave me forever marked by him.

"Kage," I breathe, my body shaking from the pleasure.

He shushes me softly. "So good for me."

The words that leave his mouth spur a reaction I never expected. One where I want to do exactly that.

To be good for him.

To please him.

To obey him.

He rolls toward me and props himself up on one arm so he can stare down at me. Meanwhile, his hard cock that strains against the fabric of his sweatpants presses against my leg—teasing me with something I never knew I wanted this badly.

"I want to hear you," he tells me. "I want to hear every ounce of pleasure fall from your lips."

My mouth falls open, and I give him exactly what he wants with a moan that would put Jenna Jameson to shame, but it's drowned out by the obnoxious interruption that is his phone ringing.

His head drops against mine as his ringtone blares through the room. "You've got to be fucking kidding me."

As he pulls his hand out, I damn near cry from the loss of contact. I was so close. So fucking close. And if the anger radiating off him while he rolls over is anything to go by, he wasn't looking for it to end so soon either.

"What?" he barks into the phone.

Mattia's voice echoes through, loud enough for me to hear. "You're not going to believe this, Boss, but I have eyes on Evgeny."

Kage sits up immediately, but his eyes stay on me. "Where?"

"He's sitting inside the Russian butcher shop on 18th."

"Is he alone?"

"No," Mattia answers. "He's with a man. About 6 foot 4. Dark brown hair. He doesn't look Russian, but he's definitely a businessman. Probably one of few who still wear navy suits."

My stomach drops as I realize exactly who he's talking about, and Kage rips his gaze away from me.

"Dalton," Kage says in hushed tones, but it's no use. I can hear him loud and clear. "Keep your eyes on them. I'm sending a couple of my men."

Just like that, my throat is so tight I can barely swallow. "T-them?"

"Yes, sir," Mattia answers.

The second Kage hangs up the phone and goes to dial another number, panic sets in. "Please don't. Not him. Not my dad."

"Quiet, Saxon," he orders, bringing the phone to his ear.

But I can't. "No. Please. I'll do anything."

"Roman," he says as he ignores me. "I need you and Cesari to grab a few other soldati. There's a couple men I need picked up."

"Ro, don't!" I scream.

Kage's head snaps toward me with a scowl I've only seen directed at the men who have crossed him. It's enough to make me hesitate, but not enough to stop me.

"Please!" I shout again. "Leave him alone!"

Within an instant, his hand is thrown tightly over my mouth, making any words coming from me sound muffled. The look he gives me is a silent threat, one that dares me to disobey him.

"Remember who your boss is, Roman," he orders. "I'll

send you the address. Mattia will be there to point them out."

I try to thrash my head around in an attempt to get free, but it's no use. So, I do what Nessa always taught me. I open my mouth as much as possible and one of his fingers presses in my mouth. Ignoring the taste of my own pussy, I bite down as hard as I can.

Kage rips his hand away immediately. "Ah! Fucking bitch!"

Blood trickles down his hand, and I run my tongue over my teeth, relishing the metallic tang that tells me I have his attention. If I wasn't a woman, he'd probably backhand me. He looks like he could murder me without a second thought right now, but I don't care. I won't let him touch my family.

"I want them alive, Roman," he says, his gaze unwavering from me. "No alternative. Call me when it's done."

He hangs up the phone and tosses it back onto the nightstand without even looking to see where it lands. With the way he's watching me right now, I'm not sure if I should be pleading for my father's life or mine, but I go with the one I feel is more important.

I'll always choose them over me.

"Please don't do this," I beg, tears threatening to spill over. "Just let me talk to him. He'll listen to me. Whatever it is, I can get it from him. You just have to let me talk to him."

His jaw locks and his brows furrow. "How could your loyalties still lie with him after everything? After he hasn't so much as—"

Not finishing his sentence, he clamps his mouth shut and stares back at me as I glare at him. The mood in the room couldn't be more different than it was just moments ago.

"Hasn't so much as what?" I urge him. "Come on, badass. Fucking say it."

But he doesn't. Instead, he looks away and runs his fingers through his hair. "I'm getting in the shower."

Getting up, he leaves me handcuffed to the headboard and heads into the bathroom. My shirt is still bunched halfway up my stomach. My panties are uncomfortably out of place, not to mention drenched. And I'm just stuck here as he walks away.

The second the door shuts behind him, I feel myself drowning in the thickness of the room. The tension lingers long after he's gone while his words play on a loop inside my head.

After he hasn't so much as…

Pieces of me start to chip away as I flash back to Enzo.

"It's your father we're after," he admits. *"He has something we need and you're the leverage we're using to get it. So, if you'd just calm the hell down and do as you're told, you might make it out of here alive."*

No.

Impossible.

He wouldn't.

But that's the thing—there really is no alternative, is there? The city was bare of any missing posters with my face on them. No one looked even the slightest bit concerned as their eyes met mine on the streets. Kage even introduced me *by my name*.

My heart shatters, and the dam holding back my tears breaks as the truth hits me at a million miles per hour, knocking the wind out of me.

My dad isn't looking for me.

All this time, I've found comfort in the thought that he would find me. That he would be the hero I've always seen him as, and he would save me from the monsters like he promised when I was younger. But he's not even trying. Whatever it is Kage and his men are after isn't worth the little girl he swore to protect his whole life.

It's not worth *me*.

THE BATHROOM DOOR OPENS and Kage steps out, steam billowing from the doorway. In any other instance, I'd probably fall to my knees and thank God for the ability to see him like this—a towel loosely tied around his waist and beads of water dripping down his perfectly sculpted abs. But not now. Not after everything I thought I knew beyond doubt turned out to be a lie.

I keep my attention focused on the ceiling in hopes of hiding my bloodshot eyes and tear-stained cheeks. As he walks to the bedroom door, I almost let out a sigh of relief, but instead, it's a choked sob that pushes its way through. And once it's out, there is no reigning it back in.

Fuck it.

"He isn't looking for me," I cry.

Kage's movements halt in the doorway, and his hand comes up to grip the trim. For a moment, I think he's going to ignore me. He stays completely silent and motionless then finally he lets out a heavy exhale.

"Goddamn it," he grumbles and turns around.

Leaning against the doorway, he crosses his arms over his chest and looks at me expectantly. I'd be lying if I said I didn't wish he was wearing clothes for this conversation, because the state of him right now is very distracting, but I'm not about to risk losing the chance for answers.

I need them too much.

"Does he know where I am?"

He swallows. "Yes."

Ouch. "And have you made your demands clear?"

"He knows what they are. Yes."

With every response, the pain gets worse, but what did I really expect?

"Has he even responded at all?"

Kage's answer is blunt. "No."

It's not enough. "What about my mom? She wouldn't just—"

My words are starting to come out choked and jumbled as he cuts me off. "We have reason to believe he's been lying to her and everyone else. He was overheard at an event saying that you transferred to Duke."

I let out a shaky breath, nodding a couple times to at least show him I appreciate the honesty while I try to blink away the tears. The idea that no one was even trying to rescue me was something that never crossed my mind. And why would it? He's been the ideal father for as long as I can remember. Now he's making a conscious effort to cover up my disappearance.

"Anything else?" he questions. His tone isn't warm, but it's not exactly cold either.

I shrug. "You could tell me what it is you're trying to get out of him."

It's a long shot. One that I don't expect an answer to. Kage is a man who never shows his cards. And after the way he snapped at me before, I doubt he has any sympathy for me at all—if he can even feel such an emotion. But instead of leaving it unanswered, he nods.

"How much do you know about your grandfather?" He walks over to his dresser as he waits for me to respond.

My grandfather? "What does *he* have to do with this?"

Kage sighs. "Basically everything."

He takes out a pair of jeans and, without an ounce of

hesitation, drops the towel. Everything in me screams to look away, but I can't. I stay frozen like a deer in the headlights as he pulls the pants up his legs. And now knowing he's going commando is damn near all I will be able to think about for the rest of the day.

"Silas was the owner of a vast amount of property in the city," he says as he comes back over to the bed.

My brows furrow. "Yeah. He was an entrepreneur."

He smirks and leans over to release the handcuffs. "Not quite, Wildflower."

Hearing my grandfather's nickname for me spill from someone else's mouth feels wrong.

Dirty.

Unnatural.

And at the same time, I wonder how he knows that at all. However, bringing it up will take us off course. I make a mental note to take on *that* battle another day.

"So, what?" I snap. "You're telling me not only is my father a fraud, but so was my grandfather?"

He raises his hands in defense. "Not at all what I'm saying. Silas was one of the men I respected most in this world, but everything he *owned* per se, was property of the Italian mafia. And when he died—"

"It all went to my father," I finish for him.

"Precisely," he confirms. "We tried to get everything transferred before he passed but…"

As he trails off, I stop rubbing my sore wrists and look at him. "But what?"

He shakes his head. "Nothing. That's enough story time for today. Cliff Notes version is that your father has around fifty-two businesses of ours, give or take a few, and as he holds them hostage, we're holding…well, you."

The whole thing is hard to wrap my head around. "But my dad is rich on his own. Why is all this so important to him?"

Kage looks down at himself wringing his hands. "He wants to give them to the Bratva— the Russian mafia, in case you don't know. One of our most sworn enemies and the people responsible for my father's murder."

Everything becomes crystal clear as the pieces fall into place, from the need to kidnap me in the first place to the conversation with Mattia last night. My father isn't just trying to become even more disgustingly wealthy—he's trying to destroy Kage's entire empire. I don't think I could ever justify what I've been through since the night I was taken, but it makes him look a little less like a monster in my eyes.

I take a deep breath, finding it a little easier now that I have a better understanding, and by the time I exhale, I've found my resolve.

"Okay," I say decisively.

He tilts his head to the side and watches me, a small smile peeking through the corner of his mouth. "Okay?"

I nod once. "Okay. I'll stop trying to escape."

His brows damn near reach his hairline. "You'll...seriously?"

"Yeah," I say, shrugging. "I mean, it's just basic logic. My father has done nothing to earn those properties, and this isn't his war to get involved in. And besides, I trusted and valued my grandfather more than anyone. If this is what he would've wanted, then I want it for him."

He doesn't say anything, but his gaze remains completely focused on me, and I'd kill to know what he's thinking right now. I run my fingers through my hair to undo some of the knots that have formed from both sleeping and our earlier... activities. When he still hasn't looked away, I roll my eyes.

"What? It's like you said. Why should my loyalties stay with him when he clearly has none when it comes to me?"

Pursing his lips, he hums. "Fair point, Gabbana."

I scoff. "It's *Dolce* and Gabbana."

The second it leaves my mouth, I know I fucked up. My jaw clenches as I realize exactly what I've done, and sure enough, when I look at Kage once more, he's already smirking.

"Don't," I warn.

His grin widens. "Gabbana it is!"

Fuck. Me. "We were having a moment, and you ruined it. It's dead now."

"Yeah. I tend to do that. It's my specialty," he quips.

"Whatever." Standing up, I walk over to where my dress from last night is draped over the chair. "If you don't mind, I'm going to change."

My intentions were for him to leave the room, but instead, he turns around and lays on the bed with his hands behind his head. "I don't mind at all."

I place a hand on my hip. "This is not show and tell, *Boss*."

"Why not? You watched me."

Every inch of my face burns as I feel it turn bright red. I yank the dress from the chair and march into the bathroom, listening to Kage's subtle laugh behind me.

Kage - 1. Saxon - 0.

STANDING IN THE ELEVATOR with Kage on one side of me and Beni on the other, I've never felt so small. And yet, now that I know the reasoning for all this, I feel protected and safe. The two men basically tower over me, and while Kage is more of a streamlined kind of muscular, Beni looks like he could fight a semi *and win*.

We step out into the parking garage, and they lead me over to a black SUV. Beni climbs into the driver's seat, while Kage opens the door to the backseat for me. I climb inside and scoot over to allow room for him, but he chooses the passenger seat instead.

I guess the agreement we came to before must have meant something to him, too. Otherwise, there's no doubt in my mind he would be back here breathing down my neck.

"Roman said Evgeny's phone isn't on him," Kage tells Beni. "He must've ditched it before they grabbed him. Pull the car into the alley, and I'll go in through the backdoor."

Beni nods dutifully, and I can't help but wonder what happened to my dad. I know I shouldn't. I should be showing him the same level of compassion that he's shown me lately, but I can't help it. I think about Kylie and my poor mother, who has lost enough lately.

Before I know it, the car comes to a halt again and Kage opens the door to jump out. "Stay here with her."

The silence in the car is deafening as we watch him walk into the butcher shop. For the first time, and for reasons I can't articulate, I'm actually worried about him. Lord knows what's on the other side of that door. For all we know, there could be an ambush waiting for him.

"Should you go back him up?" I ask, a little too eagerly.

He snorts. "Not a chance, Miss Forbes. If I go against his explicit orders to stay here with you, the only life you should be worried about is mine."

I huff. "And what about his? We don't know what's going on in there."

Glancing back at me through the rearview mirror, he gives

me a comforting smile. "Kage knows how to handle himself. I wouldn't let him go in there alone if he didn't."

The moment he says that, the door swings open, and someone is quite literally thrown outside and onto the ground in front of us. Kage steps into view, and I gasp at the sight of blood trickling down his nose. Beni jumps out of the car, ready to have his back, but Kage puts a hand up to stop him.

The guy goes to get up but gets a swift kick into his ribcage that has him dropping right back down. Kage bends over and grabs the cellphone from the man's pocket and slips it into his own. With a condescending pat on the cheek and a few inaudible words, he goes to walk away before stopping dead in his tracks.

Kage's eyes lock with my own, and an emotion I've never seen on him shows itself for such a brief moment I almost think I imagined it. It all happens in a second. Kage pulls out his gun and spins back around, sending a bullet right between the guy's eyes.

My whole body jolts like an electric shock went through it, and I throw my hand over my mouth as I scream. The body goes limp on the ground, and no matter how hard I try, I can't take my eyes off it. It was one thing seeing him kill Enzo and Carmine, but this time feels different. Although he tried to hide it, I could see that their deaths had an effect on Kage. This one, though? There isn't a single ounce of emotion to be found.

He's just indifferent.

Beni drags the body to the side and covers it in garbage bags while Kage walks back to the car. He bypasses the passenger door and climbs into the backseat beside me. As the side of his leg presses against mine, I go to move over but he stops me with a hand on my knee.

"Don't."

I don't respond. I don't think I could even if I wanted to. I do, however, sit still and not make another attempt to give him space. Cold replaces his warmth as he takes his hand off my knee, but his leg stays lightly pressed against my own.

The driver's side door opens, and Beni climbs in without saying a word, pulling away and merging onto the busy New York streets. There's a shift in both their moods. If I had a death wish, I'd risk asking them what happened, but I'm too shaken up to open my mouth.

THE WHOLE TWO HOUR car ride stays exactly the same way. No words are spoken. No glances exchanged. Kage messes around on his phone, tapping out lengthy messages and avoiding eye contact with me at all cost, but he doesn't move his leg away from mine. It's as if my touch is what's grounding him.

Keeping him in place.

Showing him he's still human.

We get back to the house just after noon, and Kage holds the door open for me to climb out. He keeps a hand on my lower back as we walk toward the front door, and a lump grows in my throat. I can't help but wonder what it's going to be like now that I'm walking in here willingly and not kicking and screaming like the last time.

The two of us linger in the foyer, unsure of what to say. It's not exactly new for us, but I thought we had turned a corner. The conversation we had in his penthouse and even the banter after, it felt good. A lot better than whatever this is.

"I, uh, need a shower," I tell him, adding, "a cold one" under my breath.

As I go to walk away, heat wraps around my wrist. "S."

He has my undivided attention in an instant, but it's quickly ripped away when a voice I've never heard before booms through the room.

"Oh good. You're back."

Kage's jaw locks, and I whip my head around to see a man standing in the archway to the living room. He's younger than Kage, probably closer to my age. He has light brown hair and matching eyes, and makes no attempt to mask the way he looks me up and down.

"Damn," he says with a smirk. "You're prettier in person. No wonder Kage has been—"

"Nico," Kage growls, cutting him off.

I look between the two of them, wondering both what he was going to say and why there is so much tension between them. "Who are you?"

"His brother," Nico answers at the same time Kage says, "No one."

Laughter bubbles out of me. "Okay, those are two very different things."

While I find humor in the situation, Kage is the opposite. He pinches the bridge of his nose and then narrows his eyes at Nico.

"Saxon, go to your room," he orders.

I groan, getting my answer. "Seriously? I thought we were past that."

"No one said we were *past* anything!" he snaps angrily. "Now go to your damn room."

The way he delivers those words is like a blow to the chest. I flinch at the verbal onslaught and don't move, choosing to stare at him instead and wonder how we got back here.

"For fuck's sake."

He waves a hand at Beni, who grabs my arm before leading me away. I keep my eyes on a deadly looking Kage and an amused Nico until they're out of view. Beni's hold on me loosens as he realizes I'm not putting up a fight, though I do consider it just on principle.

"Who the hell was that?" I ask him.

He hums. "A dead man walking if he keeps this shit up."

No more of my questions are answered as we reach my prison, and he gives me a sympathetic grin as he shuts the door. The sound of all three locks clicking shut, mixed with this morning's revelations, has me falling right back into a dark abyss of hopelessness and despair.

That small taste of freedom was a cruel form of torture.

CHAPTER 14

KAGE

I USED TO HAVE A HANDFUL OF REASONS WHY I'VE resisted putting Nico under six feet of dirt and another foot of concrete, but how rapidly those reasons are disappearing does not bode well for him. We're currently down to two.

Raffaello and Viola.

And the latter is dependent on my mood, which also does not bode well for him.

"I can see it," he says with an arrogant tone to his voice.

I push past him and walk into the kitchen. "I don't know what you're talking about."

He chuckles as he follows me. "Sure you do. You wouldn't have put her in a dress that shows off her legs if you didn't."

Ugh. I don't know what pisses me off more—that image being burned into my mind for eternity, or the way Nico got to see it too. I knew I should have sent her back into her room to change before we left. Even Mattia looked like it was taking all he had not to salivate when he saw her.

"Is there a reason you're here, Nico?" I'm really not in the mood for his antics today.

Mocking offense, he puts a hand on his chest. "Can't a guy come see his dearest big bro without a reason?"

"I'm sure you could, if you *had* a big bro," I clap back. "But you don't, so cut the shit and get to the point."

He huffs. "You've introduced Vi as your sister before."

I pull an apple out of the fridge and bite into it. "I like Viola more than you."

The only way to get through to Nico is with brutal honesty, and even that is only successful about thirty-five percent of the time. Even now, he rolls his eyes and waves me off as if I'm not obnoxiously serious.

"Fine. I was thinking—"

"That's never a good fucking idea," I observe.

"Prick," he mutters under his breath. "What are we doing with Princess Posey in there?"

My brows furrow as I try to figure out what exactly he's referring to, because it sure as shit isn't Saxon. At least it better not be.

"*We* are not doing anything with her," I growl. "She is none of your concern."

He walks over to grab a glass out of the cabinet. "I'm just saying, if Dalton isn't cooperating, we should get rid of her."

It happens in milliseconds. One moment he's going to get some water, and the next, I've shattered the glass and I'm holding a shard up to his neck. It's the closest I've come to actually killing him, and my hand shakes as my restraint wavers on the edge.

"You better make yourself very clear right the fuck now," I hiss, "because I know you're not insinuating we kill her."

His eyes nearly double in size as he tries to reach for something on the counter, but it's no use. Even if he succeeded in fighting back, Beni would slit his throat before he could reach the front door.

"Think about it," he croaks. "The plan was for Forbes to

give us back everything in exchange for her. That's clearly not happening, but we can't just let her go. It would make us look weak."

My nostrils flare, and if I bite down any harder, I'm going to damage my teeth. "You *are* weak. Saxon Forbes is off fucking limits. Not just to you, but to everyone. Do you understand me?"

Nico swallows harshly and nods, flinching when the glass pierces into his skin at the movement. I let him go and toss him to the side. He coughs violently and hunches over to take a deep breath while I flip the piece of glass between my fingers.

"Suggest something like that to me again, and you're going to learn what your insides look like," I promise. "Now get the fuck out of my house."

As he heads for the front door, I make my way toward my office. If there was a worst possible time for him to come here, spitting out his ideas like they hold some kind of value to them, it was now. After what I heard before we left the city, he's lucky I didn't slit his throat from ear to ear. I already killed one man today. I'm not afraid to make it two.

I take the phone out of my pocket and toss it onto my desk. It was only supposed to be a quick pick up, but instead, it gave me more information than this piece of junk ever could.

"Stay with her," I tell Beni as I climb out of the car and head into the butcher shop.

The phone has to be around here somewhere. He had to have tossed it right before Cesari grabbed him. And his need to make sure we don't find it only makes me want it that much more. There has to be something useful on it.

I push through the plastic that hangs down in the doorway. Ro said they got him when he was coming out of the freezer. As I look around, I spot the heavy steel door on the far wall.

Jackpot.

A table screeches as I push it across the floor and out of the way, heading for the freezer. I just want to get the phone and get the fuck out of here, before the rest of the Bratva come to inspect the damage. I know how to fight, but even with Beni, we'd be outnumbered here.

With my hand on the freezer handle, I push it down and pull open the door, but the second I do, a frozen solid piece of meat comes flying at my face. I immediately cover my nose from the impact as a blur of someone tries to run past me. He's fast, but I'm faster.

My free hand reaches out and grabs him by the back of his shirt at the last second. I yank him backward and watch as his head slams against the wall. He looks younger—closer to my age and not nearly someone I would expect to be hanging around Evgeny and the rest of the seniors who refuse to retire.

"I've met stupid people before, but if you think you're going to take me on alone, you're horribly mistaken," I tell him. "Lucky for you, I'm in a decent mood today. So just give me the phone and I'll let you off easy."

"Fuck you, Italian scum." He spits, literally spits, at my feet.

Unbelievable. "Really? I never take mercy on anyone, and this is why. You're all very ungrateful."

I bend down and grab him by the collar of his shirt. He's still clearly a little dazed by the impact to his head, but he has half a mind to try grabbing onto the leg of a table as I drag him from the room. When we get to the door, I grab him by an arm and a leg—lifting him into the air. I kick the door open with my foot and with all my strength, I throw him out into the alley.

The second I step outside, Beni sees the blood dripping from my nose and immediately jumps out of the car. My thoughts go to Saxon for a second. With no one in the car with her, she could be doing anything. Most importantly, plotting her escape. The busy streets of New York are close enough. She could get to someone and scream for help before we could manage to get her back in the car.

But she doesn't.

She doesn't even attempt it.

I focus back on the Russian piece of shit who is currently trying to get up off the ground. Beni goes to grab him but I put a hand up to keep him in place. As much as he would deserve to die, I want him to live. I want him to go back to the Bratva and tell them exactly who took their precious Evgeny.

I want them to come for me.

Just before he's able to stand, I swing a hard kick directly to his ribcage, and he falls once more. I bend over and pull the cellphone from his pocket as he tries to catch his breath and spits blood onto the ground.

"Now, was that so hard?" I tease.

I turn to walk back to the car when he chokes out the words that change everything. "Enjoy her while you can."

My gaze locks with Saxon's, and neither one of us move.

"Forbes promised Dmitri her hand. We'll be coming for her soon."

Just like that, my whole world turns an angry shade of red. It doesn't even take conscious thought. My body moves on pure rage and muscle memory as I pull the gun from my waistband and spin around, shooting a bullet straight into his brain without so much as a second thought.

Blood pools onto the ground, surrounding his lifeless body. I glance over at Beni and nod once—silently telling him to do something with the body so an unsuspecting soul doesn't stumble across it. Meanwhile, I get back into the car, this time sitting in the back seat with Saxon instead. It's not that I want to cuddle. I don't think I'll ever be the cuddling type. But after what I just heard, I need her next to me.

That part of me that has let myself indulge in the delusion that she and I could ever be a thing needs her next to me.

Had I known Dalton promised Saxon to that piece of shit, I never would have told Roman to let him get away. I would've ripped out his windpipe with my bare hands and presented it as some kind of sick trophy to Saxon—a token of what I'm willing to do for her. I would have felt nothing but pleasure as I watched him struggle to breathe until he choked to death on his own blood, a war with the Bratva be damned.

I pace back and forth across my office, trying to reason with the things going through my head. All this time, I've kept my distance from her to keep her out of this life. Silas was right when he said that this world is no place for her. She's too pure.

Too innocent.

Undamaged by all things cruel.

But all of that is shot to shit. She's in it now, and even if she gets out of here, her father has made it clear that he doesn't care. He will use her in whatever way he needs to get ahead—including making her marry the world's sleaziest scumbag. The only way out for her now is in a body bag, and that will happen over my dead fucking body. I'm not willing to live in a world where she doesn't exist.

She just had to be the epitome of the perfect, doting daughter, staying a virgin even when it wasn't being forced upon her. If only she had been like every other teenage heiress and spent her weekends partying and sleeping around. Offering anything less than an untouched virgin would be an insult to Dmitri.

My actions halt as a most dangerous idea presents itself in my head.

No.

I can't.

Can I?

Images of her from this morning play through my mind like a movie reel. The sounds she made and the way her body reacted to my touch. Fuck, she was perfect. And when I went into the shower, I barely even had to touch myself before I was coming hard to thoughts of her.

I shouldn't have even let myself touch her, but waking

up next to her being the enticing, ruthless little daredevil she is put me in a rare mood. Handing her that gun was a test. I've seen the way she looks at me. It's the same way so many others have. The question was if she valued her freedom over whatever fantasy she's built me up to in her head.

What she doesn't know is there were two safeguards on that gun. The first was the safety that she failed to check. The second was that the gun was empty. It's almost comical she actually believes I'm naive enough to sleep with a loaded gun within arm's reach of her. Still, she knew neither of these things when she pulled the trigger.

Rage flowed freely through my veins as I watched her disappointment when the gun didn't go off. But what I least expected was her reaction when I wrapped my hand around her throat. I can still practically feel as she arched her hips from beneath me, and I want the sound of her moans permanently on replay in my fucking mind.

I've always told myself I can't have her.

If Silas even knew what I was considering, he'd put me through a meat grinder.

But in the battle of us versus them, if he knew what the alternative is, would his view stay the same? Who am I kidding? He would strangle Dalton for even thinking about giving her to the Bratva. Silas was never the kind to get blood on his hands, but for his granddaughters, he'd paint the whole world red.

Fuck it.

If the choice is between me or Dmitri, I will choose myself a million times over.

He's taken enough from me. He doesn't get her, too.

Before I can stop myself, I'm out of my office and halfway down the hall. Paulo, another one of my soldati, sits dutifully outside her bedroom. When he sees me coming, he stands up and nods respectfully at me.

"I don't care where the fuck you go, but make it anywhere but here," I order.

He doesn't need to be told twice as he grabs the book he was reading and scurries off to God knows where. The keys are in each of their designated locks, making getting in easy. Not that it needs to be. I'd kick the fucking thing down right now if I needed to.

As I step inside, I see Saxon sitting on the bed and reading a book. She's changed out of the dress she was wearing and into a T-shirt and sweatpants. Her damp hair tells me she must have showered since we got back.

She pulls her eyes away from the book to glance over at me. If she's any bit intrigued by my being here, she doesn't show it. And when she turns her attention back to her book, like I'm not standing here at all, is when I realize it.

She's pissed.

"Saxon."

Nothing.

"Look at me."

Still nothing.

Not even so much as a grunt.

I walk over to the side of her bed and with my hand on her chin, I force her to face me. She tries to pull away, even attempts to push my arm away, but I only tighten my grip.

"Let go," she demands.

It's taking everything in me to keep my cool. "Talk to me."

"Why?" She's angry. That much is clear. "So you can scream at me again? Or better yet, why don't you shoot me like you did that guy?"

If only she knew *why* I shot him, but no part of me intends on ever telling her. I saw how crushed she was after finding out her father hasn't exactly been sending out search parties for her. To hear what he plans to do with her if things go his way—it will destroy her.

"Nico isn't someone you should be around," I tell her, staying far away from the topic of the man I killed today.

"And you are?" she asks, finally standing up and using all her strength to shove me off her.

As she goes to walk away, I grab her wrist and spin her back around. "No. I'm sure as shit not. But fuck if I won't take every moment I can get."

Her breath hitches just slightly, but the moment is gone as quickly as it came when her scowl returns. "You had me locked in here again."

"You could have run."

She ignores that. "You killed someone!"

"You didn't run."

"I told you I wouldn't!" Her arms are in the air as she screams the words in my face. "Unlike you, my word means something."

She tries to escape my hold once more, but this time I pull her so hard she crashes against my chest. My hand comes up to grip her cheek—a gesture that looks soft but is really anything but.

"Stupid girl," I say softly. "You should have run."

Before she gets a chance to respond at all, I crash my lips against hers in a bruising kiss. Her hands grip my shirt, and whether it's an attempt to push me off or pull me closer, I'm not sure. All I can focus on is the way her body fits with my own.

"Fuck you," she murmurs against my mouth.

My cock jumps at her words, growing harder by the second. "You're about to."

I pull the switchblade out of my pocket and flip it open. Saxon takes a sharp inhale at the sight of it. I grab the bottom of her shirt and slice it straight through the middle. I can't tell if she's mortified, turned on, or an equal mix of both, but when the fabric gives way and leaves her standing there in her bra, I don't care about anything else.

Once Saxon was in my clutches, I knew she was going to need other clothes to wear. For a bit, I just had her wearing mine. However, that wasn't going to last for long, because every time I saw her through the camera, sporting one of my T-shirts that swam on her small figure, my restraint slipped just a little more. So, I sent a personal shopper to go pick up a few things, and the lacy bras she chose make me wish I'd given her a bigger tip.

"Did that make you feel like a badass?" she sasses, pulling my attention away from her delectable body.

The corner of my mouth raises, and with my free hand, I wrap my fingers around her throat to hold her in place. Her pupils grow as she bites her lip. I make a mental note that choking is a kink of hers she clearly didn't know she had. While her eyes stay on mine, I slip the blade underneath the bra and in one quick motion I turn the bra into a useless scrap of fabric.

"No, but that did."

Saxon tries to cover herself as her perfect tits end up on display. Her hands quickly cover them, keeping them from me.

"Abso-fucking-lutely not," I growl. "Let me see them, Gabbana."

"With that nickname?" she claps back. "Not going to happen."

A growl rumbles in my chest as the knife grazes gently down her cheek. "I'm not a patient person, Saxon. You won't get far by testing my limits."

With a roll of her eyes, she lets her hands fall to her sides, revealing herself to me. My mouth salivates with the urge to suck on them until she's a mewling mess beneath me. Her nipples are at their peak, and she hisses as I run the flat slide of my knife over one of them.

They're sensitive.

They're perfect.

She grips the back of my neck and pulls me in roughly, kissing me with fervor. As her tongue tangles with my own, I spin us around and press her against the wall. My body cages her in, but I don't think she minds as she deepens the kiss even more. The taste of her infiltrates my senses and takes over entirely, until she bites down on my bottom lip. Hard.

"Fuck," I say as I pull away, the metallic taste of my own blood coating my tongue.

She smiles sweetly, as if she's not the devil herself in disguise. "You're not the only one who can be destructive."

I can't help but chuckle. "Oh, baby girl. You haven't even begun to see what I can do."

My every intention is to make her fall apart. To become putty in my hands as she goes over the edge, again and again. This isn't just a vindictive move against her father. It's a move to save her from the dark future she may end up having otherwise. Dmitri is anything but the pleasing type. That sick son of a bitch would make it as brutal as possible. But me? I get off on pushing a woman to the point where she completely lets go.

Buttons go flying as she rips my shirt open, smirking like she's secretly so proud of herself. She grazes her fingertips down my torso and inspects every dip in between my abs. Arching up on her tiptoes, she places her lips next to my ear.

"Then stop fucking talking about it and show me."

Her words spark something inside of me.

Something primal.

Something animalistic.

A low growl emits from the back of my throat as I go to my knees, ripping her pants and panties straight from her legs. In the same move, I press a hand to her stomach and hold her against the wall while draping one of her legs over my shoulder.

The second my mouth meets her pussy, it's like a four course meal to a starving man. The sound of her moans fill the room while I lick and suck on her clit with an expertise that can only be gained through experience. Her fingers lace into my hair to hold me there, and when I open my eyes to look up at her, she has her head thrown back and her mouth hanging open.

And oh, what I wouldn't give to fill it.

"Got nothing to say now, do you, Gabbana?" I tease.

Her grip on my hair tightens just enough to cause a slight twinge of pain. "Shut the fuck up and keep going."

I hum. "Bossy."

But I do exactly that. I slide my finger inside of her just up to the first knuckle, feeling how tight she is. Thankfully, she's too absorbed in the magic my tongue is creating against her clit to focus on the pain. I slip another finger in and start to stretch her open, not only preparing her for me, but making it so she doesn't completely choke the shit out of my cock.

"Fuck, that feels amazing," she breathes, and I can feel her getting closer.

Her back arches, and she pushes my head closer, grinding herself against my face. I slide my hand to one of her nipples and take it between my thumb and index finger. She looks down at me and our eyes meet. I smirk, silently telling her I know exactly how to shut her up, and that's all she needs to go tumbling into orgasm oblivion.

She screams out as her pussy convulses around my fingers.

Her body shaking.

Her breathing heavy.

I pull out of her and groan as I lick up everything she has to give me. I've never had pussy that tastes so fucking good before. I could live on only this for the rest of my fucking life. She starts flinching when everything becomes too sensitive, but I'm nowhere near done with her yet.

I lift her up with my face still firmly between her legs, and she squeals as I carry her over to the bed and toss her down on it. I wipe my face with the back of my hand and then start to undo my belt as she watches me intently. There's still a bit of a daze lingering from her orgasm, but my every move definitely has her attention.

As I drop my pants, my cock springs free, and it spurs the same reaction in her that dropping the towel did this morning. The difference, however, is how achingly hard I am this time. Her eyes widen in alarm, but she bites her lip in pure desire.

"Take your time, old man," she teases. "It's not like I'm going anywhere."

I bark out a laugh. "You talk a lot of shit, Forbes."

She sticks her tongue out at me just slightly and smiles. "It's my specialty."

A chuckle bubbles out, knowing she's telling me the exact same thing I told her this morning. "Yeah, well, I can think of a lot better things for that mouth to do than spit venom."

Licking her lips, she sits up and scoots to the end of the bed. The way she wraps her hand around my dick and blinks up at me through her lashes has me almost coming undone in a ridiculously embarrassing three seconds, but I manage to hold back.

"You mean like this?"

Her tongue juts out and she licks the tip, just enough to feel it but not nearly enough to relieve some of the pressure that's increasing by the second. I need more. More of her. More of her mouth. Just. Fucking. More.

By the third time she does it, I wrap my hand around the back of her neck and pull her in closer. "Stop fucking teasing, or you'll live to regret it."

She giggles but opens her mouth anyway and covers my cock with it. And like she is with everything else she does, it's fucking phenomenal. She sucks me like a professional, with no teeth and just the right amount of pressure. I let my head fall back as my arm twitches with the need to pull her head closer.

Like she can read my mind, she takes me as far in as she possibly can, gagging as I hit the back of her throat and swallowing around me.

"Holy fuck," I groan.

If I let myself come from this, it defeats the purpose entirely. And I don't get laid often enough to enjoy this without emptying everything I have into her mouth. So as much as I'd love to let this go on for hours, I need to stop her if I intend to pop that cherry of hers.

I use my grip on her neck to pull her off me, and before she can question anything, I drop down and cover her mouth with my own. She moans into the kiss as I lay her back and climb on top of her. Arching her hips up, my cock rubs against her, and I've never wanted to bury myself inside someone as much as I do right now.

"Kage," she says breathlessly. "Please."

Smirking, I press a kiss to her neck. "Begging? Now that's something I could get used to."

She huffs, but it quickly turns into a hiss when I line up at her entrance and begin to push in. I can feel the resistance, and judging by the way her nails are digging into my back, she's feeling it, too. Using my thumb to rub circles against her clit, I distract her while I press in a little further.

"Take a deep breath for me," I tell her.

Like the obedient thing she is, she does exactly as I say, and when she lets out an exhale, I thrust all the way in. And just like that, her virginity—the one thing that made her worth something to Dmitri—is gone. And not only will it not ever belong to him, but it will *always* belong to me.

I may not be able to have her, but I can have this.

After a moment, she wraps her legs around my waist and digs her heels into my ass—a silent plea to move, and fuck if

I'm going to deny her. As I drive into her, she drags her nails down my back and I wrap my hand around her throat.

She fucking loves it.

Getting wetter by the second, she's close to losing it again, and I'm right there with her. The headboard slams against the wall as I make sure she won't be able to move for the next few days without a twinge of pain to remind her of me.

We're both chasing our highs when her eyes widen. "You need to pull out," she pants.

"The fuck I do," I growl.

If she intended on fighting me on it, her second orgasm in the last twenty minutes makes it so she can't. Nothing else comes out of her mouth but a moan loud enough to be heard by the whole damn house. And as her pussy clenches around my cock, it pushes me right over the edge with her.

I thrust all the way in as I empty everything I have deep inside of her. The feeling of my cock pulsing, paired with how sensitive she is, is enough to keep her in a state of sexed-out bliss. Or at least it does until I pull out of her and crash onto the bed beside her.

She sits up and looks down, seeing my cum leaking out of her. The look on her face as she turns to me might set me on fire. I spare a quick glance to make sure my knife is still in the pocket of my jeans and not where she can get to it before I do.

"Are you out of your fucking mind?" she shrieks. "Or is having a baby something on your bucket list?"

Oh. I thought she was pissed I just took her precious virginity without so much as a please. If *this* is her biggest problem right now, I can live with that.

"Don't worry your pretty little head about it. There will be no babies."

She crosses her arms over her chest. "I won't take Plan B. Nessa had to take it once, and it made her sick for days."

I roll my eyes and look up at the ceiling. "I had a vasectomy when I was eighteen."

"Uh...oh," she says, and I can't tell if she's relieved or disappointed. Or maybe even both.

She doesn't need to know that the thought of bringing a child into my world is appalling to me. From the time I was ten years old, I've told myself that my purpose in life is to live out my father's destiny—but that's it. The Malvagio bloodline will die with me.

"Go take a shower," I tell her. "I'll change the sheets."

She runs her fingers through her hair that is now a matted mess and sighs. "Yeah, okay."

I watch as she climbs off the bed and walks into the en suite, a shy yet sated smile on her face as she shuts the door. Once I hear the water running, I push away the stomach-churning feeling of already wanting her again and knowing I'll never have her.

There was a purpose with this.

Something that will not only get back at Dalton but also give Saxon a fighting chance.

But that was it. It can't happen again.

I throw my clothes back on and peel the bloodstained sheet from the bed, and with one last glance at the bathroom door, I leave and turn each lock behind me.

"Get me a small box," I tell Beni as I pass him in the living room.

Once I get back into my office, I drop the sheet on the table and grab a piece of stationary and a pen.

You stole from me, so I stole from you.
Good luck getting Dmitri to want her now. - K.M.

As soon as I'm done writing the note, Beni comes in with the box. I fold the sheet in a way that shows exactly what it is the second he opens it and place the note on top of it. Then, I tape it closed and hand it back to Beni.

"I want this delivered to Dalton Forbes by morning," I say stoically.

Beni shoots me a look between shocked and amused but doesn't say anything as he nods and leaves the room. It's not the big win we're looking for, but it feels good to be able fuck up at least one of his plans lately.

Though nothing feels better than she did.

CHAPTER 15

KAGE

I've always been one to find peace in the darkness. The silence wraps around me and rocks me to sleep at night. The demons all settle down into their respective places. But tonight, it's eating me alive.

No matter how many times I toss and turn, I can't seem to get my brain to shut off. The events of today replay on a continuous loop. It's like a bipolar kind of hell, with one part of me burning with rage over the fact that Dalton wanted to give Saxon to Dmitri like some kind of fucking token, and the other wanting to constantly relive the feeling of her pussy clenching around me like I was her only goddamn lifeline.

She's intoxicating and she doesn't even fucking know it, and I shouldn't know it either.

I roll onto my back and stare up at the ceiling, smirking at the thought of Evgeny all tied up and waiting for me. Beni says I'm an impatient person who's patient when it matters, and tonight proved exactly that. The temptation to go kill him tonight was overwhelming, but the desire for him to suffer like I have was something much stronger. And besides, it's not like he's relaxing.

Roman and Cesari were given strict instructions to keep him as uncomfortable as possible, while still alive.

He deserves every drop of bloodshed before he dies.

I SWING A RIGHT hook as hard as I can, landing a solid punch to the side of Ralph's jaw. Most would recoil, but he doesn't miss a beat. He comes back just as hard, if not harder. The blow he delivers to my cheekbone is one I'm sure will leave a bruise, and it's only followed up with another to my mouth. He comes with no mercy, and that's exactly why I hired him.

Ralph is an older gentleman, and while some may see that as a weakness, his wisdom is something I admire. He's the *take no bullshit* kind, and he has that old-school way of always telling you the truth, no matter how it's going to make you feel. Legend has it he once put a fork into the back of his own son's hand just for reaching across the dinner table.

Thoughts of Saxon and what a dinner table with her would be like start to creep in. One of the unrealistic, torturous ones that show me what a life with her would have been like if things were different. One with kids filling the table while Saxon is barefoot and pregnant in the kitchen, finishing up dinner.

My head is thrown to the left as pain shoots through the right side of my jaw. I don't even have time to recover before an uppercut to my chin and a kick to the stomach has me falling on my ass. For the first time in years, I lost, and I'm not fucking happy about it.

"You're distracted," Ralph tells me as he bends down to fix the tape on my hands.

I watch as blood oozes from an open cut. "I've had a lot going on lately."

"When don't you? It's never thrown you off your game before."

And he's right. I've been training with him for five years, and the last time he beat me was the anniversary of my father's death—the year we started. Since then, I've never let my guard down in this room. Never let myself take my thoughts off of his next move.

Until now.

I'd be lying if I said I didn't know why, and it's not like anyone would believe me. Even Beni could tell something was up this morning as I avoided Saxon's bedroom like the plague. She was anything but quiet last night, so I'm sure anyone within earshot knows what happened, but the way Beni watched me, like I needed to be looked after, is not something I'm okay with.

"All I'm saying is, as a man in your position, distracted is not a good thing to be."

As he finishes what he's doing, I stand up and shake it off. "Again."

Ralph grins and gets into position. "It's *your* funeral."

But I'm anything but fragile, and the last thing I will tolerate is to be seen as weak.

MY PHONE DINGS AND lights up on my desk as a text from Roman comes through. As I open it, I couldn't be more thrilled with the image in front of me. Evgeny is on his knees, blood dripping from his lips, his hands chained to the wall. He's definitely not in good shape, but thankfully, he's not nearly on the brink of death. I want him to feel every ounce of what I have in store for him.

I type back a response, letting him know that I will be there at eleven tonight. I know Dmitri and the rest of the Bratva have been going crazy trying to find him. They have to know he's still alive; there's no body, after all. But they're looking in all the wrong places. And by the time they find him, it'll be too late.

Just as I put my phone down, I'm about to go back to the email I was typing when movement in one of the cameras grabs my attention. My eyes are glued to the screen as Saxon turns on the shower and strips down to nothing. I try to get a read on how she feels or what she's thinking, but she gives away nothing as she steps into the steaming water.

I should look away.

I can't even see her anyway, so it's like watching a scrambled porn channel. And yet I'm reverting to my youth, thinking if I stare hard enough, I might get a glance of something good.

My attention stays solely focused on the screen, and when the shower door opens, I watch as Saxon steps out. Droplets of water run down her soft skin, sliding over her tits and down to the perfect folds between her legs. There's something deliciously erotic about the way she wipes them away with the towel.

The camera angle switches as she goes into her bedroom. Standing in front of the mirror, with the towel wrapped around her body, something catches her attention. She steps closer to the mirror at the same time I zoom the camera in, and what she's looking at registers for both of us at the same time.

Bruises in the shape of my fingertips.

She peels the towel away to inspect the rest of her body, only to find more on her hips. She grazes her touch over them, and for a moment, I think she's going to be disgusted, but when she bites her lip and a sinful smile spreads across her face, I'm a fucking goner.

I press the base of my palm over the crotch of my pants, feeling myself rock hard beneath the fabric. Saxon runs a light hand down her body, her eyes closed as if she's remembering how it felt to have my hands on her. If I have any say in the matter, she'll never fucking forget.

She slides two fingers inside of herself, wincing slightly before pulling them back out and using her own juices to rub her clit. I wrap a hand around my cock, finding it pulsing and aching for release, and watch as she throws her head back in ecstasy. I don't even need to see it to picture her—pink and dripping, the same way it was for me last night.

I feel like a goddamn teenager. I honestly can't remember the last time I jerked off, but I can say it was never to someone like her. Someone so innocent, so perfect, and so fucking sinful—all at the same time.

Her knees start to shake, and like the good girl she is, she moves over to the bed and lies down. Her legs spread open, and I'm given the perfect view of her soaked pussy. The one making me feel homicidal. The one I'd kill a hundred men just to be back inside of right now. But for fucks' sake, I have more willpower than that. I *need* to have more willpower than that.

The grip I have on my dick is damn near dangerous as her motions become frantic. Desperate, even. No matter how I stroke it, nothing feels like her. Nothing beats the real thing. But watching her lips form my name over and over as her body shakes and she plunges over the edge, is pretty fucking close. And it's all I need to go with her, coming all over my hand in a disgustingly pitiful display of the man she's turning me into.

Son of a bitch.

MY WHOLE BODY IS thrumming as I pull on a black T-shirt and a pair of sweatpants. I can quite literally feel the blood pumping through me. I've waited for this day for as long as I can remember, and while it may only be one of the three, it's one step closer to fully avenging my father's death.

Walking over to the safe that is hidden behind my desk, I

tap out the code and watch the light turn green as it unlocks. The blade I pull out is a special one, my father's favorite. He had it on him the night he was killed. It was the first thing Raff gave me after getting back his belongings.

I've never used it.

Never found anything worthy of it.

Until tonight.

As I turn around to leave, my eyes land on the camera to Saxon's room. She's tucked comfortably into bed, and judging by the steady rise and fall of her chest, she's sound asleep. She looks so pure, and involuntarily, my hand flexes with the urge to run my knuckles over her cheek.

The second I realize my own actions, I regain control—forcing myself to look away and focus on the task at hand. Tonight, I get revenge on one of the men who took my father from me.

Tonight, I live up to the reputation of the nefarious prick everyone thinks I am.

I STEP SLOWLY DOWN the steps, entering the basement of the abandoned basement where Ro and Ces have Evgeny chained to the wall. It looks like something out of a horror movie, and I guess that's fitting for the bloodbath that will occur here. Roman found this place while running an errand. It's an old, massive building that's been condemned for years in the industrial park of Long Island.

Not a damn soul will hear him scream, and trust me, he'll be doing a lot of it.

The second my gaze locks with his and I see the fear he's trying to hide, my adrenaline triples. I clench my fist to keep my hands from shaking. My father always told me never to play with my victims—that it's better not to waste my time with the dead. But my father never did make time for joy in his life.

"You're scared," I tell him. "You should be."

He spits blood on the cement floor. "I'm scared of nothing, *guinea*."

I can't help but snicker at the slur and glance over at Ro, gesturing for him to pass me the metal bat. The second it's in my grip, I wind back and deliver a hard blow straight to his stomach. He braces for the impact, but no amount of flexing a set of practically non-existent abs can protect him against me. As he roars in pain, I toss the bat to the ground.

"Now, now, Evgeny. I don't think you're in the position for name calling."

Crouching down in front of him, he glares at me with hatred in his eyes. The kind that burns deep in your soul. One that holds centuries worth of a rivalry between two organizations. Only, the contempt I feel for him is much more dangerous.

It's personal, and it's fucking deadly.

"Am I really supposed to believe you're going to let me out of here alive?" he pants. "If so, you're not the brute your father was."

I chuckle and shake my head. "Not a chance, but you do have options. I can either make this quick, or it can be slow and excruciating, making your worst nightmares look like child's play. It just depends on what you're willing to give me."

He watches me intently as I stand back up and walk over to the table full of different tools to torture him with.

Knives.

Rope.

Pliers.

A machete.

"That'll do."

Gripping the handle firmly, I pick it up and start walking toward him. The horror that flashes across his face is well worth any wait I've had to endure for this moment. It's the same horror I felt when my father was gunned down in front of me. And it's only the beginning for him.

"W-what are you going to d-do with that?"

The corner of my mouth raises before I swing it and slash a deep cut right across his thigh. Blood immediately gushes from the wound as he bites his lip to try to keep in his screams.

"You're in the fucking Russian Mafia, and no one ever taught you not to ask stupid questions?" I swing it again and the blade slices through the flesh on his arm. "All those years of being Dmitri's bitch really did you dirty."

He snarls angrily at me. "I am *nobody's* bitch."

"Prove it. Tell me where he is."

The chains clank as he tugs on them, and blood drips from his arm onto the ground. "Fuck you."

Using the machete once more, this time I cut deep across his stomach, but nothing fatal. It's way too soon to end the fun now.

Evgeny hangs limp there, overwhelmed by the pain as his clothes stain red. His breathing is labored, and I can tell he's at his breaking point when I start to slowly run the machete up his pant leg.

"Next is the only thing that makes you a man," I warn. "Give me something useful."

He's silent, glancing back and forth between me and the machete. When no words come out of his mouth, I shrug carelessly and pull it back.

"Suit yourself," I murmur, but just as I go to swing it, he speaks.

"No, wait!" he shouts.

I hold the blade at my side and wait a moment while he catches his breath. "I'm listening."

"I don't know where he is right now," he says slowly, but when I roll my eyes, he rushes the next part out. "But I know where he's going. His daughter is getting married tomorrow. He'll be at the Russian Orthodox church on 37th at noon."

The machete drops out of my hand, and I laugh smugly as I grab a chair, putting it in front of the industrial-sized vice. His brows furrow as I turn to him.

"You were so close," I say.

With a nod towards Roman and Cesari, they undo the chains that hold Evgeny and drag him over to the chair. Of course, he doesn't go easily. He tries to fight his way free, but with the blood he's already lost, plus being tied up for the last day and a half, he doesn't stand a chance. They force him into the seat, and he looks up at me in a panic.

"But you said if I gave you something useful, you'd make it quick," he argues.

"No. I *said* you had two options, depending on what you're willing to give me." I open the vice with patience. "And I've always said there's only one punishment for a traitor. But thanks for the tip."

Ro and Ces position his head in the vice and pry his mouth open while I use a pair of pliers to pull his tongue out as far as it'll go. He looks confused for a second until I start to crank the vice, and then it clicks. He squeals like a hog going to slaughter as I slowly force him to bite off his own tongue.

As his teeth sink into the muscle, blood starts to pour from his mouth, but the screams of pure agony don't stop. And when he starts to gargle on his own blood, it's like music to my ears. After his jaw is completely shut, I give one harsh tug and pull his severed tongue straight from his mouth.

My men sit him up, and he's clearly about to go unconscious while he looks at me through hooded eyes, but I'm not done yet. I reach over and grab a bottle of hydrochloric acid. While I flick off the cap, Cesari opens his mouth once more. Evgeny is trying to scream something, but with a mouth full of blood and no tongue, none of it makes sense—not that I would stop if it did.

As soon as I pour the acid into his mouth, it starts to burn its way through his mouth, eating away at everything, including the massive wound where his tongue once was. He tries to spit it out, tries to pull his head away as he thrashes in pain, but we're stronger. I cover his mouth until he swallows simply because the pain of it eating through the rest of his body is preferable to it eating through the open wound.

"Lay him down," I order and as they do it, I pull my father's blade from my pocket.

Roman holds his arms while Cesari holds his feet. I straddle his stomach and rip his shirt open before beginning my artwork. The blade cuts through his flesh with ease as my adrenaline reaches an unmatched peak. I take my time and with each letter I carve into his chest, Evgeny starts to go in and out of consciousness. It isn't until I'm done that I stand up and inspect my masterpiece.

Armani.

The perfect revenge.

The first of three.

The beginning of me avenging my father's death and taking away their lives in honor of his.

Evgeny is on the edge of death as my men pull him up and hold him there. I step closer, my face even with his, and smile menacingly in the face of one of the men who stole my childhood and sealed my fate.

"You were right. I'm not the brute my father was," I growl and move my mouth to the shell of his ear. "Tell him I'm worse."

His eyes stay locked with mine as I pull back and take my father's blade, slitting his throat from ear to ear. Blood pours from his neck like a waterfall, but that doesn't stop me from reaching in and ripping out his trachea. As I hold the organ in my hand, Roman and Cesari drop his lifeless body on the ground.

What I can only describe as euphoria rushes through me. My heart pounds rapidly inside my chest as I get high on the feeling of taking Evgeny's life, like he took my father's. I inhale and embrace it all before taking a step back.

"Cut off his head and sew his mouth to his cock," I order my men and ignore Cesari's grimace. "Then I want you to nail his body to the tree in front of the church. I want him looking like a blow-yourself Jesus Christ."

As I drop the trachea onto the table, Ro's brows furrow. "But isn't that your chance at getting to Dmitri?"

I shake my head as I pull my shirt over my head, only to find my chest is covered in his blood anyway. "They cancelled that wedding the second we got our hands on him."

I'VE DREAMED OF THE day I finally got my hands on one of those bastards. I've played through hundreds of different scenarios of how I would kill them. I've pictured their expressions as the life left their eyes. But out of all the things I've imagined through the years, I don't think I realized it would feel *this* good.

The hour-long drive back isn't even enough to bring me down from this high, and when I walk inside my house to find Saxon standing in the kitchen, my whole body runs hot. As Paulo, who was tasked with keeping her in her bedroom, sees me, he starts to panic, but my eyes stay locked on Saxon.

"I'm sorry, Boss," he stammers. "She woke up and was hungry, but no one else was here, and I didn't want to leave her room unattended, so I brought—"

His voice disappears as my only focus is on the temptress in front of me, the one who has been plaguing my mind all fucking day. Hell, for three damn years, if we really want to be technical about it.

"Get the fuck out of here, Paulo," I order as she stays perfectly still, and he doesn't need to be told twice as he scurries from the room.

Keeping my gaze locked with Saxon's, I can feel my body start to react to hers. It's just her and I as I watch her attention move down to my chest that is covered in Evgeny's dried blood. She needs to see me like this if I'll even let myself consider what I want to do right now. She needs to see the real me.

I hold my breath and wait for her to make a run for it, but after she swallows harshly, she surprises the hell out of me by turning around and grabbing a towel. There's nothing in the world that can make me look away while she turns on the sink and dampens the cloth before coming toward me.

With the gentlest touch I've ever felt, she starts to wipe the blood from my skin like she's tending to the wounds of a child—and in a twisted way, she is. As she moves cloth from my stomach and up to my chest, it's taking everything in me to not take her again right on this goddamn floor.

It isn't until she rinses the cloth that I can get my mouth to form words. "Are you always so kind to the monsters in your life?"

She chuckles as she comes back with the rinsed towel and continues what she started. For a moment, I think she isn't going to answer, but then she exhales.

"Having demons doesn't make you a monster."

It's the most preposterous thing I've ever heard, and yet it was spoken with nothing but sincerity. I stare down at her, even though she refuses to meet my gaze.

"You don't know what you're saying," I tell her.

She shrugs as she runs the cloth over where my heart pounds against my ribcage. "Maybe not. Or maybe you've never considered that dark can be beautiful."

Before I can stop myself, my hand flies up and grabs her wrist, stopping her from any and all movements. She finally locks her eyes with mine, and I can see it clear as fucking day—the desire that burns inside of her matches my own. The second her breath hitches, I know she sees it, too.

And we both move at once.

Chapter 16

Saxon

THEY SAY CHAOS BREEDS MISERY. THAT THOSE WHO smile in the midst of danger are past the point of salvation. But Belle was able to save the Beast from his curse, even after everything he did to her. So why should I believe that Kage is beyond redemption?

With every move of my hips, I can feel him. His touch still lingers everywhere. The last two days have been spent learning every inch of each other's bodies, in every inch of this house. He's managed to burrow himself deep inside my brain, unrelenting and unwilling to leave as he consumes my every thought.

"I can't have you," he pants, ripping my clothes straight from my body. *"But I can't not fucking have you."*

My chest rises and falls rapidly as I'm at his mercy. "I don't think you're the kind of man who follows the rules."

There's no pinpointing exactly when we turned this corner, but I don't ever wish to go back.

I stand in front of the large master bathroom mirror, running a brush through my long black hair, and I can't help but take in how different I look. Granted, that's to be expected when you spend months locked away like some sort of princess in a twisted tower. But even ignoring that I'm not dressed in designer clothes and my makeup isn't done, I feel different.

Older.

Stronger.

More mature.

I watch in the reflection as Kage steps into the bathroom and stands behind me. Even just his gaze on me has my every nerve ending come alive. He gently runs the tips of his fingers over my chest and up to my neck, keeping his eyes focused on my own through the mirror.

"You're fucking gorgeous," he says honestly.

Using his grip on my throat, he forces me to look up at him and covers my mouth with his own. The kiss is like every one before it—demanding and unforgiving, leaving no question as to who is in control. And that's exactly how I like it.

Exactly how I like *him*.

THERE'S SOMETHING ABOUT THE way it feels when you're on top, riding a man's cock and letting it fill you completely. To know that every last inch of him is inside of me, pushing on the walls of my abdomen as my body takes all of him. Well, let's just say I now completely understand why Nessa is so boy-obsessed, except there's nothing boyish about Kage.

He lies on his back, watching me as I find my rhythm. My tits bounce with every move I make, and his hands run from my waist up to my breasts, playing with my nipples. As he takes one between his thumb and his index finger, I throw my head back and let out a breathy moan. If I've learned anything the past couple of days, it's how sensitive they are during sex. And Kage makes sure to remind me every chance he gets.

"Fuck, Gabbana," he growls. "If only your mouth could take me like this."

A small whimper bubbles out as I grind against him. "Hey, I tried."

He smirks and reaches up to wipe away my frown. "I know, baby. Don't worry. We'll get rid of that gag reflex soon enough." Arching his hips, he gives me just the right amount of pressure that already has me on the edge. "You'll be sucking me off like you were made for it."

"Yes," I mumble, lost in pleasure. "Want to make you feel good."

A low hum vibrates his chest. "You do. Such a good girl. You make me feel so fucking good."

I'm so close, literally only millimeters from leaping over the edge and diving into pure bliss, when his phone starts to ring on the nightstand. Kage groans and reaches over to hit ignore without even looking to see who it is. He slides a hand behind my neck and pulls me down for a kiss. His tongue dances with mine, and I'm so fucking desperate for release, and the phone starts to ring again.

The sound that emits from the back of Kage's throat is dangerous. "Whoever it is, I'm going to cut off their fingers and prevent them from ever using a fucking phone again."

I can't help but laugh as he reaches over and slams his

hand down on the phone with a practiced skill, putting it on speaker immediately.

"What?" he demands.

"I have news I think you'll be interested to hear." Mattia's voice echoes through the phone.

Knowing how important work is to Kage, I reluctantly move to get off of Kage, but he has different plans. His hands grip my hips tightly, and with almost minimal effort, he starts to lift me up and bring me back down—forcing me to keep riding him.

He reaches over and mutes the phone. "Stay quiet. If he hears anything from you that he can jerk off to later, I'll bring you to the fucking edge over and over, but never let you come."

Pressing my lips into a thin line, I nod and continue riding him as he returns to the call.

"I'm listening."

It takes everything I have in me to stay quiet as his cock rubs against the all-holy bundle of nerves, and he knows it as he watches me. Mattia, however, is completely unaware of what is happening on this side of the call as he goes on.

"I don't know what you did, other than the charming display in front of the church, of course, but well done for whatever it was, because things between Dalton Forbes and members of the Bratva seem to have gone awry."

I raise my brows inquiringly at the words *charming display*, but unsurprisingly, Kage doesn't share any information willingly. Instead, he pulls me down harshly and sends me soaring into one of the most intense orgasms I've ever had. As it tears through my body without mercy, my mouth falls open, only to be quickly covered by Kage's hand—keeping any and all X-rated noises inside.

"Go on," he orders.

Mattia hums. "Forbes was seen last night storming angrily out of one of the Bratva's clubs holding a package, and this morning, Dmitri and Vladimir hurried off to the airport to board the first flight back to Russia."

"That means nothing," Kage says sternly.

"I thought the same at first," he replies. "But a reliable source from inside the club said that at one point, Dmitri was holding a gun to Dalton's head. Words were spoken about distrust and not having all the power that Dalton believes he does. If I had to make an educated guess, I'd say that something happened that destroyed the confidence Dmitri had in him."

A wide grin splits across Kage's face. "Thanks, Mattia. I'll be in touch."

He swats at the phone, hanging it up, and flips us over so he's hovering over me. I squeal at the sudden movement, but he swallows it down as he presses his lips to mine once more.

"I can't believe you made me keep going," I murmur against his mouth.

Pulling back slightly, he smiles at me like a kid on Christmas morning. "Trust me, Gabbana. There is no better way to hear that news than while buried deep inside of you."

I LAY STRETCHED OUT on the couch, my feet in Kage's lap. There isn't a single part of me that isn't completely sated and exhausted. Except maybe the parts that still clench when he runs his hand up the inside of my leg. And the smirk that graces his face as I bite my lip to contain my moan tells me he knows *exactly* what he's doing.

In an attempt to keep my mind off it, I turn my attention to the TV just as the newscaster switches topics. The headline scrolling on the bottom of the screen catches my eye.

Police still searching for brutal killer.

"We have Nate over at the Russian Orthodox church, where the body was discovered. Nate, over to you."

The screen switches to a blond man standing in front of a large church with ornate spires and intricate stained glass, a microphone gripped firmly in his hand.

"Thank you, Melanie," he says. "It was almost two weeks ago when a body was discovered by a local passerby, and police still have no distinct leads as to who is responsible. There were some talks about it possibly being gang related, but that has not been confirmed.

"If you come over here," he walks over to a large single tree that sits in front of it, "you'll see the tree the body was nailed to in what police have called one of the most brutal scenes of corpse mutilation they've ever seen. It seems someone wanted to send a message and were willing to stop at nothing to get their point across."

As he continues to give viewers a phone number to call if they have any information, I look over at Kage. He stays calm, still seated on the couch with the pad of his thumb rubbing the bottom of my socked foot gently.

"Your brutally twisted handiwork?" I ask the question I already know the answer to.

His gaze meets mine, and there's a spark of something I can't put my finger on. "Does that scare you?"

"Should it?"

He grins deviously as he starts to move up my body. "Oh,

you should be terrified. Haven't you heard? I'm what all the best nightmares are made of, baby."

Lacing my fingers into his hair, I grip it and force him to look up at me. "Prove it. Make me scream."

I watch as he licks his lips and pulls my shorts and panties down slowly. He's teasing and torturing me with every move he makes, and I'm fucking living for it. My whole body squirms with the need to have his mouth on me, but he takes his time.

He ghosts his lips over the inside of my thigh, his breath warming my skin as he makes his way closer to exactly where I want him.

"Kage," I whine.

A deep chuckle vibrates out of him as I tug on his hair, and by the grace of God, he takes mercy on me. He doesn't start slow, but rather sucking my clit into his mouth and causing my back to arch right off the couch. I grind myself against his face as he eats me out like I'm his favorite dessert, and fuck, it's everything.

The talent of his tongue.

The way he knows exactly how to crook his fingers inside of me.

How he brings me right to the edge only to pull me back from it as he slows down.

My body is literally shaking in pent-up desire when Beni's voice echoes from Kage's office and ruins what may have turned out to be the best orgasm I've ever had—a record Kage makes it a point to beat almost every time we have sex.

"Incoming, Boss," he calls out.

Kage growls. "Who is it?"

"Nico."

"Oh," he answers and puts his mouth on me again, but Beni interrupts once more.

"Viola is with him."

That causes Kage to stop and pull back. "Shit."

My eyebrows rise so far they almost reach my hairline. "Who's Viola?"

Instead of answering, he stands up and walks toward the kitchen. "We're going to need wine. A lot of fucking wine."

"Kage!" I yell as I scramble to make myself look decent, but he only responds with a smirk.

Just as I get my clothes back into place, the front door opens and heels start to click across the floor.

The woman that turns the corner is every bit as gorgeous as I'd expect to see on Kage's arm. Her brown hair cascades down over her shoulders and ends just above her size-two waist that's being tightly hugged by the Chanel dress she's wearing. If I wasn't so busy wondering who the fuck she is, I'd be itching at the chance to talk fashion with her.

Nico walks in behind her and damn near crashes into her back as she stops and gives me a onceover. Kage, however, seems unfazed as he pours two glasses of wine.

One of those better be for me.

"Do you usually let your kidnapped prisoners roam free?" she asks him. "You're running a loose ship these days, babe."

Kage glances at me for half a second as Viola crosses the room toward me. "She's not your average prisoner."

Viola hums. "I see that."

She takes her time, letting her eyes roam over my body. I'm not one that lacks confidence often, but standing in front of her, I suddenly feel like every flaw and insecurity is on display.

"I'm sorry," I interrupt her silent scrutiny. "Who are you?"

"Oh, how rude of me. Viola Mancini." She introduces herself with a chuckle, putting her hand out to shake my own. The second I grab it, however, she speaks again. "Kage's fiancée."

My jaw drops and my whole body freezes as the sound of

Kage sputtering wine echoes from the kitchen. Viola, however, just smirks proudly as she turns to Nico.

"Well, that answers your question as to whether they're fucking or not, brother."

"You're engaged?" I hiss at Kage as he comes around the corner.

His eyes go dark as he watches me intently. "Would that surprise you?"

I tilt my head to the side. "I mean, given your old age, no, but being as your mouth is still covered with the taste of my p—"

"Oh-kay," he says, quickly walking forward and handing me a glass of wine.

"Pussy," I say, popping the P with narrowed eyes.

The corners of his mouth tug upward as he looks at me, both amused and fed up with my shit all at once. "Do you feel better now?"

"No," I bark. "As a matter of fact, I don't. You mean to tell me you've spent the last two weeks fucking me seven ways to Sunday, and all the while you've had a fiancée, and I had to find this out by her randomly showing up while you were in the middle of practically suffocating yourself between my legs?" I shake my head and go to walk away. "No. Fuck that and fuck—"

A hand wraps around my wrist and I'm quickly yanked back toward Kage. He holds his wine glass between two fingers and uses his palm to cover my mouth so he can actually get a word in.

"Easy, Gabbana," he scolds, his tone firm with a hint of softness. "You're playing right into her hand."

I glance over at Viola to see her watching everything go down with a smug look on her face. "O-oh."

Kage hums. "Oh is right. Now, what is it you were saying?"

205

"I was *saying* you still have a job to finish," I drawled sweetly.

He chuckles and can't fight off a grin as he shakes his head, the two of us lost in our own little world. "You're a menace."

"I know."

Meanwhile, Viola is watching Kage like he's a one-man circus act. "Did you just smile?" She turns to her brother for clarification. "Did he just smile?"

Nico looks just as amazed as Viola does. "I think he did."

Kage, however, just rolls his eyes. "As I was saying, Viola is Nico's sister, and a persistent pain in my ass. I'd sooner marry Beni."

Viola huffs. "I take offense to that."

"You were meant to," he claps back. "What are you doing here, Vi?"

"You've been MIA lately. I wanted to come see what has you so…" She glances at me once more. "…distracted."

This woman's fascination with who Kage is or isn't currently fucking rubs me the wrong way, and I find myself wanting to be literally anywhere else. Kage must sense the change in my mood because he subtly runs his thumb back and forth over my wrist while speaking.

"Oh great," he answers brightly. "So, you already got what you want. You can go now."

As if she's used to his attitude and doesn't even find him the slightest bit threatening, she gives him a playful smile and puts a hand on her hip. "Oh, come on. It's been weeks, and before that I was in Italy for a whole year. You had to have missed me a little bit."

"You're overestimating your level of importance in my life," he tells her, but you can hear the hint of teasing in his voice. There's some level of comfort between them, and I'm just not sure I want to know exactly how deep it goes.

I down my wine in one move, feeling parched all of a

sudden, and then pout at my empty glass. "Well, if they're staying, we're going to need more wine."

Correction: *I'm* going to need more wine, but they don't need to know that.

Kage smiles softly at me and nods, understanding exactly what I mean. "There's more in the wine cellar."

Ah, my favorite room in the house. Although, I will say it was the least comfortable to have sex in, but the added incentive of being able to reach over and grab a bottle once we were done made it worth it.

With Viola's attention on Kage and Nico lost in his own thoughts, I slip away quietly and head down the stairs. Brick walls line every side of the room, with a large table in the middle. There are cabinets that hold wine glasses and on the far wall are all the bottles.

I take my time, allowing my eyes to take in every bottle. Some of them are newer, while others are old enough to be worth more than a car. Personally, through all the wines my grandfather let me sneak sips of over the past few years, I've always found that the more expensive the bottle, the nastier it tastes. Then again, this is coming from someone who likes her wine sweet. The more like juice, the better.

Grabbing a bottle of blueberry dessert wine, I spin around to head for the door when I nearly walk right into Viola. I gasp and jerk back, the bottle of wine slipping from my fingers. Viola quickly catches it before it shatters on the tiled floor.

"Sorry," she giggles. "I didn't mean to scare you."

I catch my breath and shake my head. "It's fine."

She hands me the bottle of wine back and I thank her, but before I can get by to go back upstairs, she stops me.

"I was actually hoping I would get a second to talk to you," she says. "You know...alone."

To be honest, I'd rather pluck out my pubic hair with tweezers. "Sure. What's up?"

Running her fingers through her hair, she walks around the wine cellar as she speaks. "It's about Kage."

"What about him?"

"I'm a little concerned you might be in over your head," she tells me. "I mean, I get it. He's powerful. He's intimidating. He's sex on legs. But the world we live in...it's no place for a girl like you."

I scoff. "A girl like me? You know nothing about me."

"Sure, I do. You're Saxon Forbes. You grew up wanting for nothing and always had everything handed to you. And before recently, the darkest, most dangerous thing in your life was sleeping without a nightlight." She stops walking around the room and turns to face me. "You don't belong in our world."

Her words strike a nerve, one that I didn't realize existed until the words were spoken out loud. I have battled my whole life with feeling like I don't belong, but the last couple weeks I've spent with Kage, really getting to see what he's like, those thoughts haven't passed through my mind at all.

I've just been me.

"Look, all I'm saying is be careful," she says before I can respond. "You can have your little fun and screw him if it helps the time pass, but just know that's all it is. He's only fucking you because you're here and it's convenient."

"Vi?" Nico calls from upstairs.

"Coming!" Viola shouts back, then smiles at me. "I'm so glad we got to have this talk. I couldn't live with myself if I didn't warn you and you got your feelings hurt."

As she goes to walk past me, a part of me considers letting her. After all, she's leaving, and this feels like an argument to have with Kage. But before I can stop myself, I put a hand on her shoulder and keep my voice low in case Nico is within earshot.

"You know, upstairs I thought I was imagining things, but now I realize I wasn't." Now that I have her attention, I take a step back and smirk at her. "Does Kage know you're in love with him? Or is that fantasy world reserved just for you?"

Her whole body goes tense as she's called out and doesn't know what to do about it. "That's ridiculous. I'm not—"

"Don't try to deny it," I say with a flutter of my hand. "I can see right through your little act. You introduced yourself as his fiancée and played it off as a joke, when really, you like the sound of it. You crave that little fraction of space where you can pretend that you and Kage have a future together."

Her face goes red, and she looks ready to rip the hair straight from my head. I bask in knowing that I got to her, having enough experience with mean girls like her. But just like the rest of them, she composes herself quickly. She hums and smiles at me, like she already knows she won and this is just for pity sake.

"Let me make one thing clear," she spits. "The only thing *permanent* in Kage's life is the family. He doesn't do relationships. Doesn't take women seriously. Hell, the man doesn't even believe love is real, because he's never felt it. The only things that have ever and will ever hold his attention are work and the Familia. A familia which *I* am a part of. Not you and your traitorous father. So don't for a second think that you hold a spot at the table." Stepping closer, her shoulder lines with mine, and she brings her mouth closer to my ear. "You'll be gone soon enough."

She pushes past me and heads up the stairs while I grip the neck of the bottle so tightly, I'm afraid it might break.

Everything about her pisses me off. Her smug attitude. The way she acts like she knows everything there is to know about Kage, including his future. And most of all, the fact that she might be right. It's not like all her proclamations haven't passed through my mind. Hell, those worries practically live there, but hearing it come from her is different. And I don't fucking like it.

After taking a couple deep breaths, I march my way up

the stairs and straight into the kitchen. Kage watches me with a single brow raised as I slam the bottle onto the counter and grab the corkscrew.

"Please tell me she's gone."

He leans in the doorway to the kitchen and chuckles. "Didn't like Viola, I take it?"

I spin around and level him with a single look. "The woman is Satan in high heels. And I swear to God, if I ever hear her say one more thing about our sex life, like she's got some entitlement to our private information, I'm going to break off said heel and jab it into her eye socket."

Shocked, Kage purses his lips and carefully takes a few steps toward me. Once he's close enough, he pries the corkscrew from the death grip I had on it and places it onto the counter. With his hands on my hips, he spins me around and presses himself up against me.

"That's what she does," he says calmly. "She gets under people's skin and injects her poison. She's been doing it for years."

"Well, she can fuck all the way off," I growl, losing the strong-willed attitude I had before he invaded my personal space. "And you can, too, for not warning me about her when she got here, Mr. We Need Wine."

Laughter bellows out of him as he throws his head back. "Okay, fair. Let me make it up to you."

Just at the sulky tone of his words, my core tightens. "What did you have in mind? It better be good."

"You said earlier, I have a job to finish." He hooks his fingers into the waistband of my shorts. "And I hate nothing more than unfinished business."

Within seconds, my shorts and panties are back to being on the floor, and I squeal playfully as he hoists me up and sits my bare ass on the counter. He drops down to his knees, and this time, he knows better than to tease me, immediately licking a stripe up my pussy.

"Oh, fuck," I breathe.

He hums, sending a vibration right where I want it. "Patience, baby, we'll get there."

As he shoves two fingers inside of me and moves his tongue in skilled ways, I'm lost in him and the magical things he's doing to me. It's like the only things that exist in this world are us—until that gets shattered once more.

"That cannot be sanitary." Nico sounds bemused.

My head whips over to the doorway to find Nico standing there, with Viola only steps behind him. I expect Kage to stop, or at least pause. I even try to push his head away, but he's not having it. He doesn't hesitate for a second as he reaches into the knife block and grabs the first one he gets his hand on before throwing it across the room at Nico.

"Jesus, anger issues!" he shouts as he dodges it. "I'm going. I just forgot my keys."

Nico grabs them off the counter and heads for the door, while Viola's eyes stay locked on me. She's not even trying to conceal her rage as her jaw locks and her fists clench.

If she hadn't been such a bitch in the wine cellar, I may have taken pity on her. But instead, I smirk triumphantly and throw a finger wave her way before letting out a pornographic moan and pulling Kage closer by his hair.

And when I open my eyes again, she's gone.

CHAPTER 17

KAGE

THE BASEMENT OF THE PULSE HAS ALWAYS BEEN special to me. It's the first property I took control of when Raff started to let me take my place. It's where I made my first kill. And it's the place where I rid the world of sleazeballs like Brad Palmer—the asshole who thought he could give away Saxon like she was his property.

Music booms upstairs as club-goers fill the dance floor, drunk off their ass and having the time of their lives, all ignorant to the things that happen below them. Meanwhile, the men and I gather for a meeting. We all sit around a conference table, ready to discuss our next move. I thought about having this meeting at my house, but if it's going where I think it is, I want Saxon out of earshot.

Taking the last couple of weeks to myself was necessary. I needed to let the high of killing Evgeny ride out before I went on a violent rampage through Russia just to find the rest of the bastards. And more importantly, I needed to let myself get lost in the black-haired goddess that has haunted my dreams for years.

"Okay, so where are we?" I begin.

Beni is the first to answer, as he's lately taken point on keeping eyes on Dalton. "Everything has been relatively quiet from Forbes, except for the failed attempt at burning this place down."

My eyes widen. "I'm sorry, he did what?"

"It was a few days after things seemed to go south between him and the Bratva. He lit up one of the dumpsters in the back alley and a few pieces of trash near the door. I don't think he thought about the fact that the building itself is fire retardant." Beni leans back in his seat and smirks like he finds it comical.

"Why is this the first I'm hearing about it?"

He shrugs. "It was a non-issue and you were...preoccupied."

Ah. "And nothing since? What about the Bratva?"

"If I had to guess, I'd say his life was threatened," Beni says. "He's avoided all their local hangouts and has appeared to be scrambling since the night he brought the *package* to Dmitri."

"What package?" Raff questions and well, fuck.

I go to change the subject, wanting to fill Raff in on what I did, or have been doing, in private, but Nico has other plans.

"Oh, you haven't heard?"

I grip the side of the table and my jaw locks, but he's protected by daddy dearest, at least in this room anyway.

Raff looks between Nico and me. "Heard what?"

Nico smiles proudly. "Kage took Princess's V-card and had Beni drop the bloody sheet off at Dalton's penthouse."

The man who helped raise me looks caught off guard and a little angry as he turns to me. "Was that part of the plan?"

Sighing, I rest my elbow on the table and pinch the bridge of my nose. "No. What your impudent son doesn't know is that Dalton had agreed to give Saxon to Dmitri Petrov once he got her back. By taking her virginity, I made her worthless to the prick."

"How chivalrous of you," Nico drawls. "And every time after has been *what*? Making sure her hymen *stays* broken?"

I stand up, my chair flying backwards behind me, and go to lunge across the table when Beni gets in my way. Nico, however, sits there with an amused smile on his face. Ever since we were kids, his favorite hobby has been to rile me up. He's just like his sister in that regard. He just better hope it doesn't cost him his life.

"Watch it, Mancini," I growl. "The only reason you're still alive and tolerated is because I have too much respect for *that* man right there, but everything has limitations. He can't protect you forever."

He looks over at his dad, who seems cold toward both of us but especially him, and the smile drops right off Nico's face. As my adrenaline starts to calm, Beni grabs my chair and slides it behind me again. I glare at Nico as I sit back down and focus on the task at hand.

"Mauricio, have you looked into what I asked?"

Nodding, he opens the folder in front of him. "I did, and we will not disclose my methods or the fact that I managed to obtain a copy of the will, but we were correct. In the event of something happening to Dalton Forbes, everything goes to his wife, Scarlett Forbes."

Cesari looks pleased as he relaxes. "That does it, then. With the Russians out of the situation and Dalton just being a lone pain in our asses, there is nothing stopping us from getting rid of him."

Roman agrees with him, and as I look over at Beni, I find him trying to read my expression. When he doesn't find what he's looking for, he nods once and leaves me to make it official.

"Raff?" I ask, and he puts aside his feelings momentarily.

"Will you be able to get Scarlett to sign over everything once it's in her possession?"

He sighs. "I don't see why not. She and I shared wonderful memories of her father while he was in the hospital, so I'm sure she would listen to what I have to say. She just needs to be assured she and her children will be taken care of."

"She's family," I assure him. "She will always be treated as such."

Nico snorts. "A little *Sweet Home Alabama,* don't you think?"

He's fucking asking for it, and the blade in my pocket is becoming a little too tempting, but this time it isn't me who reprimands him.

"Nicolas," Raff snaps. "Like it or not, Kage is the Don of this organization, and you will treat him with respect. I will not have you tarnishing the Mancini name."

Roman presses a fist to his mouth to cover his amusement while Nico looks like a little kid who just got put in time out. I nod a silent thank you at Raff, knowing that while this won't last long, it will at least make the rest of this meeting tolerable.

"Okay," I say with finality. "Beni and I will decide on the best way to go about this, and then we will get together again to discuss."

"Something far away from Scarlett and Kylie, preferably," Raff requests.

"Of course," I agree. "I'd never consider something that would risk anyone else."

Everyone around the table agrees, and with the close of the meeting, I stand up and immediately walk out of the room. The last thing I want is to get stuck alone with Raff to explain why I've been screwing the *one* person who is supposed to be off limits. Or even worse, hear Nico make another smart-ass comment and give into temptation to gut him like a fish.

IT'S PAST TWO IN the morning when I finally got home. While Beni took the helicopter, I opted to drive—alone. The reality of what happened tonight weighs on me more than I expected. Dalton Forbes is a traitorous prick who thinks of no one but himself, and there's no doubt in my mind that the world will be a better place without him. But the part that surprises me, the part that's a real shock to my system, is the ball of worry that sits in my chest at how Saxon is going to react to it.

I walk into my room and find her sound asleep in my bed, dressed in nothing but one of my T-shirts. My new habit has become telling myself that her in my bed makes it much easier to have sex in the morning, because the reality of it isn't something I'm willing to deal with. Not now and certainly not any time soon.

Stripping off my clothes, I climb into bed. As my body sinks into the mattress, Saxon rolls toward me and lays her head on my chest. It's like her body craved the contact with my own. In the dead of sleep, she gravitates toward me instinctively.

And the only thing I can think as I close my eyes is that I hope she doesn't hate me at the end of all this.

I SIT ON THE couch, watching as Saxon tries to teach Beni a TikTok dance to impress his daughter. Honestly, I'm not sure what I find more amusing—Beni's lack of dance skills or the frustrated look on Saxon's face every time he messes up. Hell, I'm not even the one learning and I feel like I could do it at this point. No chance in hell am I ever attempting it, though.

"Kamikaze, for the millionth time, I don't know what the fuck *the whoa* is but I'm doing exactly what you tell me," Beni deadpans.

His nickname for Saxon hits a bitter spot in me, being as he came up with it when she damn near killed herself in front of me, but I tolerate it. Their friendship is entertaining to me, and if there's one person I would trust with my life, it's him.

Saxon sighs and plops down onto the couch. "I think you might just have to surprise her with candy. How old is she again?"

"Seven," he and I answer in unison.

Her eyes light up, but there's also a hint of sadness in

them. "Same age as Kylie. Definitely candy. Oh! And a pop-it."

Beni looks at her like she's lost her mind. "What in the fuck is a pop-it?"

My phone vibrates in my pocket, and as Saxon is preoccupied with explaining modern-day toys to Beni, I check it. The moment I see Viola's name, I already know what this is about, and it's not a conversation I want to have.

Viola: You told me to give you a warning next time I planned on coming over. This is your warning. I'll be there at six.

Ugh. The last time she was here, Saxon nearly wanted to castrate me. If I let her show up again so soon, there's a good chance we'll all end up bloody at the hands of a girl who doesn't realize how lethal she really is. But Viola is anything but obedient. Even if I tell her no, she'll show up anyway.

There's only one way to avoid any of this.

Kage: L'Artusi. Six-thirty. And leave the other half at home.

I slip my phone back into my pocket and look up to find Saxon smiling at me. Our gazes lock, and there's something in the air between us. Something we're both avoiding at all costs.

Her attention is pulled away from me as Beni shows her a picture of his daughter, but my gaze stays on her and the way she manages to make everyone love her.

Everyone except Viola, of course.

THE RESTAURANT IS A gem in the Italian community. High-quality food made by the best chefs around. It reminds me of a place I discovered in the Middle of Nowhere, West Virginia. I was on my way back from a funeral when I got stuck in a blizzard. I managed to find my way into this little Italian restaurant where the owners took a trip to Italy with all their employees once a year. And the food was amazing.

This place is similar, with their decor feeling like you just walked in off the streets of Venice. The light green and brown walls are accented by murals of the best places throughout Italy. There is a band in the corner, and the whole place smells like your typical Italian household—delicious. My mouth waters the second I enter.

At least I'll get to eat good food while I deal with "Satan in high heels."

Beni walks in behind me, and it's only a matter of seconds before I spot Viola...and Nico.

"Hi love," she greets me. "Oh, and Beni. What a pleasure."

He nods respectfully at her and takes a seat beside me as Viola leans closer.

"You brought protection?" she asks judgmentally.

I give her a knowing look. "I had a feeling you were going

to bring Nico, despite me telling you not to. Trust me when I say Beni is here for *his* protection, not mine."

"Fair enough," she concedes. "Where's your girlfriend? I was kind of hoping you'd bring her instead."

Of course, she was. If Viola thrives on anything, it's the ability to mess with people. Which is why I kept her away from my house tonight. Chances are, Saxon is going to hate me soon anyway. There's no point in speeding up the process.

"Getting straight to it, I see," I murmur. "Not that it's any of your business, but she's at my house. Away from you."

Leaning back in her chair, she hums. "I'm a little surprised you haven't gotten rid of her yet. You know, since the plan changed and she's no longer needed."

My eyes narrow. "Saxon and whatever the fuck the plan is does not involve you. Follow your mother's example and stick to keeping your husband happy. Oh, wait…"

It's a low blow, since Viola is twenty-eight and Raff has yet to let her marry, but she's overstepping, and she needs to know her place. Still, it's one of her few insecurities.

"Or maybe you're in over your head," she snaps back, venom in her tone.

"All right," Nico soothes. "Let's not rip each other's heads off. All my sister was suggesting is that it may be time to let the girl go free. She's not needed anymore."

Viola scrunches her nose. "Not exactly what I was suggesting, but I guess it'll do."

Ignoring her, I scoff at Nico. "A few weeks ago, you wanted her dead."

The arrogant smirk he has on his face makes me want to deck him, and that's before he opens his mouth. "I wanted to see if you had it in you. And I was right. You don't."

As I make a move to get up, Beni puts his hand in front of my chest and looks around the room, reminding me we're in a crowded restaurant. I sit back in my seat and take a deep breath as I contain my anger.

"Look at yourself," Viola points out. "You're usually the calmest person in the room, and yet the topic of her comes up and you're ready to slit everyone's throat."

"Just his," I counter.

I've said it once and I'll say it again, if it wasn't for Raff, Nico would have been checked off my hit list years ago. The guy thinks he has more power than he does and not nearly enough brains to realize he's expendable.

I take a sip of my water, then focus all my attention on the two Mancini brats. "Saxon stays until I say otherwise."

Nico rolls his eyes while Viola looks fed up. She crosses her legs and holds the glass of wine in her hand while giving me a judgmental glare.

"Do you realize the dangerous game you're playing?" she asks. "You've been screwing a girl who's overtaken by Stockholm Syndrome and daddy issues. That's why she's sleeping with you and prancing around your house like all of this is normal. It's not actually going anywhere, and even on the off chance it was, do you really think she'll want anything to do with you once you kill her father?"

"She hates her father," I snap.

Viola huffs with a smirk. "Maybe so, but being resentful of someone and being cool with their murder are two very different things."

Every point she's making is a shot to the chest. I know I should listen to her. Viola may be a ruthless bitch, but she's always been intelligent—unlike her womb-mate. Saxon has been the forbidden fruit from the start, and just because I let myself indulge doesn't change anything. The brutal truth is that things between us began under desperate circumstances on both our parts.

"All I'm saying is why wait," Vi continues. "And besides,

you're off your game lately. You've even stopped putting as much effort into finding Vladimir and Dmitri."

Okay, now *that's* not true. "Your *informant* is giving you shitty intel. They ran back to Russia with their tails between their legs."

She looks at me knowingly. "The Kage I know would have been three moves ahead and shot their plane out of the goddamn sky."

I maintain a poker face but send a silent look over to Beni, because the worst part of it all is she has a valid point.

AFTER WALKING THE STREETS of New York City for over an hour with no clearer head than I had when I left the restaurant, I finally give in and go to the one place I should have when all of this started. It feels like admitting failure as I step up onto the porch and raise my hand to knock on the door, but I know this is exactly where I need to be.

Beni waits in the car behind me, because unlike Viola and Nico, he knows this is a conversation that doesn't involve him. If only those two would take some notes and learn from him; they'd be a lot easier to tolerate.

Raff answers the door and gives me a warm smile, though I can tell he already knows why I'm here. That's why he didn't try to get me to stay at the meeting the other day and why he hasn't called me to demand we talk about everything. He knew that in time I'd come to him on my own.

"Come in, son," he tells me and opens the door further to let me inside.

I step into the house where I spent half my childhood, and it still feels the same. It's bittersweet, really. On one hand, I am so grateful that while losing both of my parents at such a young age, I still had a place to call home. But on the other hand, I hated that this never felt like home. The two people who inhabit this house love me like I'm their own, but I'm *not* their own. Though I'd never say that to Raff—he'd rip me to shreds just for thinking it.

The two of us sit down in the living room, and he gives me his undivided attention.

"So, you and Saxon," he says.

Sighing, I lean forward and rest my head in my hands. "Me and Saxon."

"I mean, I can't say I wasn't concerned about this happening. She's always been special to you, even when you didn't want to admit it." He chuckles. "Hell, even Silas saw it."

"I know. He gave me multiple lectures about her being off limits and someone I had to stay fifty feet away from at all times or he would literally castrate me."

Raff snorts. "What do you think he would do to you now?"

Even the thought alone makes me shudder. If he knew the things I've done to his innocent wildflower over the last few weeks, not even including kidnapping her in the first place, he'd set me on fire just to keep himself warm.

"I know," I answer. "Fuck. I know. It really wasn't ever supposed to go this far."

He reaches over and grabs his glass of bourbon. "You're a

smart man, Kage. You had to know you were risking a lot when you did it the first time, regardless of your reasoning."

The point he's making is clear, and it's a good one, but nothing will ever make me regret the decision to take her virginity. Knowing what would have happened to her if I hadn't…my stomach churns at the thought. The mafia life isn't one any of us wanted for her, including myself. But the Bratva life? For a woman? That's worse than being dead.

"Look," he continues. "I'm not saying it has to stop. You're a grown man capable of making your own decisions. My only concern is the future of the Familia, and at the moment, that relies on Dalton being dealt with."

"And he will be," I assure him.

"Will he?" Raff watches me carefully. "Are you going to be able to kill him without hesitation and without any thoughts of Saxon's feelings about it?"

If anyone else were to ask me this, I'd be furious. Doubting my ability to do what needs to be done is straight disrespect and a punishable offense, which is why even Beni didn't try to save Nico when I almost went at him in the restaurant. But Raff is only looking out for me.

For all of us.

Instead of answering, I drop my head and exhale, nodding slowly. He doesn't say another word as I stand up and make my way outside. The humidity in the air is so thick I could choke on it, but that's not what's making it hard to breathe.

It only takes the walk from the front porch to the car for the numbness to settle in. The same thing that saved me when I found my mother's lifeless body, and again when I watched my father get killed. The thing that makes me the brutal and ruthless killer that I am—completely dead on the inside. And just like that, nothing matters anymore.

Nothing but the Familia.

Besides, she's going to hate me soon anyway. No point in dragging it out.

I'M SITTING AT MY desk, going through security footage and learning Dalton's daily schedule better than I know my own, when Saxon's voice bellows through the house—and damn is she angry. The sound of her footsteps get louder as she comes closer to my office until there's a 5'2" ball of fire and sass standing in my doorway. Beni quickly appears behind her, but I put a hand up to stop him.

"Seriously?" Saxon asks. "You couldn't even end this shit yourself? Had to send your *boy* to do it for you?"

"Other things required my attention. And besides, you're getting exactly what you wanted." I shrug. "I don't see the issue."

"Where am I supposed to go?" she demands. "Back to my father, who left me for dead?"

While he's still around. "That's not my problem to figure out."

She doesn't need to know that I'll have men watching her around the clock until the threat against her is eliminated. It's imperative that she believes I have no stake in her wellbeing.

She goes silent and looks at me like she always has—like I'm a code she's trying to decipher. This time, I stare back at her with nothing but indifference, and only then does she see me for the villain I really am.

"You're a coward," she spits. "A spineless, weak piece of shit who thinks having power makes him a man."

It's laughable, watching her try to spark something in me with her insults. As if I haven't heard worse all my life. But for the sake of getting her out of this world and back into the lifestyle of the princess elite where she belongs, I bite.

Her eyes widen as I rise from my chair, my switchblade tightly grasped in my hand. She swallows harshly and watches me cross the room with patience. Even Beni looks worried for her safety. And maybe he should be.

"You don't know who you're messing with, little girl," I growl.

She snorts. "I wasn't so little when you were eating my pussy for breakfast, lunch, and dinner."

"Yeah, well. Every good meal goes stale eventually."

Beni makes a strained noise, like he's waiting for her to stab me in the jugular, and Saxon's looking like she actually might. Her face turns an angry shade of red and her jaw locks. If you look close enough, you'll see her whole body is shaking, her fists clenched by her side. The look she's giving me could bring a man to his knees to beg for forgiveness. But I need this to stick.

I need to make sure she walks out that door and never so much as thinks about me again.

"I'm not sure what you *thought* this was between us, but you were wrong." The lie flows from my mouth with ease, but it tastes bitter on my tongue. "You. Mean. Nothing. So take the last little sliver of dignity you have left and leave."

Saxon remains completely still. Not a single move is made. Not a word comes from her mouth.

She should be running right now.

Why the fuck isn't she running?

"Go!" I shout, making both her and Beni jump. "What are you waiting for?"

Her eyes meet mine. The piercing blues stare back at me, a perfect mix of half dead inside and half damning me to hell. And without looking away, I find myself giving in just slightly as I bark an order at Beni.

"Get out."

He sounds pained, caught between obeying and staying to protect Saxon. "Boss..."

"Beniamino," I roar. "Now!"

Sighing in frustration, he throws his head back and finally gives in. The second he's out of sight, I slam the door shut with all the pent up anger I have. Saxon closes her eyes for a moment to recover but I don't give her that chance before I pin her up against the wall.

Running my knife lightly across her neck, I'm so close I can see her pulse and feel every one of her emotions.

Confusion.

Pain.

Fear.

"I should slit your throat," I tell her. "Let you bleed out on my floor while I fuck the life out of your corpse."

Her eyes open once more, and I swear, there's fire inside them. The same fire she had when I first set my sights on her. The same fire she had when she got here. It's that fire that got me caught under her spell, which is the only reason she isn't dead right now.

"But that's what you want, isn't it?" I continue. "You want me to drill my cock into you. A goodbye fuck of sorts." As I watch her for any signs that I'm wrong, I see one stray tear slide down her cheek and I smirk. "How pathetic."

"Fuck you," she sneers. The first thing she's said since I threw her words back at her with force.

I hum and the corners of my mouth raise viciously. "No, Gabbana. That's my job."

Wrapping a hand around her throat, I cover her mouth with my own to keep her from saying anything else. Something that might make the last little bit of restraint I have disappear. I'm volatile right now, with numbness blocking every emotion. I can't have her caught on the wrong end of my rage.

As I drag my blade down the front of her shirt, she sinks her teeth into my lip. The pain that shoots through me as I taste my own blood is the only thing to make me feel since the numbness set in, and it only spurs me on. All of the rage pulsing through me makes ripping her shorts and panties from her body an effortless feat. She's panting as she stares down at me on my knees, desperation in her eyes.

She needs this.

I know better than to stick my cock back inside of her. If I do, I'll never let her walk out that damn door. Just the feeling alone would be enough to rip me out of the humanity-free state I've put myself in and have me dragging her to my bed for another few weeks without so much as a drink of water. So instead, I improvise.

Flipping the knife around in my hand, I lick the blood off my lip as I shove the handle inside of her. She stiffens. Not getting what she wants isn't sitting well with her. But as I press my thumb against her clit, all thoughts are wiped from her mind.

The blade digs into the palm of my hand as I fuck her with it, every move I make cutting me deeper. It's a punishing pain, one that's drowned out by my focus on ruining Saxon for anyone else before she walks out of my life. If anything, it's just there to ground me. To remind me why this isn't the life for someone like her. And to hurt me more than the damage her hatred towards me will cause.

"Kage," she breathes.

I know what she's saying without her needing to speak the words.

It's not enough.

She needs me, buried deep inside of her.

Without answering her, I fuck her harder. My own blood drips down my arm as the knife repeatedly lacerates my palm. Her body starts to quiver as she gets closer, and in a moment of mercy, I dive in and suck her clit into my mouth —letting myself taste her one last time and pushing her over the edge.

The scream she lets out is unlike anything I've heard come from her mouth. It's both release and pain all at once, to the point where I check to make sure I didn't let the knife go too far. But when I notice she's undamaged, at least physically, I drop the blade and it falls to the floor as I stand.

Saxon won't even look at me as tears flow down her face.

"Killian is outside and will take you anywhere you want to go." I tell her, pressing my lips to her forehead. "And if I ever see your face again, you'll be enjoying the other end of that knife."

Chapter 18

Saxon

I always thought freedom would feel different. Better. I thought when I finally escaped from the castle of hell, I'd have a new outlook on life. And in a way, I do. It's just nothing like I was expecting.

Wiping the tears from my face as I climb into the backseat of the car, they're only replaced with more as Kage's words play on a loop inside my head. He was so cold, which shouldn't be something new for him, but in a way, it was. He's always looked at me as if he could see straight to my soul. But today, he looked at me in a way that showed he doesn't have one.

"Where would you like to go, Miss Forbes?" Killian speaks with crisp professionalism and a hint of sympathy.

It's a question I've asked myself repeatedly over the last couple months, and the answer is the only thing to warm my cold, dead heart at the moment. "NYC Elite."

He glances at me through the rearview mirror. "The gymnastics center on the Upper East Side?"

I nod. "My sister is there. She goes there all summer for camp."

"Future Olympian, huh?" he says.

Giving him the best smile I can manage, I try not to be rude when I don't answer. It's not that I don't like Killian. I'm just not in the mood to make small talk, or really talk at all. Not after today.

I didn't even know Kage came home last night when I woke up to Beni beside the bed. At first, when he handed me back my cellphone and told me to grab anything I wanted to take, I thought I was dreaming. The quick pinch to my arm told me that I wasn't, which led to me thinking Beni was trying to rescue me from something I didn't need saving from. It wasn't until he told me that Kage gave the order to let me go free that I realized what was happening.

He was done with me, and like Viola said, he proved I was nothing more than a fuck of convenience.

I lean my head against the glass and look out the window, watching as we get further and further from the place I was held captive for months.

Further from all of the dangers I faced and conquered.

Further from Kage.

THE CLOSER WE GET to the gym, the more my heart starts to race. It's been months since I've gotten to hug my little sister. I think, out of everyone, she's who I missed most of all. As we pull up to the building, I'm practically jumping out of my seat.

"Would you like me to wait?" Killian asks.

I nod, smiling genuinely for the first time. "If you don't mind. I'll only be a minute."

"Take your time."

He seems to understand the importance of all this, and I appreciate that more than he realizes. A part of me wonders how Killian got into the mafia life. He hardly seems like all the other stone-cold men I've come in contact with lately. No, this one has kind eyes and makes you feel understood and respected.

It feels weird, climbing out of the car without a tight metaphorical leash. The one time I came to the city with Kage, he kept me within arm's reach for every second of it. And now, to be free of the chains that bound me to him… well, it should feel better than it does.

After I get inside, it only takes a couple minutes for me to spot Kylie. She's on the balance beam, making back-walkovers on a four-inch wide platform look easy. A wide grin stretches across my face as she lands her dismount and her eyes meet mine.

"Saxon!" she screams, and runs across the room.

If I was trying to be discreet, there's no point in that now. Everyone in the room turns to look at me as Kylie lunges into my arms. Her coach, a girl named Brittany I went to high school with, smiles at the two of us.

"I missed you so much," Kylie says, squeezing me tightly.

I breathe her in and bask in the feeling of being able to see her again. "I missed you, too."

"Wait," she says. "Put me down."

I do as she asks and feel a little pang in my chest as she takes a step back and crosses her arms over her chest. The pout on her face is enough to tell me what she's feeling, but being Kylie, she says the words anyway.

"I'm still mad at you."

"Mad at me? Why?"

"Because you didn't say goodbye before you left." Her bottom lip juts out, and her eyes start to tear. It's heartbreaking to watch.

If she knew the truth, she would never hold it against me. But Kylie is too young to be plagued by the evils in the world. She doesn't need to know a single ounce of what I went through, or what kind of man our father really is. Not yet, anyway.

I'll save that for when she's older. More mature so she can understand and deal with it appropriately.

Sighing, I crouch down to her level. "I know, Kyliekins. I'm so sorry. It'll never happen again."

She looks at me hesitantly before sticking out her pinky. "Promise?"

I laugh softly and link my pinky with hers. "I promise."

"Kylie, you're up," one of the coaches calls her.

"Better go. Simone Biles didn't become as good as she is by slacking off."

She frowns and wraps her arms around me once more. "Will I see you when I get home?"

Don't lie to her like he did. "I don't think so, babe. But I will come back as soon as I can."

"Okay," she says with a pout. "I love you, S."

"I love you too, K."

Holding back the tears as I watch her run over to the uneven bars, my chest tightens with the thought of being away from her again. But I have to do what's best for me right now, as painful as that may be.

With one last wave, I head back outside, where Killian is still waiting for me. He reaches back to pass me a tissue and I thank him. I compose myself while he waits patiently. When I finally get my emotions under control, I exhale.

"Okay," I tell him. "Take me home, please."

"Very well, Miss Forbes."

Home. I nearly laugh at the term. Home is a place where people love you. Where you can feel safe and protected. But all I feel when I think about that penthouse is the resentment I hold toward my father. It's not my home, it's where he lied to everyone about where I was and slept soundly at night while I was fighting for my life.

As Killian heads to the penthouse, I turn on my phone. An influx of text messages and voicemails come in at once, the most being from Nessa and my mom. The earliest ones from Ness seem frantic, but then she must have talked to my father because they turn to just sad. Wondering why I didn't say goodbye, or why I just stopped talking to her once I transferred schools. And my mom? Well she was clearly fed that lie from the beginning, and with the way she keeps referencing "my emails," I'm assuming dear old Dad has been sending them on my behalf.

How nice of him.

I type out a quick message to Nessa, letting her know that I'm okay and I'll be in touch soon. Just as Killian pulls up to my building, I press send and shove the phone into my pocket. With a grip on the door handle, I smile at my chauffeur for the day.

"Mind waiting one more time?" I ask sweetly. "I just have to grab a few things, and then you can drop me off at my final destination."

I've only had the two-hour drive to come up with a plan, but it starts with him dropping me off at the airport in Jersey. As soon as I grab my passport and some money, I'll be booking it out of the country for the time being. With my father's ties to the Russian mafia still unknown, and the fact that I can expose his lies, I don't trust my safety in his hands. And for good reason.

Killian smiles back at me. "Of course. I'm at your service today. Anything you need."

"You're a gem," I tell him. "I'll be right back."

Hopping out of the car, I keep my head down to avoid anyone recognizing me. However, no amount of discreetness could keep Levi, the doorman, from seeing my face. A wide grin stretches across his face as he opens the door.

"Miss Forbes," he greets me excitedly and starts walking me toward the elevator. "Long time no see! Home for a visit?"

I play along, careful not to give away anything. "Just a quick one. I have to grab a few things."

"And how is Duke? Is it everything you've ever imagined?"

"It is," I confirm. "Everything and more."

As the elevator opens, he gives me a warm hug and then frees me so I can step inside. "Well, try not to be such a stranger."

"I won't."

It's a total lie. After today, there's a good chance I won't see him for another few months, but while Levi has been a part of my life since I was Kylie's age, I need to protect myself first.

Clearly, I'm the only one who will.

When I reach the penthouse, I stop to listen for any signs of someone being home, but thankfully, there are none. As I make my way toward my father's office, I look around and notice how dead this place feels. It doesn't have the same warmth it once possessed. The couch I spent nights watching movies with my family on, and the hallway filled with pictures—it all feels fake and worthless now.

Halfway down, in the back of the bookshelf, covered by numerous first edition novels that are much older than I am, is a safe. Honestly, if it wasn't for the times I used to play in here when I was younger, even I wouldn't have realized its existence. It's been upgraded over the years, this one having a handprint scanner, but the place he keeps the key is the same as always—inside a carved-out copy of *To Kill a Mockingbird*.

I move the books out of the way and grab the key. When I open the safe, I find everything I need. All of my important documents—my passport, birth certificate, social security card—and enough money to last me a while are gathered up quickly. Just as I go to close it, however, I notice the gun. It weighs heavily in my hand as I grab it, but a package falls over when the gun is no longer there to hold it up.

Beige fabric peeks out of the opening, and my brows furrow as I wonder what piece of clothing could be so important that he put it in here. Grabbing the package, I pull out its contents and my heart drops when I recognize the handwriting on the card that falls out.

You stole from me, so I stole from you.
Good luck getting Dmitri to want her now. - K.M.

I read it, over and over, trying to understand what it means, when finally, it clicks.

"No," I breathe as my stomach drops.

The moment I unfold the fabric, reality slaps me in the face hard enough to cause whiplash. There, right in front of me, is the sheet stained with the blood from losing my virginity, and everything I knew was true but didn't want to believe when it comes to Kage.

Viola was right.

I never meant a damn thing.

My phone vibrates in my pocket, then again, and once more. I can only assume it's Nessa's reply texts coming in constantly, while my focus is locked on the damning evidence in front of me. With every second that passes, my anger builds until my blood is absolutely boiling.

I storm into my bedroom and grab a duffle bag from the closet, not even sparing a second to mentally evaluate the lack of nostalgia it brings before I march back to the office. I don't have the time. I don't have the patience. Slipping the gun into my waistband, I throw everything else into the bag and put the books back into place. And then I walk out without so much as a second thought.

Thankfully, when I get down to the lobby, Levi is too busy with another resident to do anything but wave to me as I leave. Killian waits dutifully out front, and if I wasn't so enraged, I'd almost feel bad for what I'm about to make him do.

Almost.

"Change of plans, Killian," I tell him. "Take me back to the Hamptons."

His eyes widen, as if that was the last thing he was expecting me to say. "I'm sorry, Miss Forbes. I can't do that. Mr. Malvagio was very clear with his orders."

"You let me deal with *Mr. Malvagio*," I sneer.

He sits completely still, keeping the car in place as he battles the conflict and weighs his options. He's probably trying to figure out a way he could avoid bringing me back there. After all, I should be more afraid than I am. Kage all but threatened to kill me if I ever showed my face around there again. But fuck him and fuck that.

I cross my arms over my chest and meet his pleading gaze in the rearview mirror. "I'm not going anywhere so you may as well start driving."

With a heavy sigh, he gives in and puts the car into drive. "Lord help us both."

No, Killian. Lord help him.

I POUND ON THE door with one hand while the other keeps a firm grip on the package Kage sent my father. At first, there's no answer, but when I don't relent, it finally opens. Beni stands there looking like I just gave him a piercing headache. But he's not why I'm here.

Pushing past him, I go to find Kage when fingers wrap around my wrist.

"You really do not want to do that," Beni warns. "He's not himself, Sax. He's an emotional black hole. You should get out of here while you still have the chance."

"Fuck that," I scoff. "I want answers, and I'm getting them."

He lets go of me and holds his hands up. "Suit yourself, but don't say I didn't warn you."

No longer being held back, I march my little ass into his office and slam the door behind me. Kage, having seen my arrival in the cameras I'm sure, doesn't even look up from his phone. It's as if I'm not even here.

"You're an asshole," I spit.

He exhales with a smile but still won't look at me. "You came all the way back here just to tell me that?"

Ripping the sheet out of the package, I grip it tightly in my hand as I hold it up. "It was all a lie, wasn't it?"

Kage glances up at the sheet and then back down at his phone, like it doesn't matter to him. Like *I* don't matter to him. And just like that, any bit of calm I gained during the two hour drive back here, is gone.

I pull the revolver out from behind my back and cock it before pointing it at him. While I wasn't very skilled with one when I had the chance to shoot him at his penthouse, I spent half the ride back Googling exactly how to use this thing. At the sound of the hammer, I finally have Kage's attention.

"Put that thing down before you hurt yourself."

"Answer me," I grit out. "Tell me it was all a lie."

He sighs as he stands up and steps around his desk. "Saxon. Put the gun down."

Instead of obeying, I pull the trigger. The bullet goes flying and shatters the window behind him and his eyes widen at the fact that I actually did it. Adrenaline pumps through me, and it's so fucking intoxicating. A smile pulls at the corners of my mouth as the feeling of having all the power settles in.

Kage goes to take another step toward me but I point the gun directly at him. "I'll shoot you, Kage. Don't think I won't."

A stampede of footsteps come barreling toward the room and the door barges open. The moment Beni sees me, holding a revolver pointed at Kage, he pulls his own gun out and points it at me.

"Don't," Kage orders with a hand up. "I've got this."

I snort, earning a look from Kage that silently asks if I've lost my ever-loving mind. And judging by the current situation, I'd say that's a likely possibility. After the last few months, this morning especially, he deserves to be on the receiving end for once. I won't apologize for it.

"Go, Beni. Take Roman and Cesari with you."

Like the loyal servant he is, he mumbles "it's your funeral" under his breath as they all leave, shutting the door behind them. I, however, am no less angry. Keeping his main lackey from killing me didn't earn him any points.

"Gabbana," he says softly. "Give me the gun."

A dry laugh bubbles out of me. "Why? So you can kill me with it? Do it. It's no worse than finding out all of this was a tactic to you."

"That's not what it was."

"Bullshit!" I roar. "Every move you've made has been a calculated one to get your way, and I was just your fucking pawn!"

He shakes his head. "You're wrong."

Liar! I pull the trigger again, and this time he tries to dodge it—the bullet missing him by an inch and going into his computer chair.

"Jesus Christ!" he screams. "Stop fucking shooting!"

"Then admit it! Admit you willingly ruined me to get your way!"

"Taking your virginity was to *save* you, not ruin you!" he roars, then stops to run his fingers through his hair as he tries to calm down. "The Bratva would have *ruined* you."

My brows furrow. "What the hell do they have to do with this?"

"Your father was going to give you to Dmitri Petrov," he shouts. "If I hadn't intervened, the second you were free from here, you were to be wed to a man three times your age, with seven ex-wives who have all wound up dead! They have a strict policy on marrying only virgins, especially men of his merit. Popping your precious little cherry made you worthless to him!"

My heart pounds inside my chest as I look down and away from Kage. Not only did my father leave me here for dead, but on the chance that they let me go free, he was sealing my fate for his own personal gain. I've spent weeks trying to justify in my head why he wouldn't come for me. At times, I even convinced myself he was scared. But he's not a coward —he's just a fucking sociopath.

While I'm lost in my own thoughts, Kage makes his move —grabbing the gun from my hand and taking it apart. Within seconds, it's in pieces on the floor and I'm officially disarmed. He turns around and walks toward his desk, putting his hands on it and keeping his back toward me.

"You have the answer you were looking for," he growls. "Now leave, and this time don't come back."

There it is again. The churn in my stomach at the thought of being anywhere but here. Anywhere except by his side, specifically.

A part of me is screaming to leave. With his ruthless behavior earlier, I can only imagine what he'll do if he gets his hands on me again. But then I realize, I've personally watched him kill people for much less than I just did. I shot at him, *twice,* and yet he's still willing to just let me go.

This time, I stand my ground. "No."

He whips his head around to look at me with a cocked brow. "No?"

"You heard me." With my new revelation, I feel stronger than ever toward him. "I'm not afraid of you."

Now *that* makes him laugh. The corner of his mouth raises, and the smirk he gives me tells me that he likes the little games we play.

"Not afraid of me," he murmurs, coming closer. "Do you realize letting you go was something I've never done before? I should've killed you. A lesser man would have without a single ounce of hesitation. And now you're giving me a second shot at it, after shooting at me, no less."

Feeling his eyes boring into me, I hold his gaze. "You won't hurt me."

He hums. "Don't be so sure."

The two of us stand in silence, neither one backing down. His jaw stays locked as he watches me, and I can't tell if he wants to rip off my clothes or my head. It's probably a little of both.

Letting a hint of a smile show, he nods toward the door. "Get out of here, Saxon."

"No," I answer.

His restraint starts to waiver. "Last chance. Go."

"No."

Clenching his fist, he snarls. "Fucking leave!"

"I can't!" I shout back.

"What the hell do you mean you can't?" he barks. "Just walk out the goddamn door and never come back! It's not hard!"

"I can't do that!"

"Why the fuck not?"

It's becoming harder to keep my emotions in check, I swallow down the lump in my throat and curse internally when I see him notice it. "You know why."

He stays perfectly still, almost as if he's stopped breathing entirely as he stares back at me. Goosebumps rise across my skin as I have his total, undivided attention. He takes a step closer.

"Say it," he demands.

I stay silent and unmoving, just watching him closing in on me. Even if I wanted to, I can't seem to make my mouth form the words. It's like there's a block between my thoughts and the ability to speak them.

When I don't answer, he pushes me back against the wall —the same wall he had me against earlier. "Say. It."

Staring into his eyes, with his hand wrapped around my throat, I can feel it. The shift in the atmosphere. The heat radiating off him. It's not enough that he knows it in his black little heart. He needs to hear it.

"I'm in love with you," I confess, my heart threatening to break through my ribcage.

He empties his lungs, almost as if he didn't consider it a

possibility until now. He searches my face for any sign that I'm lying, but he isn't going to find one. As twisted as it is, I've never meant anything more.

Running his thumb over my cheek, he looks at me in disbelief. "You beautifully naive woman."

He uses his grip on my neck to pull me in and presses our lips together in a bruising kiss. His tongue tangles with mine, demanding dominance in a fight I never stood a chance at winning. We grip and pull at each other like a goddamn lifeline, and my body feels like it's on fire as he grinds against me.

"You're truly certifiable." he growls against my mouth. "You're lucky Beni didn't blow your fucking brains out."

I rest my head back against the wall while he kisses down my neck. "You'd never let that happen. You act like this heartless monster, but I'm not sure I buy it."

"Ah, the hopeless romantic thinks she can rescue me from the darkness," he quips and pulls back to look at me. "Even my last name means evil, baby. There's no saving me."

With both his hands on my shirt, he rips my shirt completely in half. The tattered pieces fall to the floor and I look up at him through my lashes.

"As hot as that is, if you keep doing it, I'll never have any clothes to wear."

He stares at me, waiting for me to continue, and when I don't, he smirks. "I'm not seeing a problem here."

I throw his smug grin right back at him. "Oh, in that case, should we invite your men in for a voyeur party? I mean, since I'm a practicing nudist now and all, it's no big deal, right?"

An animalistic sound rumbles in the back of his throat, like he's meant to scare off anyone else within a five mile radius. "Let them see even too much cleavage and I'll have you wearing a fucking parka for the rest of your God-given life."

I'm not going to lie, possessive Kage is the sexiest version of him. The way he would quite literally rip someone limb from limb for so much as looking at me for too long—it pulls at the deepest parts of me.

Taking my bottom lip between his teeth, he tugs on it and earns a breathy moan from me. My hands fumble with his belt like I'm going to lose my mind if I don't get him inside me soon. He must feel the same, because the moment I push them down and his cock springs free, he lifts me up and pins me to the wall while he lines up at my entrance.

As he slides in, sounds of relief fill the room. My nails dig into his shoulders as I clench around him. With one hand firmly on my waist to keep me in place, his other travels up my back until he's tugging on my hair and forcing my head back.

His lips skim down my chin, his teeth skimming over my beating pulse. His hot breath on my neck causes pleasure to build, making my back arch more and my pelvis to thrust up against him so he's angled deeper inside me as my clit grinds on his stomach.

I feel needed, hot, and desperate, but also, I feel so fucking *alive*. I know with a few more thrust I'll be there, tipping over the edge. Drowning in the ruthless pleasure only he can give me.

"You tried to fucking kill me," he snarls, thrusting into me harder. "And now I'm going to make you wish you had."

He pulls out of me so quickly I whimper from the loss of him. From the loss of my orgasm. I was right *there*, so close I could kill him. Just as he promised.

He pushes stuff off his desk. Files, pens, even his computer goes flying to the ground.

"On the desk," he orders. "All fours, ass facing me."

His words are like a livewire to my system. I walk on shaky legs as I make my way over to his desk, bending over it seductively slow.

Kage lets out a low growl as I spread my legs further apart and my arousal slowly drips down the inside of my thighs.

I feel his heat behind me as I stare at the wall. His promise of torture has my body quivering as I wait, my eyes locked on the wall ahead of me. His calloused hands slide up my thighs, grabbing my ass with force.

I hear a wet pop before I feel him spreading my cheeks and his finger is right *there*. I tense, and then relax when I imagine what that would be like. Thoughts of him taking me that way just sparked a delicious interest I want to explore.

Slowly, he pushes a finger in to the knuckle. It's so foreign, and so tight a bead of sweat breaks across my brow as my body begins to overheat.

"One day, I'm going to fill this hole, too," he growls. "There won't be a part of your body I won't own, Gabbana."

He pulls his finger out, and it is replaced with his tongue. My back arches as he drags his tongue from my ass to my clit. He works it hard, swirling his tongue around it, sucking and nipping it between his teeth. His finger thrusts into me as he continues his assault. Everything starts to tremble, my body moving with each impact of his hand. My stomach becomes hot, and I'm so close I smile, but right as I'm about to come, he disappears completely.

"Bastard," I hiss.

"Look at you, so fucking needy you're making a mess on my desk."

His hand comes down on the back of my spine as he pushes my chest to his desk, my ass still up in the air. I feel him enter my pussy and I sigh in relief, but instead he takes slow, shallow thrusts until I'm a mess of whimpers and promises.

He won't let me come.

Won't let me find ecstasy in him.

He pulls out again and walks until he's in front of me. His cock is hard and dripping with my own juices. And I'm guessing the angry way it pulses has to do with the fact that he didn't get off earlier, when he fucked me with the handle of his knife instead of his dick.

"Finish me," he orders. "In your mouth. Now."

I rise up, greedily sucking him between my lips. Before I can begin my revenge on him, he grips my chin, the other hand in my hair, taking away all the control I had. His thrusts are hard, fast, and merciless. I focus on breathing through my nose while my eyes water, but none of this helps with the deep, needy ache I feel

It's just building, with nowhere to go.

With a final hard thrust, his head falls back as he tenses—a deep moan vibrating up his throat as he empties himself down my throat. I swallow every drop he gives me until there's nothing left.

Keeping my head down, I accept my punishment and just hope that he will take mercy on me later, but he reaches down and grabs my chin. As I'm forced to meet his gaze, I find a sinister look in his eyes staring back at me.

"I'm nowhere near done with you yet."

I WAKE IN THE morning, feeling deliciously sore from last night's escapades. True to his word, he didn't let me come for hours, until the pain of it had me begging for release. Then, and only then, did he give it to me.

Kage is sleeping soundly beside me, or at least it seems like it until I roll over to watch him. Within thirty seconds, he peeks one eye open and groans.

"Planning the next way you're going to try to kill me?" he grumbles, voice gravely with sleep.

I hum thoughtfully. "I'm thinking cyanide might be a better option. I've got horrible aim."

"Thank fuck for that."

Kage rolls out of bed and stretches his arms above his head. As his back muscles strain, I notice the scratches left there by me. My own personal claim on him.

He looks back at me and his eyes roam my naked body. "So goddamn stunning."

With a broad smile, I lean up and kiss him. "You go shower. I'll make breakfast."

Quickly throwing one of his T-shirts on, I go to leave when he smacks my ass.

"Yeah, wench," he teases. "Get in the kitchen and cook me food."

I turn around and cock a brow at him. "You know, you're awfully excited for my cooking given I just threatened to poison you."

The smile is wiped straight from his face, and I can't help but feel accomplished as I spin back and walk out. And if I get butterflies from the small chuckle I hear behind me, that's no one's business but my own.

IT TAKES ME A few minutes to find all the ingredients I need. Eggs are easily located in the fridge along with the bacon, but the pan poses to be a problem. I search high and low, in every cabinet in the kitchen, and still can't find it.

"What are you looking for?" Beni asks, making me jump.

I sigh frustratedly. "Frying pan."

A grin pushes its way through, like he's trying his best not to laugh and nearly failing, as he comes closer and pulls the pan down from where it was hanging—right in front of my face. I roll my eyes and take it from him.

"Thanks."

"No problem," he replies.

Once I get everything prepared and on the stove, I finally get a chance to answer Nessa. She's been blowing up my phone since I first texted her yesterday afternoon. And judging by the thirty-seven unanswered text messages, I'd say she's probably worried about me.

Me: Sorry. Got caught up with something. How've you been? I miss you so much.

The three little dots that show she's typing appear within seconds.

Nessa: Caught up with something or someone? When are you coming home?

I laugh quietly to myself. Leave it to Nessa to automatically assume it was sex. Granted, that's exactly what was going on, but still. I don't think there has been a single day since we turned sixteen that she hasn't had her mind in the gutter.

Choosing to ignore the first question, I answer the second.

Me: I'm not entirely sure yet, but when I am, you'll be the first to know.

I'm just pressing send when the doorbell rings and Beni goes to see who it is. At first, I don't hear anything, but then the voice that echoes through the foyer and into the kitchen is one that could ruin anyone's day.

"Beni," she greets him, but in a way that sounds like she believes she's better than he is. "Always such a pleasure."

"Wish I could say the same," he counters.

Heels click across the floor as she comes closer, and when she finally reaches the kitchen, I can tell by the look on her face that I'm the last person she expected to see. With no one else around, there's no need to be fake and hide her disgust for me.

"You're like a bad case of herpes," she says with a sigh. "I thought I got rid of you."

Taking a piece of bacon from the plate, I lean against the counter and grin smugly. "May want to talk to your doctor if you're having a flare-up. I hear there's no cure but he can treat your symptoms."

Her short fuse is already lit as she rolls her eyes and huffs. "Aren't you supposed to be smart? Stupidity doesn't seem like your style."

"And desperation doesn't seem like yours," I snap back. "What are you even doing here?"

"I was about to ask the same thing," Kage says, appearing in the doorway to his bedroom.

He looks like a Greek god with a towel wrapped around his waist. Just looking at him, my mouth goes dry, and I genuinely hate the fact that Viola gets to see him like this, too. Seeing her look at him makes me want to gouge her eyes out with my fingernails.

"Well, I was coming to congratulate you on sorting"—she

gestures up and down at me—"this, but now I see you haven't. Nico said you got rid of her."

Kage glances at me and smiles, pushing off the doorway and coming my way. "Well, Nico needs a lesson in shutting his damn mouth."

Viola can do nothing but watch as Kage grabs the bottom of my chin and bends down to kiss me. He puts damn near everything he has into it, basically sucking the breath from my lungs. And when he pulls away, the smirk he sports tells me he knows it.

"Saxon isn't going anywhere," he tells her with his eyes still locked on mine, then turns to glare at her. "She's here to stay, so either learn to live with that, or get the fuck out. Preferably the latter, if we're all being honest here."

And just like that, my every question is answered as he grabs a piece of bacon and walks away, leaving Viola shooting daggers at me with her mind.

Checkmate, bitch.

Chapter 19

Saxon

THINKING WISELY IN THE FACE OF CHAOS HAS never been my strong suit. After all, I went into my former bedroom, opened the closet, and all I walked out with was a fucking duffle bag full of personal items. Regardless of where I was going to end up, clothes would have been useful, which is why I'm in the middle of a designer boutique well past closing time.

We had planned to come earlier, but we got a little... distracted. When we finally left the bedroom long enough to get in the damn car, we were greeted at the shop by a closed sign. I tried to tell Kage that we could just come another day, but he wasn't having it. He knocked on the door and offered the very annoyed looking workers inside each a thousand dollars just to let us grab a few things.

I walk around the store, looking at all the beautiful clothes while Kage sits on a chair near the dressing room. He keeps his attention on his phone while I shop. His fingers move a mile a minute as he sends what looks to be an intense email.

"Would this look good on me?" I ask, holding up a gold dress.

He doesn't even raise his head as he answers. "I'd look good on you."

I roll my eyes. "Kage."

That makes him look at me. "What? I would. Actually, I *do*."

"Yes, babe. Glad to see your confidence isn't lacking," I quip. "Now, seriously. The dress."

He shakes his head. "Absolutely not. I brought you here. I'm not going to give you fashion advice, too."

With a pout, I exhale. "But I need someone who will tell me if something looks bad, regardless of if I love it."

Usually I'd have Nessa with me, but she still thinks I'm in North Carolina—living my best Duke University life. I can't even send her pictures from the dressing room. I've seen what she can do with the internet. The girl is a better detective than half of the FBI. She'll figure out everything has been a lie before I can even hit the checkout.

Kage leans forward and rests his arms on his knees as he smirks at me. "I could call Viola. I'm sure she'd have no problem doing exactly what you just asked."

"On a completely unrelated note, what did you do with my revolver?"

"It's at the bottom of the Atlantic," he answers smugly. "I'll buy you some scuba gear so you can go find it."

I exhale exasperatedly. "Asshole."

His laughter echoes through the store as he throws his head back, and I can't even stay mad at him for a second while I go back to looking for new clothes, with no one's approval but my own.

THE SCORCHING HOT WATER flows through my hair and down my body. My skin turns red from the heat, just at the point right before it would burn. Hot enough to feel like it's washing away all of my sins, while knowing I'm only going to commit more.

I make quick work of blow drying my hair and pulling on one of my new dresses—a black one with a plunging neckline that will have Kage wishing he hadn't left me to decide on clothes by myself. However, when I go into the living room, he's nowhere to be found. The couch is completely empty, with not even Beni watching his usual crime shows.

As I head down the hallway, I notice the office door is shut and there are voices coming from inside it. The first one I recognize is Kage, of course, followed by Beni and Nico. But then, there's another that has me wondering where I've heard it before.

"No," the voice says. "Dalton's too smart for that. He'll see it coming a mile away."

With metaphorical balls of steel and literal lack of self-preservation, I open the door and ignore the glare Kage shoots me. The room goes silent as I scan the room.

Kage wants to bend me over his knee and teach me a lesson.

Beni thinks it's only a matter of time until I get myself killed. He's probably right.

Nico's face is lit up like a Christmas tree, obsessed with the fact that I'm going against Kage's orders.

"Saxon." The sound of the voice behind me makes me jump, then sag in relief.

"Raff?"

He stands up, opening his arms for a hug, and I go willingly. My grandfather's best friend has always held a special place in my heart. The stories they used to tell me about all the mischief they got up to together were always my favorite.

I'm lost in the warm feeling of his arms when I notice the look Kage is giving me, like he's waiting for it to click.

And it does.

"Wait." I step back and out of Raff's reach. "W-what are you doing here?"

"Saxon," he says again, this time sadly, and tries to put his hand on my arm, but I dodge him.

"No," I breathe. "You're a part of all this, aren't you?"

His shoulders sag. "I tried to keep you out of this. I swear I did. But I don't call the shots anymore."

I turn my attention to Kage. "Is that true?"

He nods once, slowly. "Taking you was a last-ditch effort."

It's a lot to take in. The man standing in front of me has been in my life for as long as I can remember, and knowing he had even a small part in my kidnapping is just too much to process right now.

"So, what's the plan now?" I ask, changing the subject.

Kage cocks a brow at me. "What do you think you're doing?"

"Helping," I answer simply.

Before the word is even fully out of my mouth, Kage is shutting down the idea. "Absolutely not. I want you nowhere near this. And when the fuck did you buy *that*?"

I glance down at my dress and smirk deviously. Hopping up onto the desk, I cross my legs and run my fingers through my hair, showing that I'm not going anywhere. "Come on, Kage. Even *you're* smart enough to realize that there's no one better to help you figure out a plan to get what you want out of Dalton Forbes than his own daughter."

Nico chuckles, but it's quickly cut off as Kage glares at him, and then he turns back to me. "One more comment like that and I can promise you'll regret it later."

I bite my lip, finding that threat more tempting than frightening. "You promise?"

He pulls his eyes away from me and fixes his pants to hide his already growing hard-on. With his eyes off me, I glance around to see what everyone else is doing, only to find all the men in the room watching Kage, but of course, it's Nico who speaks first.

"You may as well tell her," he says. "If you're so adamant about keeping her around and all."

"Nicolas," Raff scolds him, but Kage interrupts.

"No," he murmurs. "For once, the idiot has a point."

I wait with bated breath as Kage turns to look at me, and I can already tell he's wondering if I'll run. At one point, I may have, but I don't know if that's even a possibility for me anymore. I don't want it to be.

"We're going to kill him." The words flow from his mouth with such indifference, it's as if he's talking about the weather. "While he was working with the Bratva, getting rid of him wasn't on the table. It would've started a war neither of us want right now. But now, with them out of the picture, it's our best option. Our *only* option."

Okay, I can see the reason for hesitation. Especially after the morning in his penthouse, when I lost it at the thought of them killing him. And while that was before I knew all of the shit he was willing to put me through, and my black heart has no place for him in it anymore, it has a massive soft spot for Kylie. He's not just *my* father, and she's too young to deal with that kind of emotional trauma.

"And how does killing him solve your problem?"

Kage keeps his head held high, regarding me the same way he would one of the men in here. "With him dead, his will kicks in, and all of our properties land in the hands of Scarlett. Your mother."

I think it over for a second, but ultimately come to the same decision.

"It's not going to work," I tell them bluntly. "You really think if you kill my dad that my mom is just going to give you what you want?"

"I've known your mother since she was a little girl," Raff protests.

"Maybe so, but even I was fooled by who my father really is and what he's really like. I can only imagine the manipulation she's dealt with for the last two decades," I explain. "If you kill him, there's no guarantee what her reaction will be. And there's no way to get rid of him without her knowing you did it. She's not dense."

Kage rubs his chin, taking everything I'm saying into consideration. "And what do you suggest we do instead? You know, being as you're the expert on him and all."

"You said the Russians are out of the deal, right?" He nods. "Offer him something he can't refuse."

"And what's that?" Nico asks.

I shrug. "Protection. He clearly doesn't care about anyone else's life, but he's too selfish to risk his own."

Beni turns to Kage. "You did just have Evgeny in your clutches. We could act as if he said something about Dalton's fate if the deal fell through."

He takes his time to process it and then rests a hand down on the armrest. "And what if protection isn't enough?"

"It won't be," I answer honestly. "That's why you give him the only other thing he wants—power."

"What?" all the men in the room balk in unison.

I hold up one hand to stop them. "You tell him that he's

starting from the bottom, but he can work his way up in your organization."

Kage's jaw locks. "Over my dead body will he ever be someone of importance in the Familia."

"He doesn't have to be..." I tell him.

Beni grins as he finishes for me. "He just has to believe he will."

I smile back at him. "Precisely."

Kage looks to Raff, pursing his lips like the idea isn't the worst one he's heard, while Beni beams proudly at me.

"Kamikaze, I have to admit. I underestimated you."

Giggling, I wink at him. "You aren't the first, and I'm sure you won't be the last."

The four men talk amongst themselves, working out small details I don't really need to be a part of, but I listen in anyway. When it's all said and done, and Beni agrees to put together a formal letter requesting a meeting with my father, everyone stands. Raff takes a step toward me, but Kage has other plans as he grabs my wrist and drags me from the room.

He doesn't stop until we're outside on the patio, finally out of the view of others. He spins around and holds my face in his hands. If I had to guess, I'd say he's still battling that internal conflict on whether he should praise me or punish me. Personally, I think he should do both.

"You, Saxon Royce Forbes, are fucking lethal," he says, and then presses his lips to mine before I can answer.

The kiss is desperate. Needy. Almost as if he was afraid he would never get the chance to do it again. Though that's how the whole last week has been. We only spent a few hours away from each other, but I came back to a completely different animal—one that's insatiable and can't keep his hands off me for longer than a half hour.

"You're like my own personal weapon." He presses a kiss

to the corner of my mouth and then my forehead. "I'm just trying to figure out if that's good or bad."

"Why would it be bad?"

He sighs and runs his thumb over my cheek. "Because it's as if you're tailored just to me, and that makes you the only one who can cause mass destruction."

I smile sweetly. "Well, personally, I think we're good for each other."

"Is that so?" His hands move to my hips and he pulls me closer. "Just know, I was serious when I said there is no saving me. I am who I am, Gabbana."

There's only honesty in his words, but what he doesn't know is I don't want to save him. Maybe I did, at one point. Maybe I thought I could. But Kage is who he is because of this world. It's dangerous, and terrifying, and nothing is sugar coated, and I fell in love with him in the midst of it all.

Wrapping my arms around his neck, I kiss him tenderly with all the patience in the world. The kind of kiss where you just want to be close. One that doesn't have any intentions or hidden agendas. It's just one to show him I'm here. That I'm not going anywhere.

"Say it again," he whispers.

It takes me a second to know what he's talking about, and then I realize. Since last week, when I was standing in the middle of his office in the middle of an epic breakdown, neither of us have talked about my confession. He never said it back, but I didn't expect him to. I wasn't telling him with blind hopes that he feels the same. Men like him, they don't love easily. But the fact that he's asking to hear it again? The hopeless romantic in me says that he's not going anywhere either.

"I lo—"

The door opens and Raff comes outside, effectively ending the moment as I take a step back. My feelings toward him are still confusing. I don't know what kind of role he plays, but

I'm sure Kage will tell me later. In the meantime, I'm left to deal with the fact that he betrayed me the same way my father has.

"Mind if I have a moment with Saxon?" he asks Kage.

Instead of answering, Kage turns and looks at me to see if I'm all right with it. "S?"

I nod, against my better judgment. "It's fine. I'll meet you inside."

He kisses me once more before going back into the house. I wrap my arms around myself in an attempt to feel comforted, but it's no use. The truth is, I'm constantly on edge if Kage isn't around.

Real healthy, Sax.

"I'm sorry," Raff begins. "For not doing more to help you. If your grandfather were here, he would never forgive me for the things I've done."

I hum sarcastically. "Well, if my grandfather were still here, there wouldn't have been an issue in the first place."

That surprises him as his brows raise. "Kage told you?"

"About a month ago. He told me everything."

He glances back at the house, seeing the way Kage makes it a point to check on me by looking outside every few seconds. It's like he can't take his eyes off me, and just knowing that makes me feel more alive than I ever have.

"I feel obligated to tell you that Silas didn't want this for you," he tells me. "This world. This *lifestyle*. He wanted you nowhere near it."

A smile tugs at my mouth. "Well, the thing I loved most about my grandfather was he allowed me to make my own choices in life."

"Not with this. He was very adamant about you not being involved in anything related to the Familia."

His tone is stern, as if the topic isn't up for discussion, and a few years ago, a few months ago even, I may have listened. Raff was one of my grandfather's closest friends and confidantes. But my nickname wasn't Wildflower because of my looks. It was because of my ability to go against the norm. I grow in the most unlikely places, and I thrive.

I run my fingers through my hair and make a promise to myself not to let the men in my life make decisions for me anymore. Most of the time, they just betray me anyway. No one has my back better than me.

"Then you should've thought about that before you let them drag me kicking and screaming into it."

With that, I leave him standing there and walk back into the house. Kage is immediately by my side, giving me a worried look and asking me if everything is okay. His fears are easily calmed with a quick smile and a kiss on the cheek, but a nauseous feeling settles in the pit of my stomach. It twists and cramps, the taste of bile rising in my throat.

"I'll be right back," I tell him.

He nods and goes back to talking to Beni while I make my way down the hall. Once I'm out of view, I run as fast as I can to the nearest bathroom and heave the contents of my stomach into the toilet. I try to keep the noise to a minimum. There is nothing less sexy than vomit. But that comes with its own set of challenges.

When there's nothing left to vomit, I sit on the floor and lean against the wall, wiping my mouth with a piece of toilet paper. At first, I justify it as anxiety—thinking about how much I've been through in the last few months. All of the betrayal. The emotions. I tell myself that I've reached the end of my adrenaline. But when I think about how every time Nessa throws up, she worries she might be pregnant, I gasp.

I scramble to pull my phone out from my bra and wrack my brain to figure out when my last period was. Days seem to blend together when you're being held prisoner, and I wasn't privileged to have my phone until recently, so my only chance is by remembering a series of events.

Kage took my virginity, and I haven't had it since then.

We stayed wrapped up in each other for three weeks before he told me to leave.

It's been a week since I came back.

I'm at least a week late.

Standing up, I walk over to the body length mirror and turn to the side to look at my stomach. It's still as flat as it's ever been, but inside, I can feel it. A woman's intuition.

"Oh fuck," I breathe, sliding my hands down my lower belly.

An exhale from the doorway has my head whipping around to find the last person I'd hope for standing there, watching me intently.

Nico.

He looks amused as he rubs his bare chin and smiles. "Oh fuck is right."

CHAPTER 20

KAGE

THEY SAY YOU CAN'T CHOOSE YOUR FAMILY. THAT they're God's gift, and in most cases that may be true. Except for mine. Whoever decided that Nico Mancini was going to end up my *brother*, for all intents and purposes, must have been Satan himself—with a fucking vendetta. I've done a lot of questionable things in my life. Enough to reserve a seat right next to the devil. It's no secret that my soul is past the point of forgiveness. There's no chance of redemption for me, but I don't think I did anything to deserve having to watch my girl sitting next to him on the couch, talking in hushed tones for the third day in a fucking row.

Even Beni furrows his brows as he walks past them and over to me. "What the fuck is up with them?"

The grip I have on my glass of whiskey is so tight it may shatter. "I don't know, but I'm about to find out."

Walking over to the couch, I sit on the coffee table in front of them. I lean forward so I can look Saxon in the eyes, and refuse to back down as she smiles at me. They both watch me expectantly, but before I say anything, I try to read what both of them are thinking. Nico has learned over the years that a good poker face is essential to our way of life, but Saxon is an open book.

I tilt my head to the side. "You know, he wanted you dead."

Laughter bellows out of Nico, but when Saxon goes to look over at him, I turn her face back to face me.

"I'm serious. He told me I should kill you. Said that letting you go would make us look weak." I snap. "Oh, and then there was the time that he suggested I cut off one of your fingers or an ear to send to your father. A message to show him I wasn't playing games."

In a surprising move even to me, Saxon chuckles and looks over at Nico. "My ear? Really? You're sick."

Nico shrugs. "That was before you won me over with all your sass and charm."

She laughs, rolling her eyes, but isn't anywhere near as angry or disgusted as I thought she would be. My plan failed. It crashed and burned and perished along with any inkling of tolerance I had toward Nico.

Before I do something I regret, like bash him over the head with this goddamn glass, I get up and walk back over to Beni. I'll kill myself before I let Nico see that he's successfully getting under my skin. Just like his counterpart, that one thrives on the ability to piss people off. It's one of the most irritating things about him.

"You good?" Beni asks.

I take a sip of my drink. "I'm going to skin him alive and feed his eyeballs to the dog."

"We don't have a dog."

"Get us one."

BY DAY FIVE, I'VE run out of patience. Dalton hasn't gotten back to us yet about meeting to talk, and for reasons unbeknownst to me, Saxon seems against the idea of killing him. If this doesn't work, that may be our only option, and I don't know what that'll mean for us. I can tell you one thing, though—if my time with Saxon is limited, I'm fucking done sharing it with Nico.

"All right," I interrupt them. "It's time for you to go."

"Kage," Saxon tries, but I'm not letting her win this time.

"No. He's been here every day this fucking week," I snap and focus back on Nico. "Get the fuck out of my house before I put my foot up your ass."

If he's learned anything from knowing me his whole life, it's when I'm not playing around. That's probably one of the few things that's kept him alive for as long as he has been. He toes the line of pushing me too far, but mainly stays on the safe end of it. And staying here any longer than the time it takes to walk to the front door would be leaping across that line.

"I'll see you later, Sax," he tells her as he gets up.

The nickname infuriates me. The fact that he is close and comfortable enough to call her anything but her name doesn't sit well with me. If it were my decision, he'd never be within eyesight of her. He's a privileged little shit with no sense of respect or loyalty, and he doesn't deserve to breathe the same damn air as her.

As soon as he's gone, Saxon gives me a disapproving look. "What?"

She scoffs. "Don't give me that. You know what. You don't handle jealousy very well."

I choke on air at the verbal backhand. "Fuck that. I can't stand the guy without you—"

Before I can say something I'll regret with the rage that's flowing through me, I get up and go to walk away, but Saxon doesn't relent. She gets up and follows me, demanding I finish what I was saying.

"Without me what?" she presses. "What the hell is your problem?"

"Are you fucking him?"

The question throws itself out of my mouth as I spin around to face her, and she looks like I just punched her in the gut. "Are you serious right now? You really think I'm sleeping with him?"

I throw my hands in the air. "Well, you haven't been fucking me."

"So clearly that means I'm getting it elsewhere," she spits. "You're unbelievable."

"All I'm saying is you couldn't get enough of me, and then you're with him for longer than three minutes and something in you changed. It's like a switch flipped or something."

Stopping to take a breath before she says anything else, she exhales all the tension and anger, then walks up and puts her hands on my chest. I stare down at her, wondering how someone can pull such a heated reaction out of me at the thought of someone else having their attention. It's not something I'm used to, and it feels a hell of a lot like vulnerability.

"You're the only man I have eyes for, Kage." Staring up at me, I can see the honesty in her eyes. "That's not going to change regardless of who I spend time with."

My shoulders sag as I deflate and press my forehead to hers. "Well if you're not sleeping with him, then the only other possibility is he's threatening you with something."

Clearly, that was the wrong thing to say as she huffs and turns to walk away from me. I immediately reach out and grab her wrist before she can get too far.

"Okay, okay," I say, putting my hands on her hips. "I don't want to fight with you."

She softens and leans into me. "I don't either. But trust me when I say Nico can be more of an asset to you than you let him be."

"Gabbana…"

"I'm done." She rubs circles against my shirt while she avoids my eyes. "You won't hear another word about it from me."

And fuck her for being my only soft spot. "Okay. No promises, but I'll try to look at him the way you do." She looks up at me, hopeful. "But only if you do something for me."

A smirk splays across her face. "Already? I thought we'd wait a little bit for that. Work our way up to it and all."

I can't help but chuckle. "It's not anal."

"Oh." She looks a little disappointed, honestly, and I file that away for another time.

"If I'm making an effort with Nico, I need you to make one with Viola," I tell her and watch as her face screws up in disgust. "I've seen what happens to those on her bad side. It's not a place you want to be."

It looks like she'd rather do literally anything else, but she reluctantly agrees. "Fine, but like you said. No promises."

"That's okay." I bend down and kiss her slowly. "Now, about where you thought I was going with that."

Reaching around, I grab her ass and she deepens the kiss. Her body molds against my own and our tongues tangle together. She tastes sweet, like candy and sin, and I'd be perfectly content if that was all I tasted for the rest of my life.

But of course, my luck is complete shit because as she moans into my mouth, Beni interrupts.

"Boss," he says, grabbing my attention. "Dalton has agreed to meet. But he wants to do it tomorrow night."

Both relief and irritation hit me at once, because while this means the plan may end up working out, it also means we have work to do. I look back at Saxon, who gives me an understanding smile and a chaste kiss before stepping back.

"Go," she tells me. "We have all the time in the world."

I nod and follow Beni into my office, wanting to get this shit with Dalton over with so I can focus solely on his daughter.

ARMED MEN FILL MY living room, all ready to follow me into war if that's what it means to protect what's ours. Mauricio is looking through the paperwork and making sure we have everything, while Saxon is planted firmly in my lap.

"I still think I should leave at least two men here," I say as I run a hand up and down her back.

She shakes her head. "No. You need everyone you can get in case you're walking into an ambush. My father cannot be trusted."

"Which is exactly why you need to be protected," I argue.

"Kage," she breathes and puts a hand on my cheek. "I'm safe here. This place is a fortress. Me and your massive boy-castle will be just fine."

Red flags, alarms, and sirens are everywhere in my head, but if I've learned anything lately, it's that there is no winning when she has her mind set to something. Hence why she's still here after I quite literally sent her packing.

"Okay, fine," I agree, just as Beni steps in front of me.

"All ready to go?" I ask him.

He nods. "Everything is in place, and we need to leave now if we want to make it there on time."

I take a deep breath and then tap Saxon's thigh for her to get up. "God forbid we keep him waiting."

Beni chuckles. "I agree with you, but we need him to accept our offer for this plan to work."

"Yeah, I get it." I look around at all the men who fill the room. Soldati from all over came to have our back on this. "Okay, everyone knows the deal? You do not even brandish your weapon unless there is a valid reason to. He has to trust us, and that won't happen if he feels threatened."

They all nod, and Beni leads them all out the front door. I hang back for a second to hug Saxon goodbye. She throws herself at me and wraps her arms tightly around my neck. I breathe in the scent of her, getting high on everything she is.

"Be careful," she says.

I kiss her softly. "I will."

As I turn to walk out, Nico snorts. "Wouldn't want *Daddy* to get hurt."

My hand flies up and smacks him over the back of the head without a second thought. It isn't until after that I realize what I did and my promise to Saxon. *Oops?*

"What about us makes you think we have a fucking daddy kink?"

"You just seem like the demanding type," he snickers and jumps away when my hand moves to hit him again. "Ooh! Spanking is only allowed in the bedroom, Daddy."

I glance back at Saxon, who's doing the best she can to hold back her laughter. Dropping my head, I sigh and shake it off, wondering what it is about her that makes me willing to do just about any damn thing she asks of me.

As we all get outside, I stop Paolo before he gets into the car. "You're staying here."

"Yes, sir," he says like a loyal soldati should.

"Stay outside and don't let Saxon see you unless she tries to leave. No one in, no one out. Understood?"

He nods. "Yes, sir."

As he goes back toward the front door, I climb into the car to find Nico and Beni both smirking at me, but of course it's Nico who has the balls to say anything about it. "Saxon is going to have your balls scrambled for breakfast if she finds out."

I roll my eyes and choose not to answer. It's better for my promise to Saxon if I don't say anything at all. And besides, I don't need to justify anything to his stupid ass.

WE PULL UP TO the building with five minutes to spare. It's an office in the middle of Long Island, a neutral ground for both of us. We're smart enough not to put ourselves in a compromising spot, which is why we got a hold of the blueprints and made sure we know the place inside and out.

I get out of the car and straighten my suit before walking in with all my men following dutifully behind. People, assumedly those who work in the building, stop to watch us as we walk by. I'd say it's a good sign that the place isn't empty, but Dalton doesn't seem like the type to care about unnecessary casualties, and neither are the Bratva.

As I enter the conference room, Forbes is already there. He stands up, sporting a cocky little grin that makes it clear he thinks he's winning here, and takes a step toward me.

"Mr. Malvagio," he greets me, putting his hand out for me to shake.

I stare down at it and then look back at him. This is the man who wanted to give Saxon away to one of the men who killed my father, for nothing more than personal gain. That alone makes it so he doesn't deserve a single ounce of my respect. And everything else he's done just seals his fate.

"I have to say, I'm glad we're coming to an agreement," he says as he pulls his hand back and we sit down across from each other. "As you can imagine, I'm desperate to get my daughter back, and I'm sure you need to regain control of the city."

It takes everything in me not to roll my eyes, but it's important not to show any emotions. My face stays firm, not giving anything away. Mauricio takes the seat beside me and pulls the paperwork out of his briefcase. When he's done, all attention turns back to me.

"Let's get this over with."

IT ALL HAPPENS IN slow motion. I run out the door with Beni and Nico close behind me, everyone else behind them. No matter how fast I go or how hard I push, it feels like I can't get to the goddamn car.

When I finally reach it, I dive into the passenger seat and pull out my phone. My hand shakes as I dial the number. Holding it to my ear, I wait for an answer as Beni peels out of the parking lot and speeds down the road.

"Pick up. Pick up," I beg. "Pick the fuck up!"

Dread and misery fill my stomach as I hear the beginning of her voicemail. I immediately call again, hoping for different results but getting the same. Despite everything I've been through in my life, including losing both my parents, somehow this feels the worst.

I'm convinced. This is hell.

Cars and buildings whiz by as Beni goes over 120 miles per hour down the road. As for me? I won't stop calling until she picks up the phone.

But like all the times before, I get her voicemail.

"Fuck!"

Saxon

The roar of the engine dies as I turn off the car and open the door. The sound of my phone ringing pierces the silence while I step out, and I pull it out of my back pocket to see Kage calling. I roll my eyes playfully and put it to my ear.

"Don't get your panties in a twist," I tease. "I didn't crash your precious Bugatti."

I can only assume he got a security alert when I left with his most expensive car. But what else was I supposed to do? I had to get here somehow.

His breathing sounds labored. "I don't give a flying fuck if that car is in a thousand pieces. Where are you?"

The worry in his voice is adorable as I walk into the small house. "I take it you didn't get my message? Viola texted me. She needs my help with something. Because God forbid she does anything on her own. Princess might break a nail."

He starts talking before I'm even finished. "Saxon, listen to me. Get back to the house, now!"

"And have her pitch a fit because I stood her up?" I scoff. "Not a chance. Besides, you didn't want me to be alone, and now I'm not." I look around the room for signs of her. "Or at least I won't be when I can find the bitch."

"S!" he shouts. "It's a trap! It's a fucking trap!"

"What?"

The sound of a gun cocking behind me has me spinning around on my heels. A woman stands in the shadows, her face covered by the darkness. The only thing I can make out is the shape of the gun she's pointing directly at me.

My breath hitches as she pulls the trigger, one after another. The loud bang is deafening but nothing is worse than feeling the bullets lodge themselves in my stomach.

The phone falls out of my hand and clatters onto the floor, only for my body to do the same. The pain that shoots through my arm as I land on it is just something else to add to the damage.

"Saxon!" Kage roars through the phone. "Saxon, answer me!"

But as I open my mouth to speak, nothing comes out. Blood pours from my lower stomach and pools around me. I can't move. I can't make a sound. I'm going to die, and there's nothing I can do about it.

A single tear leaks out as my assailant comes over and picks my phone up off the ground. She hangs up on Kage and steps over my body, walking toward the door. Just before she leaves, she lights a match and drops it on a chair by the door. All I can do is watch as the flames creep over the soft fabric, throwing light into the dark room.

Everything starts to go blurry as I lose consciousness, but at least the pain is starting to fade. Deep down, I think I knew it was always going to come to this. From the moment I ended up in Kage's grasp, there was no making it out of this alive. I was going to die, either at someone else's hands or my own. The only regret I have is that I didn't get to tell him about the baby. Though maybe that's for the better.

Darkness starts to tunnel around my vision as my body goes cold. Death is setting in, and yet the only thing that passes through my mind before everything goes black is that I know who did this.

I'd recognize those Balenciaga heels anywhere.

To be continued.

Screams in Symphony
Coming January 21st
Preorder Now

There once was a girl,

tarnished and ruined by the actions of others.

Some are born plagued by darkness,

but she was doused in it by those she trusted.

Like Lucifer himself,

she fell from the heavens and landed amongst the flames.

Now she wears her crown black,

with diamonds coated in the blood of her enemies.

This isn't the story of a girl who saved the villain.

This is the story of a girl who became something much worse,

and the man who loved her for it.

ABOUT THE AUTHOR

Kelsey Clayton is a USA Today Bestselling Author of Contemporary Romance novels. She lives in a small town in Delaware with her husband, two kids, and dog.

She is an avid reader of fall hard romance. She believes that books are the best escape you can find, and that if you feel a range of emotions while reading her stories - she succeeded. She loves writing and is only getting started on this life long journey.

Kelsey likes to keep things in her life simple. Her ideal night is one with sweatpants, a fluffy blanket, cheese fries, and wine. She holds her friends and family close to her heart and would do just about anything to make them happy.

Books By
KELSEY CLAYTON

Malvagio Mafia Duet

Suffer in Silence

Screams in Symphony

North Haven University

Corrupt My Mind *(Zayn and Amelia)*

Change My Game *(Jace and Paige)*

Wreck My Plans *(Carter and Tye)*

Waste My Time *(Easton and Kennedy)*

Haven Grace Prep

The Sinner *(Savannah & Grayson)*

The Saint *(Delaney & Knox)*

The Rebel *(Tessa & Asher)*

The Enemy *(Lennon & Cade)*

The Sleepless November Saga

Sleepless November

Endless December

Seamless Forever

Awakened in September

Standalones

Returning to Rockport

Hendrix *(Colby and Saige)*

Printed in Great Britain
by Amazon